PLAYING

HIS GAMES

COPYRIGHT

Cover by Book Cover by Design
Photograph by Wander Aguiar
Editing by Editing 4 Indies

© Donna Alam 2017

ISBN: 978-1977501189
ISBN: 1977501184

Other Books by Donna Alam

The Pretty Series

Pretty Hot
Pretty Liar
Pretty Things

Trouble by Numbers
One Hot Scot
Two Wrongs
One Dirty Scot
Single Daddy Scot
Hot Scot Christmas

The Morning After

One

LOUISE

I'm going to wrap my fingers in your hair, and like a good little girl, you're going to open your legs and let me see what's mine. . .

'Oh, God.'

I press my head deeper into the pillow as my dream fades, replaced by an annoying buzzing that takes me a moment to comprehend. *My phone.* My hand shoots out from under the covers in a desperate attempt to *Make. The. Noise.* Stop! It can't be morning—not yet. I can't have been asleep for very long. But the sun piercing my eyelids seems to contradict my theory.

'Oh, Lord.' Okay, so I'm not entirely comfortable. I lick my parched lips, still groping for my phone as it dances just out of reach. 'Curse you, Flo,' I grumble as several thoughts wash through my wool-filled head.

Tequila is the Devil's water, and I'm never drinking again. If this is what it feels like to be twenty-six, fast forward me straight to middle-age.

The sheets rustle as I shuffle closer to the edge, muttering and heaping blame on the woman who'd forced me from my comfort zone and onto the dance floor last night. My roommate and friend, Flo. The woman who's right at the top of my shit list today.

'You're old before your time,' she'd taunted, a flash of light from the dance floor making her smile look malicious. *'Darling, you know what they say; people who don't dance are terrible in bed.'*

I'd rolled my eyes, but her ridiculous gauntlet had roused my competitive side. So, of course, I'd headed for the dance floor . . . just by way of the bar. Never let it be said I'm not up for a challenge, but dancing required the loss of inhibitions, and the removal of those required tequila. And by the way I feel this morning, it seems to have taken a bucket of the stuff.

My eyes are uncooperative as I continue the search for my phone, patting blurry items with my hand when the thing suddenly stills.

'There is a God,' I mumble, though the declaration is more a groan than words. I flop back against the pillows with a sigh, not caring who called.

I pull the duvet over my head to ward off the light, wondering how I'd left the drapes open last night. *Typical, the one day I'd welcome a grey London morning is the day spring decides to arrive.* As the duvet settles on my body, I note I'm naked under it. I wonder if I flashed the neighbours last night?

Oh, well. Maybe if I was less tired, I might care. But as my brain is currently preserved in tequila, it seems like a matter for some other time.

I'm not usually such a morning grouch, still waking with the excitement of someone who has only been living in London for three months—someone who'd transplanted their life over four thousand miles. The city is still strange and so new, I find I don't mind waking to the muted sounds from the café next door. It's almost comforting; a sort of acoustic urban backdrop. And nothing remotely like back home.

It strikes me then how unusually quiet it is this morning. Is it a long weekend? And if it is, how come I don't know? A singular car trundles along the road outside, the sound of children's voices drifting up from below. They're familiar sounds but not quite right.

At least the heat is on; London hasn't yet agreed with the spring calendar, and my bedroom is usually freezing cold. Reveling in the unexpected comfort, I arch my back and yawn, wriggling my toes to a cooler part of the sheets before stilling mid-motion because something feels wrong.

The sheets. Egyptian cotton. Thread count in the thousands, like the ones my mother uses at home. The sound of my phone on the nightstand hitting wood, not glass. The warmth of the bedroom. And, more telling still, the extra leg my foot has just brushed in bed.

I push the duvet off my head in a hurry, and there, on the other side of the mattress, lies the very nice, but unfamiliar, rear view of a man. His masculine shoulder lifts along with a deep sigh and my heart almost stops, though the shock of the motion is fast lost as his large hand reaches to push the comforter down his body until it's coasting his hip. Muscles. So many muscles. Cording his neck, a bulge of bicep, the flex in his lats. The dimples low on his back. Wow. I think this is what's called an athletic build.

Seems I'm not at home, and I'm not alone, and the realisation jolts me awake like a slap.

Laughing. *So much laughing.*

Dancing. *And not by myself.*

Drinking. *Definitely more than I should have.*

The man. *All of him.*

I'd gone out straight from the office last night—in my work clothes, no less— in celebration of a record week. My colleagues had also somehow found out my birthday was the week before, so as much as I hadn't wanted to go, it seemed impolite not to attend my own birthday celebration. Plus, you can only refuse an invitation so many times before comments turn to back stabbing. So I'd accepted and drank tequila, of all things. Far too much tequila, apparently.

It began innocently enough—it was only supposed to be dinner and a few drinks—when one of the finance guys, with mischief in his eye, had mentioned a local club. He'd said he'd heard it was a club for kink.

'You know, S and M?'

'You wouldn't know kink if it paddled your arse,' answered someone from another department; acquisitions, I think. The table erupted into laughter, the comments becoming bawdier by the minute. I'd sipped my wine, obviously being

sensible at that point, trying to laugh along, even as my heart sat in my throat. It was just a bit of a joke to them but not so to me. I'd tried not to flinch as the questions turned my way.

'What do you think, birthday girl? Should we go see what it's all about?'

All eyes were on me. I was sure the staccato beating of my heart could be heard over the music, the restaurant noise, and chatter. Dominance. Submission. Sex. The words were so darkly tempting yet so complicated, and tied in the roots of my psyche somehow.

I've had lots of theory learning—Anais Nin and Anne Rice, and I've watched all the movies; The Secretary, Maitresse, and the classic Belle de Jour. And okay, maybe a little porn, too. But I shouldn't. Not least because . . .

'Sure, why not.' I'd answered, setting down my glass. Cool, calm, and collected, my answer hit the air on a wave of wine bravery. And I'm not sure who was more surprised—me, or them.

Uptight Louise. The Ice Queen. I'd heard their names for me, not that I've ever cared. I developed my armour years ago and carry it everywhere.

And just like that, we'd finished our meal and headed to the club.

Once inside the place, I recall the mild disappointment, expecting something different, though what, I wasn't sure. Maybe something tawdry. Freaky. Something less tasteful and . . . ordinary? The interior could've been any high-end bar in any city in the world. Dark, sumptuous tones and smoky mirrors, crystal chandeliers juxtaposed by raw brick. It was sophisticated but not long the focus of my attention. Because that was pulled almost magnetically to a man in dark a suit. A man in a suit watching me.

At first, I'd thought him a tourist. Not necessarily a London tourist—he looked too sophisticated for that—but maybe a tourist to the club seeking similar thrills. I'd still been considering the same thoughts much later when he'd slid a hand around my neck. He couldn't have known how the placement had affected me, but he read my reaction instinctively.

Yearning inside. Wet panties outside.

But how can I recall these very visceral reactions, yet can't remember his face? And how did I come to be sitting with him?

Did I . . . did I really lick spilled Patrón from his neck?

Oh, God. In a sudden rush, I remember almost falling onto his lap and spilling my drink all over him. He'd been very gracious about being my landing place, even laughing as he agreed I absolutely should buy him a drink by way of an apology. After all, he was wearing mine. And his voice? Caramel, dark chocolate, and all the smooth, dark things. And his accent? Panty-melting posh.

Thoughts and images of the evening rise like sudden wisps of smoke. Offensive promises whispered in the darkness, anonymous hands caressing my flesh.

From the corner of my eye, something else catches my attention. A set of leather restraints dangling from the edge of the iron bedstead. Did I wear them? And if I had, oughtn't I feel at least a flickering of shame? It's strange, but I don't seem able to summon a suitable sense of disgrace. And that feels . . . odd.

Hangovers tend to make me melodramatic, only I don't really feel hungover anymore. Best cure for a hangover? Shock, apparently. Sure, my mouth is dry. Okay, nasty. But the wool hampering my head seems to have gone. I feel lucid, almost. Headache free. Though there are other aches. Ones I expect I'll be delighting in for days . . .

So it had happened. I'd experience the forbidden—my ultimate fantasy—and I hadn't been forced to pass go, missing my two hundred and shooting straight to hell. But better to blame the tequila than to admit responsibility. *Because intention is everything.*

The sheets rustle as the man stirs again, bringing me back to my predicament pretty quickly. As it becomes clear he's still asleep, I use the opportunity to reacquaint myself with him, as best I can, when faced with the back of his head.

His dark hair I recall clearly, thick and glossy, tamed by an expensive cut. And blue eyes, I think. Well-dressed, blue eyes, dark hair, but what else? Judging from the feeling between my legs, pretty well endowed.

I inhale, counting to three then release the breath over the same count. That he's a deep sleeper is a plus because escape is just a few steps away.

Awkward greetings and morning breath would be bad enough, but I'm almost certain we hadn't exchanged names. *Because I would've remembered that, surely?*

Besides, after my behaviour last night, I think I'd rather not face him right now. Whoever he is.

As my phone chirps with a text, I swipe it from the nightstand, sore in places I'd rather not think about. Sliding my legs from under the covers, I peel the sheet back. Not daring to drag it with me even the shortest of distance, I find my toes are not the only thing exposed to the morning air. Trying hard to remember where I'd abandoned my clothes, I scan the room as I swipe my thumb across the screen of my phone.

I find a missed call and a text from Flo, the woman whose demise I'll schedule sometime later today.

The text reads:

Wassup, bitch? If the bubbling spots on the screen are anything to go by, another text would be following shortly.

Come on, Loo, answer da fone!! I'm well jel of the stud you pulled. I need deets!

Sorry, Louise is dead. Lots of love, last night's serial killer, I reply, typing with both thumbs, surprised not to see matching bruises on my wrists. I rotate them, savouring in the silent bruising, wondering how long it would be before the colour shows. Then I spot my panties hanging from the post at the end of the bed. Seconds later, I've wiggled them up over my hips, my thumbs then continuing our conversation as I search the room for my bra and the rest of my clothes.

How could you let me go home with a stranger?

What kind of a friend are you?

How could I have NOT let you? comes Flo's retort. *The stud was wearing you like a coat.*

I snort, regretting the action immediately, but as I turn my head, sleeping studly hasn't stirred.

Flo likes to pretend, at least by text, that her first language is street. No one would guess from her texts that her accent is more Knightsbridge than Newham, or that Flora, as she's known at home, is the daughter of someone in Parliament. Or that her mother possesses the title The Right Honourable. There's a strange sort of symmetry in this, considering Flo is definitely more *dishonourable*.

Don't get your knickers in a knot, darling, Flo's next text read. *Get them up your legs and meet me at the coffee shop on the corner. I've known where you were all along. Turn left out of his front door. I'll be the one wearing a rather natty fedora I've snagged from the back of your bedroom door. Ciao x*

God knows what else she's "borrowed" from the visit to my room. My smile doesn't last very long, replaced by a frown. His front door. How did I allow myself to get here? And how does she know where I am?

It might not exactly be my first, but one-night stands aren't a regular occurrence for me. In fact, the last time I'd woken in a stranger's bed, I'd been eighteen and miles from my college dorm. Tequila had also been to blame then. But this time is . . . different. Items checked off my bucket list.

A night of kinky sex ✓

A night of Fifty-Shading fun ✓

I shake my head and the absurd thoughts away, spotting my black bra hanging from a chair on the other side of the bed. A chair very close to my companion's head. Stealthily, I creep around the edge, stepping over a couple of torn condom wrappers with a silent sigh of relief. *At least someone was paying attention to such things.*

I gingerly pull the lacy strap, unravelling it from inside a man's oxford shirt, and fight the urge to look at him as I turn. It's not that I think I'll be disappointed—in my mind, he's definitely handsome. But it's maybe better to leave it that way; a vague impression of the man. Memories of a dark-haired stranger. And I might've managed it had Flo's words not echoed that moment in my head.

I've never been to bed with an ugly man, but I may have inadvertently woken up with one or two.

My reluctance to look at him isn't vanity—I'm not afraid of tequila goggles. It's more a feeling that, in looking at him, I'll validate my recklessness. If I don't look, it might be easier to ignore the night I've spent with a stranger, doing things that, this morning, I . . . I can't exactly recall.

But for all the lies I tell myself, my eyes are drawn to him as I turn.

He's instantly familiar from last night rather than any prior acquaintance. Flashes of complete images follow. Lounged in his chair, one hand wrapped around his glass, the other wrapped around me. The flash of white teeth as he laughed. The way he whispered in the cab how he couldn't wait to be inside me. Images of us in this bedroom, his dark hair entwined in my fingers, his mouth between my legs. His hand on my breasts, the warm sense of being held in his arms. In his hands. The sensation his body against mine.

His hair is unruly in sleep, neither black nor brown. His profile, though still chiseled, is softer than in my head, sleep blurring his hard edges. His mouth is ridiculously sensual for a man, though a strong jaw balances his features, dark stubble completing the near perfection. Heat crawls from my belly as I remember the bristling sensation at my shoulder. *The echo of it between my legs.* My blush only deepens as I realise my fingers are absently tracing that same path.

I fold my arms across my chest, aching to touch myself yet not ready to move or look away. The skin of his bare torso is porcelain to my gold, the muscles in his shoulders and arms, from what I can see, highly defined. One bare ass cheek peeks from the sheet across his hips. From what I can discern from the sum of the parts on display, it's safe to say this man keeps very fit.

I shake my head, rousing myself. No matter how handsome he is, I need to leave before he wakes and the inevitable awkwardness of a second meeting sets in.

Silently slipping on my bra, I suffer a sudden flashback of dropping my blouse and skirt to the floor of another room. *A striptease? No. I don't have that sort of confidence.* Picking up my phone once again, I swear my heart touches my tonsils as I reach for the door handle when he speaks. I swallow past the lump of discomfort, not daring to turn, but he isn't awake. *Thank you, Lord, for unintelligible sleep ramblings.* Without turning, I slip from the room like a thief, the echoes of his sleep-roughened voice conjuring other memories . . .

In the club, he'd ordered a bottle of tequila, smiling as I'd directed the waitress to take away the limes and salt.

'Serious tequila doesn't need embellishments,' I'd said. He'd chuckled darkly as I added, 'And all bets are off after a couple of shots.'

Curled into his liquor-damp shirt, both our sets of friends were quickly forgotten as shot after shot was poured. I'd heard of the strong, silent type, though never experienced the thrill of attention accompanying this. Dark eyes watching. Weighing. Seeing right through me. And when he did speak, his words hit almost viscerally. Like a sign from the universe, I'd thought. It wasn't long before our tentative flirting became a hot and heavy make-out session, right there in the club.

I close the bedroom door behind me with a *click*, finding my fingers at my lips as I recall how the stranger's lips emancipated my reasoning. Last night, I was someone else. Someone a little reckless. *Someone drunk off her ass.* That's my story and I'm sticking to it, especially as I recall what happened next.

As I'd come up for air, kiss-drunk and so aroused, I'd whispered a question so daring, my cheeks still burn with the memory.

'Do you want to go someplace else?'

My tone was so sultry, he couldn't have misunderstood. I may as well have had a neon sign saying, This Girl is DTF.

His answer? In my experience, men in real life don't say the sorts of things that make a girl ache with need.

He told me he'd love to.

That he'd take me home in a heartbeat.

But that his tastes were rather hard edged.

He'd sought to shock me, for sure, unaware of the pulse of pleasure beating between my legs. Because I wanted to be sure—because I'd wanted to hear those words again—I'd lowered my gaze and asked him quietly asked to elaborate.

And he did.

He said he got a kick out of marking beautiful skin. That he liked nothing more than to see a woman's body tied, every line taut and elegant in her distress. And that, for him, this wasn't just a prelude to sex.

In my whole life, I'd never been so turned on, and in my haste to have him inside me, I would've forgotten my purse if it hadn't been for him. Then outside as we'd waited for a cab, I couldn't stop myself from touching him. Kissing him. Pushing my body up against his. When his fingers tightened suddenly around my wrists, it had taken me a moment to appreciate he was restraining me physically. Rather than a warning, it was a green light for direction—a green light for go. Excited didn't come close to how I was feeling, and I think, without his strong hands wrapped around mine, I might've gotten down on my knees in that dirty street, promising to swallow him whole.

Fuck. If I can recall his answer, does that really mean I said those things?

Because he'd said the first time I got on my knees for him, I'd be naked with my hair wrapped in his fist. That he'd take his pleasure from me like a gift.

And I wanted it. I wanted it all. By the ache in my jaw, I guess I received it. And then a little bit more.

'This isn't like me,' I'd whispered just moments after we'd climbed into the cab. A moment of lucidity? Was I scared or making excuses for myself?

As he'd bent to kiss my forehead, he seemed to be fighting a smile.

'Are you trying to tell me you're leading me up the garden path?' His voice, low in register, rippled down my spine.

'Yeah,' I'd replied, suppressing the shiver. 'The lady garden path.' I'd made a drunkenly lewd gesture in the vague direction my crotch when he'd grabbed my hand in one of his, moving the other to the nape of my neck.

'All roads lead to Rome?' I murmured weakly, not wanting to appear cowed. His predatory gaze caused a flare between my legs, drowning out every one of my thoughts.

'I take a path less travelled,' he'd whispered, his lips brushing my face. 'I like to be in charge.' The flare turned molten, my insides dissolving as his thumb stroked the thundering pulse in my neck.

Back in the stranger's house, I try to force the sensory memories away. How can I still feel the effects of his words dancing down my spine? Pulsing between my legs?

I follow the weak sunlight spilling down the unfamiliar stairs. My feet are light as I tiptoe along the hallway, opening the door to what I think might be the living room.

Jackpot.

In an unruly heap on the floor, I find my skirt and blouse. And underneath, my shoes. Dressing quickly, I slip back out into the hallway, picking up my purse and jacket from an antique hall stand. Clothes to door, I'm out of the house in two minutes flat.

The path to the garden gate is unremarkable. An Edwardian terraced house, it's quite large. A dark red door with brass fittings leads to a pebbled pathway leading to a wrought-iron gate under an awning of neat vines. I remember the footpath crunching beneath the soles of my shoes, thinking how comfortingly ordinary his house appeared to be. I'd stared at the door in the darkness while he spoke with the cab driver. Comfortingly ordinary, at least, until he'd pushed me against it, the handle unforgiving at the small of my back, his hips—his hard-on—pinning me there.

'The point of no return.' In contrast to the discomfort of the large handle digging into my

back, he'd smiled sweetly, and all I could think was how much I'd wanted to run my fingers against his mouth. Slide my tongue between his lips. 'I do think you'd let me fuck you right here.'

I made a noise; it didn't resemble a denial, my head filling with images of just that. He'd fuck me hard, my legs wrapped around him, his fingers hard, hot points against my hips as I—

He chuckled. Was it my expression? It sounded dark and bitter and sweet. It matched the man. It matched his accent. And what he said next was my undoing.

'You like the sound of that? You're wet for it. You want the feel of the night air on your nakedness as I fuck you hard and fast.' But then he'd gestured behind to the cab. 'Before he leaves, you need to decide. I want to fuck you until you can't stand, but you leave your wants and desires at this door. You understand? I like things my way.'

'Are you going to hurt me?' My question sounded like pure encouragement. I didn't consider the implications as I slid my lips against his. Tongues tangled as our kiss deepened, my fingers grasping his shirt as though to hang on to my sanity. It was a kiss like I'd never experienced before. A kiss that was hot, wet, and heavy, and a promise of things to come.

He'd groaned as he pulled away, signalling silently for the cab to leave.

'My way.' As he'd turned back, his eyes shined black in the moonlight, his fingers finding my chin. 'Means you wait for an invitation.'

He'd kissed me again. Hard this time, his choice, and my further undoing. I leaned against the handle more heavily, the ache between my legs loosening my limbs. As our mouths parted, he'd slipped the key in the lock before leading me inside. Meek and disheveled, my mouth tingled as much as my back ached, but I was so fucking aroused.

Back in the morning light, and in the shade of the hedges surrounding the garden gate, I push away the recollection before I drown in sensation overload. Rousing myself, I pull an ever-present elastic from my purse, gathering my blonde hair into a messy topknot. Then, pulling down the hem of my skirt, I push my shoulders back and swing open the gate to step out onto the street. If I'm doing the walk of shame through whichever London borough I'm in, I'll do it as I do everything. With my head held high.

Two

LOUISE

'My slutty senses are tingling!' Flo rises from the café outdoor table setting just around the corner as she'd promised. My borrowed hat sits on the table, her black hair loose around her shoulders, shining almost blue in the sun. 'Where've you left your horse?'

I glance down at my crumpled clothing, taking a beat to decipher her non-sequitur. I suddenly feel a little old. Old enough to know better, at least.

'It's my shoes,' I answer belatedly, realising she's teasing me. Anyone who'd worn four-inch heels one full day and part of the night was bound to have an awkward gait. And here I was, wearing them again. There were, of course, other aches, but I wasn't about to share those details.

Collapsing into the chair opposite, I swipe Flo's cup and swallow a mouthful. My grimace is instant. 'Green tea?' When I so need a coffee. When she doesn't respond, I look up; I'm greeted by one highly defined and eloquently raised brow. It's the kind of look that demands details. The kind of look hard to ignore.

'It's true,' I protest. 'My feet *are* killing me.'

Flo's response is a dirty, sniggering laugh. 'Only your feet, sweets? And do leave my tea alone. I've no idea where your mouth has been.' Ignoring my shocked expression, she passes me my canvas tote. 'Here. I've brought those god-awful plimsolls you wear. And a cardigan.' Somehow, I sense she isn't done, proven right when she breaks out into a sing-song tone, 'Because appearances are everything!'

'Only to the vain and shallow,' I mumble, placing the bag on the empty chair next to mine.

'Just ninety-eight percent of the city's population, then?' She lifts her cup as she stands. 'Make yours a latte and a banana muffin?'

'You know me so well,' I reply gratefully, shrugging on the long-line sweater. I look down at my feet, realising this isn't the case at all. After last night, I barely know myself. I slip my feet into my favourite pink Chucks and wrap the pale scarf around my neck. While I might be in desperate need of a shower, at least I'm now more suitably dressed for a Saturday morning, though a little cold.

Adele begins to croon from the café shop door as Flo pushes it open from the inside, cups in hand.

'Anal,' she states certainly, flopping into the metallic chair opposite. 'It had to be.'

'What?' I splutter, my gaze darting around. Lowering my voice, I hiss, 'I would ... I ... never did *that*.' But would I have said no? The pulse between my legs isn't the answer I'm looking for.

'Not you, silly. The song.' She breaks into a couple of surprisingly melodic lines from Adele's hit; words about the delights of a new lover and the things unshared. 'The other tart gave him things she couldn't. It had to be anal,' she repeats with certainty.

'I worry about what goes through your head sometimes.' My tone is disparaging.

'Only my head?' Along with her response, she shoots me a bawdy wink.

'It's too early for sex talk.'

'And don't knock what you haven't tried,' she adds, ignoring my plea with a narrowed gaze. I feel the full weight of her scrutiny as I concentrate on the contents of my cup. 'If I were a betting girl, my money would be on last night's piece of hotness.'

'Money? For what?' I ask, glancing up from my cup.

'I bet you'd have given him a backstage entrance pass.'

'I'm not a concert.'

'You're sure? Because last night looked like his audition, but the question is, will he be getting a call back?' When I don't dignify this with an answer, she points an accusing finger in my direction. 'I do hope so because you never show interest in anyone, and last night, I think you'd have shagged him on the dance floor!'

'Can we *not* do this now,' I groan, my mind filled with horror—flashes of movement, silhouettes flaring as though lit by a black light. 'I'm not hydrated enough for a debrief.' I regret the words as soon as they leave my mouth. 'Stop!' I say, holding up a hand. 'That's not what she said.'

Flo laughs. 'Such movements. You should totes put them on your résumé.'

Her pronunciation sounds terribly French as I groan and plant my head in my hands. 'I don't know what came over me,' I mumble.

'I think I do.'

'Please make it stop,' I say, throwing both my eyes and hands heavenward.

'You're such a drama queen,' she says, still laughing and thoroughly enjoying my pain.

'Me? You're the queen of drama. If you hadn't made me dance, I wouldn't be sitting here in yesterday's clothes!'

Without dancing, there would've been no need for tequila. Without tequila, there would be no indiscretion to report. No stranger.

I'm not sure I welcome that thought.

'You should be buying *my* breakfast as thanks.'

'Where did you go, anyway?' I ask, hoping to shift the conversation to her favourite topic. *Namely Flo*. 'I can't remember you being around much after I fell on him.'

'Fell on his cock, you mean?'

So much for that plan. And why does the word sound so much naughtier in her accent? 'Shush. Not so loud.'

'Hungover, sweets?'

'I can't believe I went home with him.' I also don't realise I'm chewing my thumbnail until Flo pulls it away.

'Don't worry,' she says, cutting me off. 'I was there, keeping an eye on things.'

'How did you know where I'd be?' I ask, the thought occurring belatedly. The phone call is one thing, but meeting me here, nearby?

'I insisted on seeing his driver's license.' Flo keeps her eyes on her tea as she stirs. 'I knew exactly where you'd be.'

'And you stayed—in the club?'

'Of course. I was rather taken by the barman. Don't you remember? He was a bit of a sort.' London English was sometimes like another language. Why couldn't she just say the barman was hot?

Folding her arms across her chest, Flo begins the dissection of our evening—the bits I'd missed. The problem started with an open tab at dinner; things had gone downhill very quickly, apparently. As she imparts last night's hot gossip—who did what and with whom—I try to stay focused on the details, though my mind is overwhelmed by other things . . .

In the stranger's house, after leading me down a hallway, he'd opened a bottle of wine and poured us both a glass. Soft music played in the background; the lights were low. His manner solicitous, throwing me off balance at the change of pace. What happened to the man who'd pushed me up against the door? I wanted him back. Hard. Fast. More.

He's an academic, I thought he'd said. Something about teaching, maybe? That didn't make sense today. There was a certain reserve about him; a power underneath. Something kept on a tight leash. I've known teachers in my life. People in the profession usually have an obvious authority about them, not one restrained. A need to be heard. The love of a captive audience.

Captive. My mind slides back to the question of the handcuffs again.

'Tsk, tsk. A one-night stand,' she admonishes, chuckling as she pilfers a piece of my breakfast and pops it into her mouth. How she can manage to chew and smile, I don't know. Oh, for a toothbrush this morning. And a couple of Tylenol.

'I'm not a virgin,' I retort half-heartedly.

'Oh, I know. Maybe just . . . revirginized.'

'God, you're so . . . ' *Perceptive?*

'Crass? Yes, so my mother says. But you haven't had sex since you moved in with me, other than with yourself.' Jesus, are the walls that thin? 'What? Am I not supposed to notice?' I open my mouth to protest—my vibrator cost me a fortune; its motor is as silent as the dead! 'You work. You run. You knit furiously. Don't tell me that's not repressed sexual energy.'

'That's not true,' I manage finally. 'I've been out with you. Besides, knitting is a fashionable pastime.'

'The pertinent word was "furiously". And yes, we've been out, but you turn down drinks offered. And you ignore the studs at work.'

'I never mix business and pleasure.'

She sends me a look that suggests I've no idea what pleasure is.

'Sweetie, I find there are few things you can be certain of in life. But, in my experience, three things never lie.' She begins to count off the items on her left hand. 'Drunk people, small children, and leggings.'

'Thank you, Flora. Why, that clears up everything!' She can be so abstract at times.

'Last night,' she begins solemnly, 'you said you didn't want him. You'd said you needed him. If that's not repression, then I've no idea what is.'

'I did not.'

'You mumbled something else about a bucket list. God knows what,' she adds with shrug.

'My bucket list? I'm only twenty-sex—*six*.' Lord. 'I'm only twenty-six, I mean.'

'I know exactly what you mean.'

Ignoring her, I carry on. 'At this age, a bucket list is a bunch of vague notions of places I'd like to visit . . . things I'd like to do.'

'Then I guess you can check off doing a sexy stranger. That man is hot. I like this new Louise,' Flo asserts. 'She should get laid more often. Emotional outbursts suit her.'

'No,' I reply quietly. 'I've told you. Being in London isn't about those kinds of experiences.' Truthfully, I've been hit on plenty since I'd arrived from the States. I'd just promised myself I wouldn't fuck, get involved, or any of that stuff.

I want culture, experience, and perhaps a promotion. Last night, I strayed from the path I'd set for myself.

Flo sighs. 'You'll have the memories. Good ones, I hope?'

Was he good? My bodily aches tell their own tale.

'That was a hint, by the way. You Americans are so literal.'

'I *literally* don't know what to say.'

'I know he was a good lay. Your turn. And don't spare the detail.'

Elbows on the table, she cups her cheeks in her hands. Meanwhile, my latte turns sour in the pit of my gut. She knows he was good in bed? Does that mean she's had first-hand experience? I can share breakfast but not my men. *Or proclivities*, I think more frighteningly.

'What do you mean *you know he was good*?' I ask casually.

'Because, not moments ago, I was recounting some hilarious tale, and you were somewhere else—staring off into the distance. There wasn't even a flicker of recognition as I told you I'd recently taken part in an orgy at the local rugby club. I told you I'd screwed the entire team. Then both of them—home and away! You were totally zoned out. Face it, you're still fuck drunk, Louise.'

My relief is swift as I grab my cup, grimacing at the taste of cold coffee.

'I imagine your vagina has had a thorough seeing to.'

'And it's now closed!' The cup clatters against the saucer as I duck my head.

'He was that good?' replies a laughing Flora, her hand gesture the universal sign for "too hot to touch".

'I mean the topic of my sex life is closed!'

The next hour passes without further comment on last night, though I sense Flo is just biding her time. I've never spoken to her about my past, not that I've much to tell, but this morning's breakfast seems to have signalled to her that things are about to change. I'm sure she isn't done with her interrogation.

As we walk home, the familiarity of the area surprises me. It seems my stranger and I live in the same borough. The realisation causes me a disconcerting thrill, especially as new memories and sensations continue to arise.

Last night, after he'd led me into his house, things had seemed stilted and awkward for a few minutes, at least from my side. Somehow, we'd begun a silly word game, and I'm not sure if we'd gotten off track, or if he'd meant things to happen as they did because not long after, he'd led me upstairs.

The Night Before

One

LOUISE

'You seem nervous.'

The prospect seems to amuse him, but he's right. It had seemed much easier in the club—easier in the dark of the cab. It felt natural to play along with his promises, the kind of promises that might sound like threats to other girls.

I want to fuck you until you can't stand.

Sign me up for some of that, but do so quickly because my tequila bravery won't last forever. Maybe the change of pace has me feeling off balance. His reaction is like the tango; quick-quick, slow. Is it natural to want to be pinned against the door? Held tight in his hands and fucked hard on all fours? And why is he watching me so? Whatever the reason, his eyes remind me of a tiger. And I'm feeling deliciously like his prey.

'Do you play?' I ask, my eyes alighting on a chess set. Expensive looking and highly polished, the set appears to be in the middle of a game. 'What?' I look up at his low chuckle. 'What's funny?

'Oh, nothing,' comes his reply, though his expression clearly says otherwise. 'I do play. Chess and . . . other things.'

'So cryptic.' I take another sip of my wine as I continue my examination of the room. Pale, sumptuous sofas, a large oriental rug, and abstract, original artworks. From a chair, he watches me with a dark-eyed confidence as I move around the room. 'I like games,' I say, filling the silence. 'Or at least I did when I was small. Mostly.' At the incline of his brow, I realise my tone is tinged with bitterness. 'My brother and I are the kind of *fight to the death siblings.*'

'I prefer games of an adult nature and find wagers add to the appeal.'

'*I'll bet* you've made that an art form,' I say, ignoring his meaning. 'Such a sultry purr,' I tease, my wave of wine bravery carrying me on. 'I imagine you're very popular with the ladies.'

'I do okay,' he answers, his eyes heated and hungry as they travel over me. 'And some nights I do more than okay.'

A little overwhelmed and a lot turned on, I plant myself on the sofa opposite him. I have the insane desire to say *let's fuck*, but instead, I manage, 'Then let's play.'

'I don't think you're ready for the kind of games I play.'

'Then why do you think I'm here?'

'To fuck.'

'And you're quite particular in your tastes?' Despite my cool demeanour, nerve endings seem to pulse at the surface of my skin as I recall his earlier words. *I'll tie you up. Watch every line of your body grow taut with an elegant distress.*

'I believe I said I like hurting pretty girls.'

'Maybe I'm a pretty girl who likes to be hurt.' I don't think my voice has ever sounded so sexual.

'Maybe you are,' he answers reasonably. 'Or maybe you just think you are.'

Oh, God, I am—I want to be. 'Oh, a dilemma. Am I kinky or vanilla? Where would your money lie?'

'I'm trying to decide.'

'Play me to find out,' I challenge, swirling the wine in my glass. 'Cards . . . poker . . . you decide. The winner gets to decide how we fuck.'

'To the victor goes the spoils?'

That sounds a little open-ended. I'm not sure I'm ready for that—all my openings would probably be ended, for sure.

He's smirking as I look up. I hadn't said that out loud, had I?

'Terms to be negotiated following defeat,' I add, ignoring the possibility.

'I look forward to it,' he purrs.

'Don't fret. I won't be *too* hard on you.'

His deep burst of laughter resounds through the room. 'I like a woman with confidence. Though I'm not sure I have any playing cards here,' he says as his eyes drift from mine, scanning the room. 'Something simpler, perhaps.' His gaze moves back to me. 'A word association game.'

'That sounds like . . . ' *something my brother and I would play on long journeys in the car*. Or in other words, not the kind of adult fun I was expecting.

'Trust me.' His smirk reappears. 'It'll be fun.'

'If you're after a glimpse into my psyche, you'll be disappointed.'

'Sweetheart, by the end of this evening, I'll know you inside and out.' His tone drips with innuendo, but before I have a chance to parry, he lays down the rules. 'The first word that comes into your head, and hesitation earns you a forfeit.'

'What kind?' I ask, frowning back at him.

'You lose clothing.'

'Oh.' My frown eases. 'Prepare to get naked, then.'

'Peach.' There was no hint of challenge in the word; I almost didn't realise we'd started. I was expecting something smutty—rude or risqué.

'Fuzz?' Unsettled, my response sounds like a question. I get the sense he's enjoying my reaction, laughing at me somehow.

'Knife.' Eyes are bright with amusement, and his tone gives nothing away as I think, *I don't recall Christian Grey playing these sorts of games*, and almost forget to answer.

'Oh, er, edge!'

'Oh, dear.' This sounds more taunt than a consolation. 'That's your first one.' His gaze touches my mouth then dips to my breasts, his smile growing in depth and deviance, halting the breath in my chest.

'What? No way!' I more hot than bothered by his bold attentions. I find myself squeezing my thighs, desire coursing through me like an uncertain thrill. *New feelings—powerful, too.* 'Well, barely,' I add, tucking my calves closer to the chair as I reach for my glass.

'Don't mutter. It's unbecoming.' His accent seems to clip the words into a command, the admonishment making my stomach twist. I have to force myself to sit still—to not squirm in my seat. But, God, I want to. Far too much.

'Rules are rules.' He leans further back in his chair, spreading his arms across the back of it. His gaze dips from my face to my chest again. 'Take it off.'

Nothing in the history of me has every sounded so darkly tempting.

'Rules *are* rules,' I agree, albeit a little breathlessly, as my fingers reach to loosen a pearly button on the placket of my blouse. 'Even if I do think you're making them up.' My fingers shake with the weight of his instruction—with the position I'm about to place myself in.

It's been a while since I'd had a one-night stand. Hell, it's been a while since I'd had a man between my legs at all. Surely, it wasn't supposed to be this unravelling. Surely, I wasn't supposed to feel this pull to him. This isn't the tequila; I'm lucid enough to know what I'm doing. Sober enough to feel the subtle zing of our chemistry, the electric-like pulse dancing in the air.

This night is confusing—his intentions hard to decipher—but the bulge in his pants suggests it'll be worth it in the end. So worth it.

His dark eyes watch on as I pop the last button of my blouse. Unfurling my legs, I stand and slide it from my shoulders. It flutters silently to the carpeted floor. Half undressed, I perch myself back on the very edge of the chair, resisting the urge to hide myself by folding my arms across my chest.

And he just . . . stares. Doesn't give me a hint to his thoughts, just watches silently. I don't know what to think, and I don't know what to feel, though my body seems to speak for me as my nipples pebble under the pale lace and between my legs begins to throb.

'Come.' The word is low and raspy, and my response is almost instant.

'Yes! Please and often.' As though magnetized, my eyes flick to his crotch. 'Or I could lend you a hand?' My mouth waters at the prospect, and that little snippet is new. I don't usually think of blow jobs like lollipops. 'You didn't strike me as a brat.' His brow furrows. 'It's a little late in the evening to start acting like one now.' His gaze alights briefly on his watch as he slides his arms from the back of the chair, reaching to a side table and his own glass.

'I thought it was an invitation.' My words are flippant; I don't like his cool expression—not one bit. I want to force a reaction and desire, quite viscerally, his hands on me.

'An invitation to put you over my knee, perhaps.' Taking a sip of his wine, he hides a slow smile behind his glass. 'You're making this too easy. Anyone would think you want to lose.'

'No one likes to lose.' As I cross my legs, his gaze follows the motion.

'You'd be surprised,' he replies cryptically. 'I'll say again, *come.*'

'Here?' I try not to cringe as the word trails off to a question. He's barely touched me since we entered the house, and the longer we play this silly game, the more desperate I feel. I have the insane desire to push him back against the chair and climb all over him, to take control . . . But before the thought is fully formed, he speaks again.

'Good.'

'Oh, thanks,' I answer automatically, sliding a lock of hair behind my ear, my head simmering full of half-thoughts. An instant later, I bring my mouth to my hand to swallow my giggle. '*Oh-oh,*' I sing. 'I did it again.'

He sighs quietly as he places his glass back. 'I'm beginning to think you aren't taking this seriously at all.'

Despite his weary tone, I can almost see the cracks in his composure. So I goad. 'Come on; this is supposed to be a game. Lighten up! I just—'

'Thought you'd manipulate the situation?' In an instant, his fingers are on my chin, his face so close that his breath blows over me, bringing warmth and whisky and want. 'Were you hoping to make me laugh? Get me to fuck you on your terms?' His lips brush my cheek so lightly in contrast to his words. 'Try again, love, and this is your last warning. Good.'

My heart stammers as he leans away, my mouth following suit as his finger trails down between my breasts. 'G-girl.'

'And that's your second.' His mouth curls fully this time, his smile like sin itself.

I close my eyes and swallow, my competitive streak rising to the surface immediately. 'No. No way.'

'You paused,' he replies, amused. 'That earns a forfeit. I feel his smile as his mouth slides against mine, once more in the barest of teasing touches, and my eyes flutter closed in the anticipation of more.

'*G-girl*, while adorable, means you forfeit.'

He pulls back, eyes almost level with mine, and I realise they aren't actually dark, but a shade of blue a little less intense than indigo. My breath halts as he draws his index finger down the length of my skirt from thigh to knee. His fingers toy with the edge before slipping under the hem.

'My lovely loser.' As his thumb begins trailing soft circles on the inside of my knee, it takes every ounce of my strength to stop from leaning back against the chair and opening my legs. 'Take your skirt off.'

I'm nobody's loser, lovely or not, even if a part of me wants to lose to him. Against the desire swimming through my veins, I place my hand around his wrist and slide it free. Leaning back, he follows my movement as I cross one leg over the other, bending forward to unfasten the buckle of a singular, though spiked heel, red Mary Jane. I flick it from the ends of my toes to the floor, and as it lands between his feet, I lean back on my hands.

'A pair constitutes one item of clothing,' he purrs with the shadow of a smile.

'No,' I begin, preparing my argument. 'A shoe is a shoe; one shoe, one item.' I add a light shrug as if this were the sanest of discussions.

'So let me ask you; when you're down to your bra, will you lift out an individual tit?'

I stifle a giggle, though I can't halt my growing smile. The few months I've been in London have been confusing. While I hadn't expected to become a sucker for every guy in a sharp suit, I'd expected to be swooning hard over Englishmen. It hadn't happened that way—some of the accents I've encountered are downright undecipherable! But his accent, this nameless stranger? It's enough to make a girl's ovaries quiver.

Despite this strange game, this evening is exciting, seducing, and sort of illicit. An item to check off my bucket list?

Trade good reason for the chance of kinky sex. ✓

But this? This is priceless. The last time I'd heard someone say tit in that accent, I'd been watching TCM. A guy in tweed plus-fours with binoculars hanging from his neck. I say, there's a lesser-spotted tit in that tree, he'd proclaimed.

I have a small patch of freckles across my chest; did that make me lesser-spotted or more? This time, a giggle escaped along with my ridiculous thought. Judging by his expression, there's not much point in letting him in on the joke. Instead, I sigh softly and bend forward to loosen the other shoe.

'Remind me never to play Scrabble with you,' I complain.

His response is one word. 'Body.'

Now we're talking.

'Butter,' I reply instantly, images flitting through my head of creamy, soft skin.

'Shiver.'

'Delight.' *Delightful shivers in the dark, skin sliding against skin.*

'Quiver.' Was it my imagination, or was his voice a little rougher that time?

'Naked,' I whisper, yearning to be the same. *Naked and in his arms.*

'Throbbing.' He swallows deeply, and *that* I don't miss.

'Pussy . . . I mean, ache.' My cheeks burn instantly. It's hardly a sophisticated choice of word.

'*Tsk, tsk, tsk.*' He draws out the admonishment with a slow shake of his head. 'Hesitation number three. Though I could let that one slide, if you show me where you *ache.*'

Without answering, I stand and pull on the zip of my skirt and, with an exaggerated shimmy, slide it over my hips, anticipation chasing the fabric across my skin. As I step from its dark pool, his look of dark triumph makes my insides churn.

'I'm pleased you aren't a sore loser.' His voice is low in register, his words smooth, like water running over rocks.

'Who says I'm losing?' In two sensuous strides, I'm standing between his splayed legs. 'And who says I'm—'

'Sore?' he finishes as I climb astride his lap. 'Maybe not yet.' He brushes the hair from my face, an act so very tender compared to what he does next. Hand wrapped around the back of my neck, he pulls me down to him. 'Because a gentleman can always be tempted.'

My eyes roll closed as his mouth moves to my neck where he groans the word, 'Deep.'

'Water,' I answer as, his hands on my hips, he swallows my word with a kiss.

'Chastise.' His tone is even, but I'm not fooled. That isn't indifference I feel between my thighs.

'Thrilling.' And I mean it. I want it all—I want him.

'Im—*pact*.' He punctuates the word with a slap against my ass, our bodies clashing with the blow. My arms slide around his neck, for fear I'll be swept away.

'Whimper.' My voice sounds strangled as I peel away from his chest when his hand tightens on my numb yet smarting skin.

'Bruise.' The word is almost a question as his large hand squeezes again.

'Badge.' This one is on instinct as I close my eyes and imagine it there. A handprint, red and distinct. Fingers splayed. To be viewed the next day for private pleasure another day.

'Arse.' His hand tightens against my flesh as if he can't get enough of it.

'British.' Another answer purely on instinct; I school my face, expecting a pithy comment, but I'm startled by his laughter instead.

'Are you trying to tell me something?'

'I like the way you say ass,' I reply simply.

'And I like your *arse*.' He grabs it again, this time with both hands. 'What I would do to it,' he growls, running his fingers down to where my cheek meets thigh. 'Fingers.' This sounds like a deliberation. I want certainty.

'Get off,' I reply somewhere between a groan and a sigh. This isn't an instruction to stop.

'That's two words,' he chastises, teasing the slip of lace between my legs. *Teasing the edge of my control.*

'Don't care.' I offer him two more. Desperate, my lace-covered chest heaves under his nose as his fingers catch the elastic seam of my panties and slip inside.

'Wet,' he growls as his finger sweeps my seam. We both feel the evidence of it—hear the slick sound of my desire.

'Wanting.' The atmosphere around us thickens, banding us together with lust.

'Wanting what, I wonder?' He barely moves his finger, yet wetness still pools between my legs.

'You,' I moan, lowering myself onto his hand.

'Fuck.' Savage and hard, he spits the word out, his need rising along with mine.

'Heaven!' I cry out as his fingers push deep inside.

My arms still linked around his neck, I melt into him, over him—cling to him like glue. He holds me there with one arm tight around my waist. His fingers work between my legs; my muscles tightening in testament to how much I want this.

His hand slides from my waist and grabs my ponytail, pulling and tilting my head to one side.

'Sadistic,' he grates out, his jaw flexing and his eyes burning bright.

'Affection.' Another word on instinct, my mind purely absent, my body in charge of *all* the things.

'Bedroom,' he growls, and all I can respond with is a hissed, *'Yes.'*

Two

LOUISE

I pause as we reach the bedroom door, the heat of his body almost burning me from behind. There's no turning back—not that I want to. I just like how close he is and how he crowds my space. As his finger grazes my hip, desire rolls across my skin, and I'm brought back to the fact that I'm clad in only my underwear while he's still fully clothed. *He's playing power games*, I think. *And for once, I'm in the mood to lose*

'Are you sure you won't tell me your name?' His hands curl around my hips, his lips finding my shoulder with a gentle kiss.

'No.' I whirl around to face him, bringing me into the room. 'It's my turn to choose—bed.'

'You don't want to know my name?' he purrs, ignoring my direction. Biting the inside of my lip, I shake my head. Because that would be too easy and a little too real. I'm relieved when he doesn't press me again.

'Stead,' he answers. He leans back against the doorframe, sliding both hands into his pockets. I think he's playing it cool until I see where his gaze lies.

There, above the bed, hang a set of leather cuffs—seeing them was partly the reason I'd spun around to face him in the first place, my heart jumping with a mixture of fear and delight.

The cuffs, their leather patina seems polished to a mahogany stain. Well-used, well-worn, and obviously cared for. I try not to smile, my current aspirations being almost the same. Would he use me well? Wear me out? Meet my needs and care for me tonight? All without even knowing my name?

As his eyes remain level on the leather, I begin to wonder what he's seeing there. Is he remembering other women wearing them? More experienced women—those who know instinctively how to play these games? The thought lingers and expands as images of my own making play through my head. This man with a redhead—a blonde. A harem of women of which I'm just one.

'Should . . . I mean. Maybe . . .' My words are halting and flustered, spoken to drown out the images and jealous thoughts.

As his eyes rise, I realise my mistake. He smiles, equal parts beautiful and brutal, but it's a smile that doesn't extend to his gaze.

'I thought we were done,' I almost whine.

'Darling, you need to choose which piece you're losing next.'

His tone is filled with desire; my skin burns where his eyes touch, and I find my stance changes immediately as my hip cocks in attitude. Outwardly pissed but inwardly thrilled, something inside me flares instantly. *Rebellion.*

'From forfeits to consequences.' He sighs quietly. 'I do believe you're trying to force my hand.'

I can't restrain my smile, quite liking the sound of that. Force his hand on me. In me. Around the base of my neck. But then I realise my behaviour isn't aiding my cause but hampering it, so trail my finger down my body between the two garments in question as though I've not yet decided. The natural progression would be to lose my bra. It's what he's probably expecting, and the opposite of what I'll give.

I bend forward and, with a slight wiggle that's purely for show, slide my panties from my hips.

'Stop,' he demands suddenly; his words clipped and concise.

I partially straighten with a questioning look. Stop the action, or does he want my response to the word?

Stop, go? Stop, clock? Stop messing about and let's fuck?

Panties around my knees can't be a sexy look, yet one glance at his heated expression tells me that can't really be true. Something warm and liquid blooms deep in the pit of my belly, spreading out under my skin. Maybe this is like the cuffs—like a restraint? I widen my stance a little to hold the fabric in place, or at least that's what I'll tell myself—feeling awkward, embarrassed, and more than a little wet.

He pushes off from the wall, stepping so close our bodies almost touch. The moment is endless, the heat in his gaze like a brand. His hand rises almost in slow motion as one fingertip brushes my sternum.

'Temperance,' he murmurs.

'Overrated,' I rasp, leaning into his touch. We both watch as his fingers travel down my body, grazing the soft skin on my stomach down to my open thighs.

'Restraint,' he cautions, pulling gently on the small strip of hair between my legs.

'Trying.' The word hits the air between a sigh and a tremble.

'Would that be trying for restraint or just trying to *be restrained*?' He steps around me, circling my body slowly as his hand trails my waist, and I feel the weight of his gaze. 'Well?'

'What?' The word is strangled—garbled—somewhere between an actual word and a cry as, at the very same moment, he brings his hand to my ass. Hard. Fast.

His arm catches my elbow as I stumble, the sound of the impact echoing in the room. My cheeks sting like shame and the impact ricochets straight to my groin, lingering there in a gratuitous throb. I think I might whimper, moan—something.

As he steps away, I lurch toward him, the flimsy garment tying my limbs forgotten in lust. No one has ever had this effect on me as every cell in my being screams for more from him. Desire replaces anger and shame as I wrap my hands in his pristine shirt and whisper, 'Again.'

His response is wrong by yesterday's standards, though everything that's right for tonight as he grasps my forearms. *Held in his hands, not in his arms.* This isn't an embrace as he kisses me slowly, kisses me tenderly, an action as soft as his next is hard.

'You're trying my patience.' Twisting me around, he pushes me forward and down against the bed.

My heart is in my throat, my pulse thundering everywhere as he pushes himself between my legs. Leaning into me, he forced my body to sink flat, and the pressure of his teeth on my shoulder is a sign of my position. A sign of his control. I give it to him gladly, whimpering as his lips trail and graze my neck as his hands lift mine above my head.

The loosening of his pants. A rustle of foil.

My panties slide the rest of the way from my legs.

I think to myself, *he'll loosen my bra at any moment*, when he slides one knee between mine, spreading me wider. A hand under my hips, he lifts me in readiness from the bed.

'Fuck,' he growls, all civility gone from his tone.

'Pleasure.' Is my response required at all?

'For mine. Not yours.'

Too late, I think, hoping this time the utterance isn't out loud.

Grabbing handfuls of sheet, I anchor myself, moaning loudly as he pushes inside. I'm so wet that my body offers no resistance to his power, unless you count the small smile I curl into the fist by my mouth.

'Fuck.' His tone is low and rough as though he's fighting for control. 'I can feel you pulsing around my cock.'

If his words weren't enough to make me moan aloud, his next action is. I cry out in pure ecstasy in response to the snap of his hips.

'You're. So. Fucking. Tight.' He punctuates his growls with his movements as I begin to soar.

I thrust my hips backwards, my arms still near my head in my desperation to please him. In my desperation for more. For harder, for deeper. For his teeth against my skin. His hand snakes around my waist, pulling me upwards and back onto him. In my desperation, my movements become frantic, his fingers curling around the fragile column of my neck, stilling me. I know I shouldn't like it, and that I should say so right now. But at this moment, the action feels more like an embrace. Especially as his fingers tenderly touch my jaw, turning my head. Somehow, my breasts balance free above my bra; he teases the hard peaks as we kiss. A moment of slow, tender lips and wet swipes of tongue before he begins to move again. Small, precise, yet powerful thrusts. I feel him deep inside—feel his every muscle twitch and flex as he holds me close. I'm a doll in his arms—something fragile and delicate. Something to be positioned at his whim.

His, my body screams. *His for the night.*

At the thought, my breathing becomes shallow, my muscles holding him tight enough to make him groan.

'That's right,' he rasps. 'Let me feel your pleasure. Give it to me.'

From china doll to animal, I buck against him, desperate to take it all. Frantic to get to that edge— the feeling is white hot, pulsing through my limbs and under my skin as he holds me there, but the friction isn't enough as he stills his hips.

'You need this, don't you, sweetheart?' In the absence of words, I moan as I writhe against him. 'But good girls say please.'

With one hand holding my neck, he slides the other between my legs. His fingers are light and deft and something other than what I need. I buck against him, desperate for pressure—for fast and hard fingertips. For his teeth at my neck. For his cock to sink into me. To push me into the bed.

'You're so *slick*.' His words are as soft as a caress, his strong arms holding me tight, preventing me from moving, from slamming into him. *From using my own fingertips*. My breath is short, my chest heaving as need tightens my skin. I do need it—I need it all. But a good girl? Can I be? For him? 'I can feel your need pulsing around my cock. Your clit pounds against my fingertips. I can make it so good for you—'

'Please!' I cry, the word expelled in a sob. I close my eyes at how desperate I feel. How desperate I sound. 'Please. I'll do anything.'

'Like that, yes,' he hisses with one hand on my neck, one sliding between my legs.

I see stars, the universe, as his fingers slide through my wetness, touching where we meet. I detonate—coming so hard that my cries sound anguished and desperate. I writhe against him, singing his praises and chanting my relief.

One minute, I'm in heaven, and the next, I'm pushed down to my hands and knees. There's no time for post-coital bliss as he tears another climax from me. His hands hard on my breasts, the man rides me, driving inside over and over again. A harsh advance. A pounding. A pummelling. And I love it.

No kissing.

No stroking.

No endearments.

No words.

Nothing but our pleasure and surrender melting us across the bed.

Playing His Games

Chapter One

DAN

Hello, my name is Dan. And I own a kinky sex club.

That's not how I introduced myself to her last night. Nor did I mention I was the owner of Mede, the club we were sitting in. We'd never met before, and she wasn't aware of my reputation, my past, or proclivities. She didn't even seem to know about the club next door, let alone my ownership. The Lion's Den is . . . an exclusive lifestyle club, or sex club, some would say. For most, it's a place perhaps more myth than anything. A place where an assortment of appetites and tastes are catered for by way of a rigorous vetting system. And, of course, an extortionate membership fee.

I push away from my desk. After spending hours looking at figures, and not the mathematical kind, I'm done. I'd spent the morning interviewing for new staff for both clubs. Some would say it's unethical to ask candidates to attend our group interviews in their underwear, but it's important to know our future employees are comfortable in both their sexuality and their own skin. Wait and bar staff within the Den need to be unfazed by nakedness as well as prepared to see things that cannot be unseen.

The afternoon had been taken up by meetings with a couple of talent management reps. Patrons of the Den pay a pretty packet to be members, and I like to make sure they're provided with entertainment beyond their fellow member exhibitionists.

The sun is setting, the club a hum of activity in preparation for Saturday night. Still in my office overlooking the main salon, I'm still trying to clear my head of last night. All day long, my mystery blonde has occupied space in my head, leaving me little else to concentrate on. It's odd. I usually find a little dominance leaves me in a productive mood, but the opposite has been true today.

Last night was . . . different. And for that, I'm glad. She may not have given me her name, but she gifted me her secrets.

As I'd stirred from sleep this morning and sensed I was alone in my bed, for once, it didn't feel like relief. I was oddly disappointed not to wake wrapped in strange girl and cotton sheets. It was an unusual and unwelcome realisation for someone who, more often than not, will order his bed partners a cab shortly following the deed or scene. Quite honestly, I don't often have use for a bed when fucking. But last night had been different. Despite my reputation, I haven't found anyone who had interested me like this girl.

Louise. An American from Massachusetts, or was it Maine? I can't recall, not that she'd given me her name at all. We'd both had a bit to drink before we'd gotten to those details, and I'd been both intrigued and amused when she'd pressed her finger to my lips when pushed.

'It's better this way,' she'd whispered.

An unusual point of view, but maybe anonymity added to the experience for her. But there are other ways to skin a cat. *Or find a name.* I'd watched her last night in the public bar, dressed more for the office than a club. She'd looked carefree and a little reckless and, as the evening progressed, in the mood to fuck.

The whole evening was a step out of the ordinary for me. Let's just say, the past two years has put me off casual fucking. That's not to say I don't play the odd scene or screw the occasional woman when the urge arises, but on the whole, I've become more solitary lately. *Not that most people would believe this. They like the myth, not the man.*

Last night was uncommon for a lot of reasons. I'd intended to spend the evening at work and, as such, had planned to check in on both managers before heading to my office next door. Plans had changed when I'd met a client on the way in to the more mainstream of my clubs. He's a regular at The Den and was in the mood to chat. Perhaps client doesn't cover it. Kit Tremaine is a hotshot hotelier I'd been talking my expansion plans over with. So I'd gone to the bar to have a quick word with the bar manager on duty but also to order a round of drinks. As I'd waited for my order, I found myself eavesdropping on the conversation of two girls at the bar. Like piano keys, one light, one dark, and although they weren't looking my way, I sensed they were talking about me . . .

'*He's pretty cute,*' the blonde had said in an American accent that was hard to place. '*But aren't they all? Over here, I mean. Especially when they talk.*'

Her friend replied with something so ridiculous I found myself fighting a burgeoning laugh.

'*How many times must I tell you? That's not what we want them to use their mouths for.*' The dark-haired girl threw her head back, laughing throatily.

I found myself smiling along, something that doesn't happen much these days. Maybe I'd become cynical. Maybe that's what owning a sex club meant. That and . . . well, I'm not thinking about *her* today.

But I like a woman who knows what she wants. One who isn't afraid to say or admit. And last night? Louise certainly did.

'*Sweetie,*' the dark one called out to the new barman, Trey, gesturing to both of their glasses. '*Two more of these, if you wouldn't mind. And if you're a good little boy, I'll buy you a nightcap later.*'

I doubt she'd have been the only one hitting on Trey. I'd heard he was quite popular with both sexes. Good looking and affable. And apparently incredibly well-hung. Trey's expression barely altered but for the incline of one fair brow. I wondered what his response would have been had his boss not been present while also considering giving him a trial shift at The Den.

'*That man?*' said the dark-haired girl. '*The best sex I've ever had. He made my eyes roll so far back*

*in my head I swear I could see the Farrow and
Ball.'*

*'Dare I ask?' Trepidation filled the blonde's
words.*

'The wallpaper, love.'

*'Come on,' Louise, as I'd find out later, pleaded.
'There's a booth free. I need to sit down; my feet are
killing me.' She'd turned quite suddenly, her blonde
ponytail swinging over one shoulder, and fuck if
the sight of that didn't do something to my dick.*

I love a ponytail wrapped in my fist. Love how the
first tug creates a resistance and crave how quickly
it melts when accompanied by a kiss. *By teeth
against her bottom lip.* As she walked away, my
eyes followed her high heels, her tanned and toned
legs, and her round arse . . . all the way to the booth
next to where Kit was sitting, putting the girl in my
direct line of sight.

I took my seat and watched, waiting for her to
return my gaze. Observed as, menu in hand, she
narrowed her eyes as though experiencing trouble
reading it. I wondered if she'd left her glasses at the
office—they were dressed so. I wondered if she were
the kind of woman who wore cotton or lace.
Wondered how she'd feel wrapped around me. At
some point, she'd responded to her friend—I hadn't
heard the question, but assumed they were still on
the topic of the barman.

*'Not really my type. I prefer someone a little
more . . . professional looking. My downfall? A
man in a sharp suit.'*

The pitch of her friend's response had been too low for me to catch, but when Louise raised her head, our gazes met. Lifting an enquiring brow, I'd pointedly glanced down. Yes, my shirt was open at the neck, but my suit? Tailor made. Saville Row all the way. Her mouth formed a soft *"o"* at my suggestion, eliciting a twitch in my pants. I'd felt the urge to introduce myself—I do have a soft spot for disconcerted women—but I'd managed to curtail the urge.

Lately, I've found it's best not to get involved, no matter how tempting the prospect sounds. She seemed to make a concerted effort to ignore me from then on. And she was good at it, too; her eyes didn't meet mine once. And I watched. And stayed, telling myself I was enjoying Kit's company and the change of scenery. More drinks were ordered, others joining the pair shortly after; men and women, all dressed similarly. My theory of an office outing confirmed. One guy—grey suit, fair hair— made a play for Louise, but she rebuffed him easily as though his interest was a long-standing joke. I could see at once it wasn't, for one party, at least, but grey suit played along then moved along to other more willing prospects.

I couldn't make myself leave after that. Not even as Kit left for next door and his assignation with the married couple he's currently fucking. I sat alone, observing the group dynamic from a distance while biting back the need building inside me. I'd like to think fate rather than tequila pushed her into my lap. Despite splashing me with her cocktail, she wasn't what I'd call drunk, but uninhibited. Definitely well lubricated, her attitude a complete turnaround. Together, we'd drank more, and it was she who'd suggested, rather euphemistically, that we retire to somewhere quieter.

My mouth curls into a half smile as I recall her coy suggestion. And her reaction as I'd answered.

I told her I'd fuck her, but that I enjoy sex a certain way. While I hadn't expected her to run from me screaming, I had foreseen her at least drawing away. And true to my experience, her smile faltered as was often the way with the inexperienced. No matter how daring they think themselves. I'd leaned back in my chair, allowing her to move from my embrace, but she didn't move. She'd just stared at me from under her lashes, the light from the dance floor turning her hazel gaze from a mild flicker to a flame. To my absolute surprise and delight, she'd asked me in a small voice to elaborate.

Fuck. I have work to do. I can't sit here reminiscing all day. I head to my private bathroom and throw a couple of handfuls of water against my face. In the mirror, my tired expression stares back at me. Tired and behind on work, but so worth it as I get lost in the feeling of my abdomen tightening against the roundness of her arse.

'It wasn't real,' I tell my reflection.

Just because I can recall every tremble and shudder doesn't mean we had a connection. And she didn't tell me her name for a reason. We were each just fulfilling a primal need last night. She was merely walking on the wild side, and I was breaking a dry spell.

And we'd both been pretty clear on our desires.

She'd wanted to be bound. Tied like a sacrificial lamb. I'd told her I'd fuck her for my pleasure. And to both of our satisfaction, I had.

I'd fucked her thoroughly while limiting her movements and not allowing her to contribute to the act. *Which isn't strictly true*, my expression reminds me, an almost rueful smile reflects back. My cock stiffens as I recall the sensation of her insides tightening greedily, almost pushing me over the edge. And that was all *her* pleasure, the lines blurring further as I'd slammed into her again and again. Unbidden, my mind slips back to that precise moment . . .

As I'd fast approached the last point for lucid thought, I'd gripped her tits tight, and she'd groaned. Sweat glistened against her neck, and I'd bent forward, tasting it with my tongue before biting her perfect flesh.

I'd drawn my body lower against hers as she'd climbed higher, imploding powerfully, calling out, her body willing mine on. I'd pushed her arse higher, my hands tight on the flesh of her hips, pulling her back, her body pounding to my very hilt. I'd come hard, shooting hotly, snarling and grinding, growling obscenities and calling out abhorrent words.

Her delicate hands were gold against the pale of the sheets, balled into fists as she writhed under me in the last throes of her own ecstasy, milking sensation from me. Collapsing next to her, I'd held her, my body already mourning the loss of her wet warmth. My heart beat wildly as I'd moved the mass of tangled hair from her cheek. She was smiling, her eyes almost closed, and on the very edge of sleep.

'Was awesome,' she'd murmured, her tone filled with that uniquely sleepy satisfaction that only comes from one kind of physical exhaustion. She'd kissed her own fingers then placed them against my lips. The action was unexpected and somehow more intimate than what we'd just done. I caught her retreating hand and brought them back to my mouth, kissing the tips before returning her hand to the bed. 'Didn't use the cuffs,' she murmured, so sleepily subdued.

The truth was I hadn't thought; I'd just needed to be inside her at that point. Instead of admitting this, I'd just growled, 'Maybe you weren't a good enough girl.'

She snorted, might've even rolled her eyes, but when she didn't rise to the bait, I kissed her forehead and murmured, 'Next time.'

In the bathroom mirror, my expression blinks back as I recall that, to both our satisfaction, they'd been used later during the night. But I'd expected—wanted—there to be at least one more next time before morning fully broke and we parted.

In my arms, she shifted, and her eyelids became heavy. I hadn't wanted her to leave. She'd rolled away, seemingly not the type for post-coital canoodling. Ordinarily, this would've been more than fine, but for some reason, this time it didn't feel right. I'd pushed the thoughts to the back of my mind, wondering if I should loosen her bra, but then she'd sat up, feeding her hands behind her back. Pulling the bra down her arms, she'd shoved it against my chest and immediately lay down again, releasing a very soft breath.

Standing and stripping completely, I'd dealt with the first of the night's condoms then slid back under the warm sheets. Pulling her body to me, I'd breathed out in relief at the touch of her warm skin. Settling into the soft pillow, I was utterly content.

Back in the softly lit bathroom on this cold Sunday, I suddenly realise something monumental. Something I'd hereto missed. I'd taken her back to my house—my place of sanctuary. I hadn't fucked her in my apartment, here, above the club. How come I'd only just realised that?

Chapter Two

LOUISE

Everyone has one-night stands

At home on Sunday evening, I curled into the arm of the sofa with a glass of wine by my side and a pile of work reports on my lap, my mind still lingering over last night. The thoughts are seductive, and my physical reactions to them very real. I rub my bare arms, telling myself my skin still tingled from my second cold shower of the day, the result of Flo using all the hot water, rather than some kind of sensory memory.

'You're sure you wouldn't like to tag along?' Flora asks, fastening the clasp of her earring. 'You know what they say about all work and no play.'

'Who's they?' I counter, not really expecting a response.

'Luke from the office, for one.'

Flo's use of an even tone causes me to lift my eyes from the row of columns holding my attention. Sliding my glasses higher on my nose, I realise she's wearing my Michael Kors dress. *I knew she'd been hunting for more than my fedora yesterday.*

'You don't mind if I borrow it, do you?' she asks, smoothing the material against her thighs.

'Would it matter if I said yes?' I remonstrate.

'You wouldn't because you're a darling and I love you for it.'

'And you're the bitch who stole all the hot water. Again.'

Laughing, Flo murmurs something about it not being her fault the boiler was old, and that she'd mention it to her father. I decide not to point out she already had, spending the money on a long weekend in Marbella because *she longed to feel the sun again.*

'Well, I'm off,' Flo says, sliding her clutch from the console table. 'You're sure I can't tempt you to a couple of glasses of pinot noir in the company of a cute venture capitalist?'

'You know he's likely *investing* in a quick fuck later on, right?'

'That's what I'm counting on, sweets,' she responds, her words followed by a tinkling laugh. 'And he has a friend.'

'Feel free to pass on my heartiest congratulations. And no,' I reiterate as she looks about to speak again. 'Money men have no soul.'

'No, but they have plenty of coinage,' she replies, rubbing her index finger and thumb together to emphasise her point. Flo spends her life perpetually overspent, even working full time and receiving an allowance from her dear old dad. She's the essence of high maintenance. 'Lou?' she questions.

'Please don't call me that. It makes me sound like a public convenience.'

'Fine. *Louise.* Please don't tell me you're going to spend your evening staring at work reports?'

'Then don't ask.'

'How about I—'

'Oh, no thanks,' I retort as quick as a flash. 'Not after last time.'

'What? Is it a crime to ask one's friend if she'd like to see some penis pictures? It's what I look at when I'm bored. Anyway,' she adds, pretending to be annoyed. 'I was only going to loan you that book I told you about.'

'The book of dicks? Not thanks. I'll be fine.' I make a shooing motion with my hand. I don't need to borrow literature. My Kindle is kind of heavy with a very specific kind. 'Get gone.'

'Fine,' she responds, sticking out her tongue. 'Some people just refuse to be helped.' She giggles, ducking as the scatter cushion I throw narrowly misses her head. 'Ciao, darling. Don't wait up for me!'

I return to the row of numbers, trying to find my place again. I've never taken Flora up on her offer of arranged dates, but for once, I feel a little out of place. But I'd promised myself this year in England would be one of focus—of culture and promise—not about me. Yet my mind can't help but return to one man in particular. A man of good looks and urbane charm. A man with a dominant streak that called to me.

And I hadn't even asked him his name.

I'd hoped last night would help not hinder how I've felt lately. I'd expected to feel unwound rather than the other way around. Taking off my glasses, I rub my eyes and sigh. What was it he—my stranger—had said?

There's freedom in a little bondage. Sometimes, a person needs to be tied to feel free.

Must be wonderful to allow yourself, I find myself thinking. And remembering how freeing it had been.

Chapter Three

LOUISE

The last thing I want to do is hurt you.

Friday afternoon. The week has passed so quickly, the days blurring like scenery viewed from a travelling car. I tried to put the events of last weekend behind me as best I could, but the memories are like waves that rise suddenly, engulfing me. Leaving me breathless and even a little wet. Even now, in this professional setting in a room full of my peers, my mind wanders back down that track. The meeting turns to inconsequence, and my thoughts return to his bed, though come back abruptly as my phone buzzes with a text. I stare at my phone for a beat as the meeting carries on around me, the message not making sense. A misdialled number? A threat meant for someone else? My mind is still working on delay as the text is followed immediately by another.

Though I'll get to it eventually.

My heart scarcely has time to flutter before the arrival of the third. I slip the phone under the table, almost sure I'd set it to silent, not vibrate. As I lay it against my thigh, it vibrates again.

Dinner first. You'll need the energy.

Rolling my lips together, I curtail an embryonic smile. I know who this is but don't have time to consider how before my phone buzzes again.

The very last thing I want to do is hurt you. I'm going to take my time getting you there. You'll come so hard and so often the pleasure will blend with the pain.

Everything south of my navel clenches with deliciousness. I studiously keep my eyes lowered for fear my colleagues will be able to read my thoughts via my expression as another text comes through.

The cuffs. You'll look so beautiful in them.

Heat flares everywhere, my nipples hard and aching in the confines of my bra. And I'm sure if I were standing, I'd need to sit down. I need a moment. A moment with him. I almost laugh aloud.

My house. Saturday after 6. Do you remember where?

He wants to see me again. My skin sizzles and my heart soars—a repeat of the experience is the chance I hadn't foreseen. Fully zoned out from the meeting going on around me, I contemplate an appropriate response.

Yes, yes, please! Too eager. *Yes, sir?* Hilarious, though sort of appropriate; the address, at least. *Could he be a little Dom?* Just considering sending that as a response is laughable, isn't it? *Dammit, I need to read better books.*

Who is this? Too coy, as well as too easily misconstrued. I don't want him to think I'd forgotten our night already. Or make myself sound like a slut. At that particular thought, I choke back a laugh, turning it into a dignified clearing of the throat.

Redundant. I went home with him after only knowing him a few hours. He probably already saw me as easy.

What am I worrying about? It's not like I have to see him again. Wasn't that the point of creeping out from his bed last weekend before he awoke? The reason for not exchanging names and numbers, too. I'd planned on saving myself the discomfort. The awkwardness and his assumptions of me.

Far better to just fuck . . . then fuck off. Or at least, that was the plan. And how in the hell did he get my number, anyway?

In not telling him my name, I'd felt mysterious. A little powerful. But more than that, I'd begged him to fuck me. To bruise me. Perhaps I thought anonymity would provide me with the excuse that those desires weren't really mine. That it was just an experience. Something to get out of my system before slamming it back in the closet with the other rattling chains. If we each remained anonymous, maybe I could pretend it never happened—that it wasn't me. He'd probably remember me as some hot, nameless fuck, and I could continue telling myself I'd been pretending that night. That it was an experience that had nothing to do with who I really am.

And what better place to do this in than a country far away from my own? Someplace I'd be gone from in a year.

Yet on the brink of another weekend in London, I allow myself to feel the first stirrings of regret as I read his texts. *Words and promises burning my thigh.* A tide of reckless rises in my mind; excitement accompanied by a tremor of fear as I consider seeing him again. I slip my phone under my leg and try to focus on the meeting—the litany of performance indicators and projections—even as my mind strains to return to a performance of his. But a second chance of the experience. Should I? Could I really?

What would Flo say? That, at least, is easy to anticipate. *What's the problem, sweets? Wasn't he fun? Wasn't he hung? Hit that till you're done.*

If only it were that easy.

I shouldn't really.

~*~

Waking the next morning in my cold and soulless room, I stretch and decide I'm going to stop kidding myself. Why shouldn't I go? At the fairground, everyone revisits their favourite ride, right? But as a get out, or fate's opportunity to screw this up, or maybe a strange kind of punishment, I find I can't answer his texts.

I leave it in fate's hands, and if he isn't home because I don't confirm . . . well, that would be that. The universe will have spoken. So fatalistic. And while I feel like a coward, I still don't call.

Driving out of the city, I spend a mindless morning at Ikea buying useless shit for my room. My giant blue bag is full of candles, towels, and other household stuff when I spot something that, on instinct, I think I might buy for him. *Him. My mystery man.* Despite cowardice interfering with my manners, and a reply, a good guest never arrives empty-handed. I could take wine or chocolates, but those gifts seem too familiar or commonplace. Maybe bland? But I would take something, even something that felt like a prop.

In arriving with a gift, would I feel more or less like a whore?

Flo's out again this evening, so I don't have to prepare any explanations. As the evening rolls around, I take a cab after casually asking Flo what street I'd spent last Friday night on. I arrive at his house a little after six, the butterflies in my stomach the size of albatrosses. The gate squeaks, the gravel crunches, and then I'm at his front door, staring at the huge handle. I look down at my outfit of casual sexy chic; a light boyfriend jacket, a white tank, dark, tight jeans, and heels. *I'm not trying too hard to look sexy, right?* Sick with nerves, I ring the bell just once, squeezing my fingers tight against the package in my other hand, half hoping he won't be home. *The other half of me tight and tingling.* But as the door opens, his handsome face welcomes me, wreathed in such a wide smile that my whole body is awash with relief. *And other stuff.*

'What a surprise.' The light barb in his tone is clear as he bends to kiss me on both burning cheeks. I should've called. I've been childish, but it's too late to do anything about it now.

Taking my hand, he pulls me over the threshold, and I'm compelled to follow as much by the strength of his smile as his hand. We walk the generous hallway—no creeping for me this time— and down a short flight of stairs to a large, airy kitchen. Shaker style cabinetry, butcher block work surfaces, and a high-end Aga stove, of all things. Something delicious is cooking—something fragrant with herbs. I recall I've been invited for dinner, but find I'm still surprised I'm here. It strikes me that this isn't a bachelor's kitchen and I can't help but look for the tell-tale signs of a wife. Thankfully, nothing obvious. Sliding my butt onto a stool as directed, I place the tissue wrapped parcel on the island bench.

'Balls?' He laughs sort of quizzically upon unpackaging them as he holds the wrapping and ribbon in one hand with the brightly coloured balls balanced on his other palm.

'Juggling balls,' I clarify. 'You like games.' I shrug, feeling childish. *I should've stuck to wine or chocolate*, I think, when the reality is more that I should've confirmed. Still, an unfamiliar rush of pink creeps into my cheeks as I consider the randomness of my gift.

'Perceptive girl,' he replies, his smile taking on a cryptic edge. 'I'm very fond of games.'

As though sensing my discomfort, he steps closer, taking one of my hands in his. Wrapping the unravelled ribbon around my wrist, he ties it in a bow, kissing the point of my pulse below. The soft touch might've taken the power from my knees had I not been sitting. It's just as well that he turns at that point to open a bottle of wine.

From my position on the other side of the kitchen, I study him. A dark, fine knit sweater clings to his defined back; his dark hair somehow tousled yet tame. The pale skin on the back of his elegant neck, and as he turns, those brilliant dark blue eyes that seemed to see right into the core of me last weekend. He's just as good looking as I'd remembered; pale and strong though lean. Very well groomed with just an edge of something louche. Because despite his hundred-dollar haircut and his handmade shoes, something is just a little bit wrong about him.

The thrilling kind.

'Louise.' He smiles as he hands me a large glass with a very generous pour. I contemplate the liquid as he leaves me for a moment to place the bottle on the table on the other side of the room. It's set for dinner, I notice for the first time. Dinner for two.

'Where did you get my number?' I ask, inhaling a sharp breath. 'And how do you know my name?'

He slips his hand into the back pocket of his dark jeans, pushing one of my business cards along the wooden countertop in front of me.

'I didn't leave that on purpose,' I respond immediately. I raise the glass to my mouth—both something to hide behind and something to quell my nerves. The wine is cool and tart. I instinctively feel little of the first and much of the last.

'Did I say so?' His perfectly arched brow matches his tone. 'I'm afraid I have a small confession to make.' Confession or not, the look he sends me isn't contrite. 'I'd taken the card from your purse while you slept.'

'You went through my things?' My voice is incredulous, my shoulders around my ears in distrust.

'You can tell a lot about a woman by their bag contents,' he responds blandly. 'Keychains with pictures of unmentioned husbands and children. Credit cards with names other than the ones they've told.'

'I think that's beside the point,' I bluster even as his words make sense. Invasive, maybe, but wasn't he also protecting himself?

'Is it?' he counters calmly. 'I'm afraid my depravity knows no ends.' His words drip with innuendo that heats between my legs.

'Look, I've never . . . I don't do this usually. I know how it looks.' I duck my head, unable to look away fully. At least, not when he's looking at me that way.

'I don't think your vision quite meets mine.' His gaze slides from my face, lingering quite obviously over my tank covered breasts before travelling the length of my legs. 'Because what I see looks pretty fucking exquisite.'

The words, his attention, turn my nipples to pebbles. Makes my panties a mess. The atmosphere changes, the air between us sparking with electricity. And it's all him.

I swallow more wine, feeling off balance. It's a strange sort of feeling, both loving and loathing my body's reaction to him. I've never felt someone's attentions weigh so heavily on my skin. My past is . . . confusing. I've dated, of course. Slept with men. But somehow, those faces pale next to him. This is a man, not a boy. He isn't to be toyed with unless I'm prepared to feel the sting.

Deep breath. Don't cow.

'Why did you call?' I manage eventually, surprised by my cool tone.

Ignoring the fact that he hadn't, he shrugs lightly. 'Would you prefer I hadn't contacted you at all?'

He steps closer, and I notice how much taller he is now, and even from the perspective of a high stool, something is dangerous about him.

Contradicting my thoughts, he holds out his hand, palm up in invitation. Without even thinking, I take it, sliding down from the stool.

'Would you prefer to have forgotten last Friday? Ignore that part of you until the next time it grew too big to ignore?' I open my mouth; heedless, he cuts my words off. 'I've known women like you, reluctant and full of denial. Until someone holds fistfuls of their hair.'

The threat and the promise lights every one of my nerve endings, and his admonishment shouldn't turn me on . . .

'And that someone is you?' What sounded like a challenge in my head comes out as more of an invitation.

He smiles a dangerous smile as he steps to me. On instinct, I back away, inwardly cursing my reaction. My body craves being caught, but my head would like it to appear as though I desire the opposite. Something ingrained in me feels I should hold my ground—resist—but as he steps closer still, and I move again, it's like we're taking part in some kind of dance. One he's all too familiar with. But then, my bottom hits the edge of the scrubbed wooden table behind, and I realise there's nowhere else to go.

'Are these evenings always anonymous?' he purrs.

'I told you. I haven't . . .' I curl my lips inwards, cursing myself. I'd lay money on that was what he'd expected me to say. *What they all say.*

As he catches my wrists in his, the flush of nerves and excitement seems painted across my chest. *He's enjoying my disconcertion. He thinks I'll bend for him.*

'I want to hear you say it.'

My wrists in his hands, I look at the floor to conceal my expression, not wanting to be that person—be secondary to him. 'I told you already,' I murmur. 'I don't usually do this.' Why do those words sound so tired? Even to me? When my gaze rises again, I fill it with defiance. 'I *don't.*'

'Yet here you are. Again.' This time, his smile is kinder. 'Daniel. You haven't asked. My name is Daniel. I'd like to hear you say it.'

'Why?' Did he notice me raise my chin a fraction more?

'Because I want to hear my name on your lips.'

His mouth, those words, lick right between my legs. I close my eyes, struggling with my feelings and the dynamic, and for reasons I don't understand, I revert to type. And sarcasm.

'And to what do I owe this . . . pleasure, Daniel?' Will this attitude level the playing field? Hide my crumbling self-control around him?

'The reason for my invitation?' he repeats, one brow curled in question. 'Unfinished or extended business. And let's be honest, your being here proves the pleasure wasn't only mine.'

He leans towards me, and I meet him halfway, grabbing fistfuls of his shirt. Our kisses are hot and heavy, fingers urgent, fumbling, and grasping. He moans into my mouth, and I feel it everywhere. My hands fall to his belt, grasping the fastening. I need his cock in my hand. In my mouth. Inside me. In my haste, it takes me a moment to realise his hands cover mine.

Our mouths separate as he pulls them to my sides, and as his eyes slowly rise, his intentions are written in a measured smile.

Slowly, so slowly, he begins to peel me from my clothes. His attentions are so thorough and his words so sweet as he slides the jacket from my arms, kissing my cheek.

'Your skin is like silk,' he whispers, sealing his lips over my collarbone, popping the button of my jeans. 'You taste like honey.'

Lifting my arms around his neck, he sucks on my bottom lip as he glides them over my hips. 'And your cunt is heavenly.'

I barely notice the items dropping to the floor. Until I do. Standing in the warm kitchen in just my underwear and white tank, I shiver. But not because I'm cold. I feel exposed. Sort of dirty next to him and his clothed self. And wired, so wired. More so as he looks at me. Just looks. His gaze appraising and making me feel like just a . . . a thing. His thing.

I feel all those things along with the unravelling pulse between my legs.

I grab for his belt again, but he lifts my hands away with a low laugh.

'My rules, you remember?'

His rules suck.

Of course, I remember, but that was then, not now. Why strip me half naked in his kitchen to remind me he likes to be in charge? Now is the time for action, not games.

Never in my life have I felt so desperate; doesn't he understand?

Very deliberately, he lowers my hands to my sides, and my heart misfires as his fingers then lift to his black leather belt. In the silence of the room, the buckle clinks open. I want not to watch. I don't want to be so effected. I feel I ought to look away—to not play these games—as he pulls slowly on the zipper. *To tantalise.* But watch I do—my panties are wet and sticking to me, my chest moving in heavy breaths—as he lifts his cock, swollen and thick, free of the seams. It looks at home there, the weight of it in his palm. The feeling of skin on skin.

'Kiss it.' His voice is soft and low and so tempting. 'Lick it. I want you to make it . . . *wet.*'

Not a command nor an instruction but compelling enough to make me fall to my knees against the hard flagstone floor. Moving his untucked shirt, I push the sides of his trousers wider when he tilts my chin. His eyes roam over my face, dark and tense as I stare up at him. I'm not sure what he hopes to see, but then rests his hand on my head like a gentle benediction. Like he's granting permission. And like a good girl, I do as I'm bid, bending forward and kissing his silky tip.

Dan sighs softly as I slide my mouth down his length, pausing only to look up at his face. His expression is exquisite, a mixture of suspense and agony, of awe, and as I take him deeper, he exhales a rasping gasp.

In my mouth, he's satin, steel, and musk, and in my ears, he's intense. He tells me how I whisper to him as he stirs from sleep. How he can't stop thinking of me during the day. Of how he'd touched himself in the shower this afternoon, thinking of me. Wanked, he says, the coarseness of the word rushing through me like the blood in my veins, my brain spilling over with his pornographic montage. *One hand on the glass, the other working himself, my name on his lips as he comes.*

His hand strokes my hair as he speaks, his words now low and hoarse, driving me to move faster. Further. Pushes himself further into my mouth. Makes me wet. Needy. Makes my mouth sloppy. Makes me want to touch myself as he whispers breathless words about the gold of my skin and the velvet of my cunt. As he growls that I'm cock hungry for him.

His hands tight in my hair, I moan as he begins to move himself, sliding deeper as though he can't stop. As he grazes the back of my throat, my gag reflex reacts, my eyes smarting and leaking as I pull away and look up at him. His wet cock still in my hand, my chest heaves as I try to catch my breath.

'For me,' he whispers.

And when he asks so beautifully, what else can I do? Mascara stings my eyes as I bend forward, allowing him to lay his steady hand on the back of my head, my insides pulsing and twisting as he tangles his fingers in my hair.

I've known women like you, reluctant and full of denial. Until someone holds fistfuls of their hair.

God, he was right.

'Take it all.'

And I try. Oh, do I.

'That's it,' Dan hisses, his hips jerking, the sounds of my pleasure humming in the back of my throat. I'm going to do this. *Make him come for me.*

Suddenly, his hands are under my arms as he pulls me up from my knees. Turning me swiftly, he folds his arms around my waist, turning me to face the kitchen table. His cock twitches against my ass, his lips on my neck as he whispers,

'I can't wait. I want to be inside you when I come.' His hands slide down my back and over my ass, pulling at the band of my panties, causing the fabric to dig tight between my legs. He isn't gentle, and my voice comes out strangled, shocked by the sudden action—stunned as he pushes himself against the crack of my ass. I breathe a sigh of relief as he moves back.

Taking my hands in his, I allow the weight of his body to bend my body across the table. My torso pressed against the solid wood, he curls my fingers around the far edge.

'Don't let go.'

His hips press into me, holding me against the hard edge to remind me of my position. Remind me of my Friday's expectations—all the things I'd tried to ignore. *Well used. Well worn. Well fucked. I want those things. I want them all.*

'Such pretty decoration,' he murmurs as he pulls back a little ways, running his hands across the rounds of my ass. 'Did you choose these for me?'

My body jerks as his finger slide between the fabric-covered ass cheeks.

'What?'

My tone is terse, maybe a touch panicked, as I turn my head over my right shoulder to try to look at him. Need burns in my gut, fanning out further down. But what he didn't know—what he hadn't experienced yet—was that I'm prone to go off the boil quite quickly. Off the idea of sex.

Concentrate the fuck on what's bent over the breakfast table, not my underwear.

If he notices my frustration, he doesn't say.

'They're virginal, almost.' His tone is tinged with humour, accompanied with a feigned widening of his eyes. 'I wonder why you chose white?'

'I didn't.' My frown deepens. 'They were on top of my underwear drawer.'

'You expect me to believe you never gave it a thought?' Dan's amusement deepens.

'Well, yes,' I reply, embarrassment deepening colouring my mood. 'Because it's true. Do you think this is special or something? You and me, tonight?' I move to straighten, to address his almost derisory tone, but find myself prevented by a large palm placed low on my spine.

It isn't intimidating or a threat, but it's definitely an instruction. I surprise myself by remaining quiet and keeping still.

'That's quite disappointing,' Dan drawls, leaning forward and expanding my limited view. 'I feel very much put out.'

Put out. I snigger lightly. I wish he would. I'm seriously cooling; the thought of faking an orgasm before going home to finish the job myself is almost heartbreaking. I had such high hopes—

'*Ow!*' His hand meets my right ass cheek at speed, the dishes on the other end of the table rattling. His hand is censorious, not sensuous like I'd expect it to be. This isn't kinky fun—now I'm just startled. And very annoyed.

'What the hell?'

'Do you think this is some kind of joke?' His words are spoken quietly, yet the chastisement stings. *A lot like my ass.* 'That's not how this is playing out. You don't get to pull my strings.' His hand tangled in my hair, he pulls to emphasize the point. Right at that moment, every strand seems wired to my core.

I whimper—at least, I think I do—but it doesn't sound quite right. The noise is heavy and loaded with something I don't recognise. As he pulls away, smoothing my knotted hair off to one side, he pools it over my shoulder and onto the wood.

'This isn't just about you, and what you want,' he says quieter still. 'This isn't just about reaching the point where you come or where I get off. Tonight should be far more than baring just our skins. We are more than just the sum of our sexual parts.'

Despite his earnest tone and my near nakedness, my mouth was speaking before I'd engaged my brain.

'Don't tell me you're going to go all Holism on me,' I said through a strangled laugh. I lay my cheek and embarrassment against the wood. Why can't I help my smart mouth? Sarcasm is unbecoming, or so my father says. That aside, it makes me sound reactionary, not like someone who'd actually read Gestalt. Drunk on my stupidity, I can't seem to stop. 'Get it? Holism? 'Cause I'm all—'

'Holes.' He answers for me, his tone cold. 'Yes, I understand. You have three of them, available for anyone willing to put up with your attitude.'

I resist the *fuck you* balanced on the end of my tongue, replying lightly. 'You know, that wasn't very nice.'

'If it's nice you're after, go next door. Ask for Charles.' His body barely touches mine, his hand splayed on the table next my face. 'My ex-wife tells me he's an adequate lay, though a little straight-laced. He doesn't do arse.'

My first reaction is to assert that I don't either. But I don't—can't. Not with his mouth at my ear, his words snaking down my spine and ending in a shiver. Even as I mentally slot away the small insight into his life.

He doesn't move, and he doesn't speak again, though I'm aware of the sound of his breathing as I focus on the hand in front of me. Long, elegant fingers. Strong wrists. For a fleeting moment, I imagine the veins in that beautiful hand strained and standing to attention, his hand wrapping around my throat. Inching forward, I lick the very tip of his thumb, sliding my hand to almost circle his wrist. Wriggling a little for leeway, I pull on it, bringing it between the table and my chest.

'I won't be manipulated,' Dan says, though he offers no resistance.

'Bear with me, please,' I whisper, pushing to a stand.

His body moves with mine, one hand still pressed flat against the table. The hand I hold captive, I cover with my own, slipping both down my body as I widen my stance. His breath hitches as his fingers brush the triangle of white lace between my legs. His hand curls instinctively to cup, but he doesn't move an inch more, maybe waiting for me to make my point.

I wriggle a little against him, one part discomfort from what I'm about to admit, and one part needing to feel his touch again.

'Be my marionette,' I whisper. 'For just a minute, let me lead.' I slide our hands under the waistband of my panties. 'My underwear choice may have been more conscious than I care to admit. Or maybe I was just trying to hide this.'

As his fingers meet my bare skin, they curl in a caress.

'Bear with you because you're . . . bare.' A low cavernous laugh rumbles against my back.

'Maybe,' I say, trying to bite back a giggle. On a whim, or so I'd told myself, I'd made a waxing appointment. But it seems to appeal. Truthfully, to more than just him. 'Do you think I'm trying to disguise the wickedness within?'

'I should say more like match the inside to the outer.'

His finger rubs against the newly waxed skin, satin soft. It's just the most delicious of feelings—I can barely think. Drowning in a sea of silk, of sensation, I moan a low sound.

The finger stops its teasing, dipping between my smooth, wet lips. And my knees almost give way as he whispers into my neck, 'Turn around. Let me see.'

As I do, he slides my panties over my hips and down my legs, his body following suit. Sunk into a low squat, his eyes are hot on my skin.

'Sweetheart,' he murmurs, his breath a caress on the space between my legs. 'Get your arse up on that table. Let me see if this tastes as pretty as it looks.'

Chapter Four

LOUISE

'Beautiful.'

His words hold a reverence I'm not used to as his hot breath blows over my skin. With my butt cheeks parked against the edge of the table, I want to be bold—to spread myself out for him—but I just can't seem to find the courage. I shouldn't have worried as, hands on my knees, he presses them wider.

'No need to hide.' My thoughts scatter as his warm tongue licks along my inner thigh. 'Sit back. That's it,' he murmurs as I move myself more solidly against the wood.

'Daniel,' I start nervously. My fingers grip the table edge tight as he lifts my legs wider again.

'I like it when you say my name.' His gaze travels up my body. 'Don't worry, darling. I've got you. You can fall on my watch.'

My thoughts scatter, robbing me of sense. Is it his endearment, or the way he looks at me as though I'm edible? Whatever the reason, I find fingers uncurling as I lean back. Allowing myself to be positioned, I watch him, propped against the table on my forearms.

Cool air and warm breath brush my bare skin, and I bite my lip to stop myself from moaning, my stomach muscles taut in anticipation of his lips. I want this—I can't remember the last time I felt like level of need for anything. I don't know—

Anything. I don't know anything, my thoughts turning to dust at the swipe of his tongue, everything taut and aching from just one lick.

'Don't stop,' I demand quickly. 'Oh, God. Do that again.'

His response is a low rumble before he licks me once again. 'You taste so sweet,' he whispers, groaning as he kisses me as he would my mouth. I throw my head back, the vibration ricocheting through me like a blast. The long swipes of his tongue and the scratch of his stubble against my inner thigh, it's not long before I'm writhing against him, begging for him to be inside.

'Not yet. I haven't finished tasting you yet.'

He bends around me, bringing the wine bottle he'd placed on the table after pouring us both a glass. My insides tense with nervous anticipation. The wine is chilled—what will that feel like when he pours it over me? But then he kisses me again, long and deep, his tongue working magic over my clit.

I cry out. Curse. I try not to ride his face—try to get a grip on this desperation. This throbbing need.

'What did you think of the wine?' His mouth pulls away from my pussy, his gaze tracking up my body, his mouth glistening and wet. The sight of him there, kneeling between my legs, his tongue flicking out to taste me from his lips, is obscene. I can't look away, and my thoughts are like marbles, rolling about. He can't really expect any sense.

'It went down really well.' Innuendo I haven't the bandwidth for makes him smile anyway.

'You're fucking perfect.' The corner of his mouth hitches in a secretive smile. I startle as he pushes two fingers deep inside my body, his mouth latching onto my clit. 'And you taste like cream.' His words are whispered between flicks and sucks.

'Oh, God. I need . . . ' All of it. I need all of him.

'You're so warm and so fucking wet,' he finishes . . . dousing me in wine from the forgotten bottle between his legs.

My body bows in shock, but he holds me in place as the wine flows. The coolness is startling, and I cry aloud, my cries drawing out as his hot tongue returns to my flesh. He licks the spilled wine with murmurs of appreciation. Words of encouragement as he licks my pussy and thighs. *Tart on his tongue. Slippery. Cool. Warm. Fucking irresistible.*

Wetness sits under my thighs as he pulls back, raising the bottle again. For a brief second, I think he's returning to the table. But then, I read his intent. The cool neck touches my heated centre as he drags the glass the length of my core.

'How does it feel?' he demands, his gaze bright and avid as he watches the progression of the bottle until the opening is balanced at mine.

'*Hard.*' My word is pure encouragement, my teeth gripping my bottom lip against the urge to tell him I want it. *Do it. I want you to. Fuck me with it.*

'What else?' His gaze is hungry, desire shining there as he teases me with the very tip. In and out, he drags it, my desire to be filled absolute.

'It's cold.' My word comes out more groan as he slides it in a little deeper, my insides clenching around the neck.

'Not for very much longer,' he replies, dragging the bottle out. Bringing it to his lips, he drains it of the remaining liquid, his eyes intent on mine. 'I know which taste I prefer'. He pulls the bottle away, his tongue licking a drop of something from his top lip. My breath hitches as he returns the bottle between my legs.

'And now?' he asks, teasing me with a slide and retreat.

'Not fair,' I rasp in return, dropping my head back as my insides scream for more.

Dan pushes the bottle a little deeper, and I'm wanton in my acceptance, spreading my legs and moaning. I welcome the invasion—crave more—as his lips return, sucking my clit into his mouth. It's almost too much, too much visually, at least, as my eyes fall between my legs and the dark thatch of hair. As though sensing this, his eyes track up my body, the midnight blue darker with the weight of his intent.

He pushes it farther still, where my body has warmed the glass. The pressure is sublime, the feeling intense as he fucks me with it slowly, my nerve endings firing white hot at the sensation of the smooth glass and his hot tongue. Licking, tasting, his mouth—his actions—push me to the brink of climax, my gasps all vowels and no sound. I want to push my hands in his dark, silky hair. I want to gather him to me so he finishes the job.

'Do you want to come?' he asks, his smile leaking between my legs.

'What kind of question is that?' I groan then squeak as his teeth find my clit. *A warning*. 'Yes—yes, I do,' I pant, my words much more contrite.

'Not badly enough, perhaps.'

'No, I do. Please, I do want to come!' My arms will no longer hold me, my head banging against the wood.

'Ask again,' he taunts, giving my clit a sharp suck.

'Please, Dan. Make me come.'

'I thought you'd never ask.'

The world closes at the touch of him. There's no Dan or Louise. There is only my pussy, this table, this bottle, and his lips, pulling my orgasm from me.

Chapter Five

DAN

Silence stretches out between us, much like my ex's adored cat. I have other secrets. But how to begin? Naked and in bed, warm, and sated, there's something about the moment. Something more than the glow of great sex. Is it comfort? Happiness? Whatever it was, I'd happily drown in it.

'So ex-wife, huh?' Folding her arms across my chest, Louise rests her head just below my chin. I find myself smiling. Though I can't see her expression, I don't need to, to hear her curiosity.

I make a vague, noncommittal sort of noise in answer, wondering how long it would be before she presses again. Divorce is never a pleasant topic of conversation. Problem was, this is just the tip of the iceberg. My personal life, my businesses; she has no idea what a fucked-up state I'm in.

'What's this from?' Her voice brings me back to the moment. I'm thankful she hadn't pushed further, though I'm not entirely comfortable with her current train of thought.

'Ah.' She no doubt heard my consternation as I look down at the faint scar running across my ribs.

'*That* is the result of being on the wrong side of edge play.' I tuck my chin to my chest in order to see from the odd angle. So much for modifying the conversation.

'Definitely some kind of edge.' Her tone sounds pondering, and it tickles as she runs her finger across the pale ridge. I sit up a little to better see her, warmed by the small, worried frown on her face. 'What happened? Did you have an accident?'

I laugh but not at all pleasantly, slightly disconcerted she didn't get the terminology. Was she that unexperienced? I wouldn't have thought so up until now, perhaps.

'An accident? I suppose you could say that. If accidents have names and last a number of years.' I inhale a deep breath. 'Annabelle, my ex.'

'Ouch,' she murmurs. 'Must've been acrimonious if she tried to stab you.' She purses her lips, almost as though she'd said too much

Acrimonious is true, but she didn't stab me, not that I'm certain she wouldn't, if she thought she could get away with it. 'Well, yes. She is a bit of a nut.' Attempted murder or not, this was true.

'But how ex?' she asks, scrunching her face. I shake my head, reluctantly finding her expression adorable.

'*Acta est fabula.*' Breath rattles in my chest. I believe it's what's called a laugh.

'Daniel?' There are questions in the softly spoken word. It was the first time she'd said my name, discounting sighs and moaned utterances. And the bit where she'd almost screamed it at the end as she came. It had been a rush; the bottle, my mouth. Her reaction. I'd have happily eaten her out all night.

'The drama has been acted out,' I translate, the words expelled with a sigh. 'The marriage is well and truly over. It had been for a long time, apparently. It might've been kinder if she'd just said so, rather than finding them in our bed. Not this bed, obviously.' I reach up and rattled the cuffs, not missing the hitch of her breath and the gleam in her eye. *Kinky all right, just not well versed.* 'What's left between us is a little paperwork and, of course, the customary awkwardness of things.' I brush the hair away from her face, twisting a lock around my finger. 'I made dinner. I hadn't consciously planned to debauch you on the table the minute you walked through the door.'

'I'm disappointed.' She laughs softly. 'Here I was thinking you'd put a lot of thought into this evening. Selected the bottle, especially.'

'The bottle was one on instinct. A lot like taking your business card.'

'You wanted to see me again?'

'I was sorely disappointed when I woke, and you weren't here.' I keep my voice even, trying not to chastise.

'I panicked. I'm sorry. For both then and now.'

'Now?'

'For not responding. You couldn't have been sure I would come.'

'Couldn't I?' This one was pure salaciousness, along with my slap to her arse.

'Ouch! Be serious.'

'Oh, I am,' I reply darkly. 'I've put more thought into this than you'd probably care to know.'

She shivers. Perhaps, it's nervous excitement. Perhaps, it's the finger I draw along her spine.

'Are you cold?' I ask, the thought just occurring as I attempt to pull the abandoned quilt from the bottom of the bed with my foot. She begins to giggle at my attempts, so I give up, rolling her underneath me instead.

'Shall I be your blanket?' I whisper huskily as she spreads her legs around me. 'I could cover you. Keep you warm.'

Her groan is pure pleasure that I taste on my tongue. Lips move and tongues caress as, between us, her stomach rumbles.

'Hungry?' I graze her jaw with my teeth, wondering how long before I can have my fill of her again.

'For you, maybe.'

I flick my tongue across the seam of her lips, light and deft. Because, God, it turns me on to hear that. As she tilts her head, exhaling a shaking breath, I take her lip between my teeth to hear her moan. To hear her hunger for me.

Teeth grazing, hips lifting, skin rubbing skin. How long had it been since I petted heavily while naked in bed? For added effect, I take her hands in mine and lift them to the pillows. Her breath hitches; her fingers close enough to reach out and graze the cuffs. All telling pointers to slot away as I bring my mouth to her ear for some sadistic whisperings.

'Get up.' I as good as plank above her, delighting in her lust-suffused confusion. 'Come on; let's get you fed.'

'I'm a different type of hungry,' she complains, her tone petulant.

'Food now,' I repeat, rolling from her. I slip from the bed and slip on my discarded jeans. 'I promise, you'll need your strength later.' As I turn my head from her shoulder, she peers out from under the weight of her bed-messy hair.

'Who says I'm staying?'

'You should. I think you'll enjoy what I have in mind for dessert.'

'Why do I feel like it isn't going to be cake or ice cream?'

I laugh, throwing her my shirt. The majority of her clothing is still in the kitchen, and as much as I'd love to see her walk around my house naked, I don't think she's quite ready for that yet.

'The kitchen will be colder now, the floor especially. Help yourself to socks or whatever from the dresser.' I point in the vague direction, not wanting to take my eyes from the golden creature lying across my bed like some temptress. I clear my throat and run my hand through my hair, all things to distract me from making her stay there indefinitely. *And under me.* 'The bathroom's through there.' Again with the pointing. 'I'll be waiting. Don't be long.'

I hope it sounds like a warning as I stride from the room.

Chapter Six

LOUISE

Sometime later, I make my way down the two flights of stairs to the kitchen, thinking maybe Dan didn't know what cold was because the flagstone floor is warm on my toes. *He must be spoiled.* His back is to me as I enter the kitchen, still naked to the waist. Ink peeks out from his low-slung jeans, and I wonder how I hadn't noticed that, mentally adding it to my list of curiosities.

As he hears me, he turns and smiles, holding some kind of implement in his hand.

'Please, sit,' he says, conducting me to a seat in the large bay window as if the spatula is a conductor's baton.

I do as I'm told, though I feel pretty odd sitting here in his window in nothing but a shirt—his shirt, no less. I curl one leg under my ass in the odd way I usually sit, my eyes drawn to the garden. *Is that a swing set?* I can't be sure as I don't have my glasses on. I mean, it's green and so far away that it blends into the lawn. But could it be that he has a kid? My dangling leg begins to bounce minutely against the panelling in anticipation of my question.

'Wine.' *That* isn't a question as he hands me a glass. My eyes slide to the scrubbed table, the spilled wine and bottle from earlier nowhere to be seen. My cheeks burn pink with the memory as his voice pulls me from my head. 'What shall we drink to?' I shrug; I have no idea beyond the trite kind of toast. His eyes slide over my shoulder to the window and garden beyond. 'How about to ex-wives and sweethearts?' He raises his glass. 'May they never meet.' I've no idea what to make of that as he turns back to the kitchen. 'Do you like venison?'

Do I? I have no idea. I'm overcome with the ridiculous need to snort; *oh deer*. I'm not even hungry anymore. Just confused.

Dan turns his head over his shoulder, sliding me a sly smile. 'Well, I know you like meat.'

I roll my eyes, bringing the glass to my lips and swallowing a large mouthful. 'I, er . . .' I clear my throat. 'I see you've got a cat,' I say, making bland conversation and pointing at the matching pink bowls on the floor.

His answer is a noncommittal murmur as he turns away, but surely, the bowls spoke for themselves? Unless . . . no. *I've definitely read too many books.* The man is a little bossy and a little commanding in bed, but not a dominant. He didn't look the type to keep those sort of pets.

And no way am I interested in playing those kinds of games. I shake my head minutely. *What was it Flo said? I must be fuck drunk?*

'What's her name?' I ask. Pink bowls? I'm guessing *her*.

'Depends who's calling.' As he pauses, I see the bunch in his shoulder, the muscles flexing before he forces them to relax with an exhaled breath. 'If you must know, her name is Pussy. Or Twat.'

I choke a little on my next sip. 'You're kidding!'

'She's a sort of a salmon pink colour.' Was that supposed to be some kind of explanation? As he turns, the spatula is still in his hand. 'Annabelle, my ex, calls her Pussy, and I . . .' His words trail off, his eyes gliding down to my seated but barely covered crotch.

'You got custody of a cat; a cat you don't even like?' No one would call a treasured pet such a horrible name. I can't imagine taking the thing to a vet with a name like that; both were equally awful. Maybe he's the vindictive type?

'Who says I don't like the thing? Maybe I just like twats.' His short laugh has a hard edge. 'Besides, we have a sort of joint custody agreement, instigated by the cat. It's not like she moved very far away, and the damn thing keeps coming back.'

The implement—spatula, flip, or whatever the name was for that thing—waves in the direction of the window I sat in.

'What?' I turn my head in the direction his pointing, trying to make sense of his words. 'The cat lives nearby or . . . ?'

'Annabelle, and by default, the cat, live next door.'

Un-fucking-believable! Yet, by his face, apparently true. Trying not to show any reaction, I definitely refrain from turning my head to look out of the large bay window I'm currently back-lit in.

'I think I mentioned good old Charles, the bloke from next door. She had an affair with the neighbour.' He tries to sound unaffected, an effect ruined as he adds, 'The clichéd whore.'

'I thought you were kidding.' Wow. Why would he stay?

'About her leaving or about him not doing arse?'

'You said she'd shagged him.' The word feels unfamiliar and a little false. 'Not that she lives with him.' Not that she lives next door. *No matter. Not my business.*

'Obviously, one preceded the other, not that I care anymore.'

I hold out my hand in prevention, suddenly hit by the inappropriateness of my enquiries. Two-night stand etiquette didn't extend to this. 'I'm sorry. I didn't mean to pry.'

'I'm fine with not talking about it, as you'd imagine,' he replies, a touch droll, before stalking back to where I sit. 'If bigamy is having one wife too many, then marriage, in my opinion, is tantamount to the same.'

I laugh in spite of myself. Easy to do as he seems to bear no scars. Well, other than the one at his ribs. *Sheesh.* He stands next to me, staring down, but I can't make out his expression in the light.

'Take it off,' he purrs. I frown. I'm only wearing one item of clothing; he can't possibly mean that. But as he slides the edge of the spatula down the inside of my arm, I realise he does. 'Would it help if I said please?' The edge of danger in his tone makes my stomach flip deliciously.

But no. Nope, not happening. Not happening at all.

Sliding the implement across my waist, he pushes it down between my bare legs, sliding it farther until he's caressing my inner thigh. 'You weren't shy earlier when you were on the kitchen table, spread across it like a feast.' His words bloom deep in my belly. Why does this turn me on? It was much lighter earlier. We could've been seen. *I could've been seen.*

'You're thinking about it, aren't you? The prospect of being watched. Driving your audience wild as you writhe under my mouth.'

Damn him for being right. The scene he paints is so darkly tempting, the words like silk against my skin.

'You are so very beautiful, you know.' His words are heavy with awe.

'I bet you say that to all the girls.' My response sounds husky and encouraging, probably to us both.

He brings the metal down on my outer thigh swiftly, leaving my skin pinked and smarting. *Leaving me aching in other places.*

'That's for being saucy. When I pay you a compliment, you are to accept.'

I find myself nodding, washed away in this world his words create. He places the spatula down next to me, kneeling on the floor in front as he pushes my legs wider, forcing me to unfold my awkwardly placed legs. His hands slide the length of my thighs, thumbs curling inwards as he reaches the very apex.

I tremble, a mixture of desire and distrust consuming me. One hand reaches up and loosens another button at my chest—the shirt wasn't fastened well to begin with, I'd sort of made sure of that. Dan spreads his long fingers to span my collarbone, sliding the shirt from my shoulder a touch. Just a little . . . then a just a little more.

'I thought we were going to eat?' My words are more breath than true words, my back relaxing against the cool glass. His eyes seem darker, heavier, though mischief lurks in his smile before he speaks.

'I thought we'd established earlier we're beginning with dessert.'

Chapter Seven

LOUISE

Dinner lay abandoned in the kitchen as we lay once more in his bed. As Dan lies on his back, my head rests in the hollow of his shoulder as his thumb absently strokes my hip. Outside, it's begun to rain, the room silent but for the soft patter against the glass. My skin is chilled as the duvet pools across one corner of the bed, hanging down onto the floor. But sated and comfortable, neither of us are disposed to move.

'Oh, my Louise, if I take you home, I'll make you plead.' His lips against my hairline, his song is half whisper, half sultry tune.

I laugh softly, placing my hand flat against his chest as I look up at him. 'My pop, my grandfather, used to sing that to me. Though *he* used the right words.'

'You think my words are wrong? I think they're perfect.' Continuing in a low, husky tone, his song makes me shiver. 'I know *just* what you need.'

'Neil Diamond won't be happy with what you've done to his song. How old did you say you were, anyway?' My hand shakes against his chest as it rumbles with laughter.

'Old enough,' he replies softly, kissing my head again.

I could get used to this; used to being kissed for whatever his reasons. *Desire. Comfort.* With a deep breath, I remind myself that's not what this is. This is a one-night stand extended. Neither are us are looking to get involved beyond sex. *This isn't a relationship.*

'What is it?' Dan asks softly. I shake my head rather than answer. 'Come on; I can feel your frown against my lips.'

'I can't believe we're here in bed again,' I say, picking the first thing out of my head to say.

'I'm not complaining,' he answers, tipping my chin with his index finger, when he adds quite suddenly, 'Though I can't make out if you've done this before.'

'This thing?' I repeat, moving an indicative finger between us. 'Casual sex?'

Laughter rumbles through his chest. 'What strikes you about this situation as casual? Casual implies unintentional . . . a sense of happenstance. These were no accident,' he almost growls, brushing his hand along the back of my thigh to where my leg meets ass. 'I can't believe you're still red. I barely touched you.'

Downstairs, he'd licked me into oblivion by turning me to face the window and working me from behind with his mouth. I can't recall ever coming as much as I have today, and if you'd asked me before, I'd say it wasn't possible. Maybe it was something more to do with the way he'd used his hand intermittently to smack my ass.

Best. Dinner. Ever.

'I agree,' I say, burrowing closer. 'You were very . . .' What were the words?

'Particular about their placing?' he offers. Try intense. Commanding. I'm sure I could come up with a few others given time. 'I'm particular kind of man,' he murmurs, pulling me closer still and tipping his head over my shoulder to gaze down at my smarting cheeks again.

'I probably should've mentioned I bruise easily.'

The idea seems to delight him, but after a moment of silence, he speaks again. 'You didn't answer.'

'About what?'

'If you've done this kind of thing before. You like being spanked, you've enjoyed my hand around your throat, and you've a thing for being held down.'

'Are you asking me if I'm kinky?' I keep my words light to hide how I really feel. *Conflicted.* It's easier in the moment, easier when my synapses are drunk on endorphins. *Or half pickled by tequila.* Stone sober and after the fact? I can't explain. *Won't explain.*

'No, I'm pretty sure you are.' His words come out in a rumble, but I've not time to protest as he carries on. 'What I'm asking is if you've played before. Dabbled in the scene.'

I know these words from movies—from books. It's all been theory up until now.

'No,' I answer quietly. 'This is a first for me.'

'For a complete novice, you seem pretty adventurous.' It isn't a statement of disbelief, but I still wasn't sure what he could mean. Was it that I'd complied with his earlier demands? That I'd lain pliant and semi-naked in the large window as he'd gone down on me? That I'd made all the right noises as he'd bent me over that same window seat? That I'd allowed him to spank me? With his hand? With the metal spatula?

'I hit you quite hard.'

'I liked it.' Disconcertingly, I feel my face reddening. It would probably match my ass on a colour chart.

'Yes, that much was clear.' His low laugh rumbles hollow against my ear.

'While hating it at the same time.' My voice is low as I impart this.

'That sounds very normal.'

I snort because that can't be true at all. More like abnormal. Who likes and dislikes being hurt? Pulling my head away from his chest, I prop it on my bent arm.

'Maybe I've watched a lot of porn.' It was a truth I hadn't meant to share. I should've started by mentioning the books.

As he laughs heartily, I cover my eyes with my hand.

'And how was it for you, darling?' he asks, once his laughter becomes manageable.

'It wasn't exactly satisfactory, but it took off the edge.' My skin tingles with the admission, but at least I can laugh at myself. Even if I'm laughing alone. I'd started watching mainstream porn some time ago and, in a moment of feministic defiance, subscribed to a woman-centric site. It was there I'd found the delights of bondage. A little S&M. Fifty Shades has a lot to answer for, though truthfully, I can trace my interest farther back than that. *Much farther back*. With a small shrug and a smile, I try to disguise how hard the admission is.

'What else?' Dan asked, his sultry tone encouraging our game of show and tell. 'When did your interest start?'

'I think, if I'm honest, it's always been there.' My answer is quiet, and I find I can't look at him, instead pulling at a loose thread on the pillow holding Dan's head. 'When I was a little girl, I wasn't much interested in dolls. I loved the rough and tumble, games of cops and robbers where I was always the bad guy, cuffed to the fence. Tied to a tree, that sort of thing.'

'You weren't a very good bad guy then?'

'No,' I reflect, a smile peeking through. 'Somehow, I always seemed to get caught.'

'Funny, that,' Dan says, amused. 'And now?'

'I'm a little old for games.'

'Really? I thought you played rather well.' He strokes a finger across my cheek, no doubt following the red blaze. 'Have you pursued it in other ways?'

My head comes up quickly as I send him a look that I hope says, *what is this we're doing here?*

'You just jumped in the deep end?'

'I might've joined some websites. Sort of.'

'You *sort of* joined some websites?'

'Okay, I joined some sort of websites,' I repeat, giggling. 'God, I can't believe you've needled that out of me.'

'I'm not much into needle play,' Dan sates plainly, not giving me time to ask as he speaks again. 'These websites? I take it they're the kind where people don't list their places of work?' I shake my head. 'Post photographs of their lunch? Their pets?'

'Well, they post pictures . . . just not of what they had for dinner.' My shiver is tinged with revulsion as I recall some of the things that I can't now unsee. 'And some do include pets.' Mask-wearing folk in cages, eating from bowls at their Master's feet fills my mind. Women and men on all fours, of ponytails sprouting from butts, presumably plugged.

'I can imagine.'

'I just bet you can.'

'But you found no satisfaction in the internet?'

I shake my head again. 'You know the term *keyboard warriors*?' He nods. 'Well, I attracted a lot of keyboard Doms. Lots of instruction of how to get down on my knees and worship.'

He chuckles crookedly, his hand stroking the hair from my shoulders, tender touches against my back. 'And that didn't do it for you?'

'Funnily enough, badly spelled demands are kind of a hard limit for me.'

'You've even got the lexicon,' he teases.

'It's all book knowledge. Haven't had much practical.'

'So you read dirty books, too?'

'Very funny,' I deadpan. 'My God, how have you gotten me to spill this stuff?'

'Good sex wipes out everyone's bullshitting skills.'

'Your turn,' I say. 'You're into this stuff?' His answer is the incline of one brow. 'Do you play and stuff?'

'You know I like games,' he purrs. 'But we're talking about you.'

'And it's making you hard,' I note with a sly glance.

'That's all you. Now, books you say. But what else?'

'That's pretty much it. What you have on your hands here, friend, is a brand spanking newb.'

Ignoring my spanking reference, he almost purrs, 'Experience can be very overrated. *Facta non verba.*'

'Show off. Deeds, not words. Yeah, we learn Latin in America, too.' I can't help but smile down at him. He's like a peacock displaying his plumage. It's easier to joke. To ignore the bad memories these feelings might invoke. 'And I'd have settled for proper sentences.'

'Erotica, porn, and kinky social sites. Anything else to confess?'

Blinking heavily, I bite my tongue against the urge to answer *you*. 'Nothing,' I say instead. What else was there? *Reparative therapy and forced Christian camps.*

'Haven't you ever . . .' Was he going to ask me if I'd been to any clubs? And if he did, would I tell him that was what I'd hoped would come of last Friday night? 'I don't know, perhaps asked a past boyfriend to rough you up a little?'

Without regard for my nakedness, I pull myself upright and cross my legs as my voice takes on a perky edge.

'Hey, Brad?' I say, flicking the hair from my shoulders with exaggeration. 'Will you, like, wrap your hands around my throat? Maybe grab my ass when we kiss? Slap me a little before, before . . . fucking me real hard?' My shoulders sag, my expression marred by a frown. 'You have no idea.' And I'm not telling him.

'So tell me,' he suggests softly.

I can't spill the words. How can I explain the line I'd walked back home? Socially? Morally? Instead, I feed him half-truths.

'You're looking at a small town girl with the same boyfriend from high school through college. A couple of casual relationships afterwards.' A father who is a pastor, but I'll leave that out for now. 'That's my tiny world.'

'I'm certain kink isn't exclusive to cities.'

'I got close.' My eyes fall to the sheet, and I chew my bottom lip as I recall. 'With a boyfriend one time, I got close. I was in college. He noticed how I held my hands above my head when we were in bed, I think.' On the rare occasion neither one of us had a roommate. 'Then he bit me. As he was, you know.' My eyes flick to his, hoping I don't have to spell it out for him. 'He left a bruise.' I smile at the distant memory, the sensation of teeth that are more accurately Dan's. 'I couldn't stop examining it as it faded. Even he thought it pretty hot. The next time, he bit my lip in the middle of sex. Now, *that* was definitely hot.'

Maybe I've said too much; Dan looks less than pleased. Lying down again, I hide my face in his shoulder once again. 'Somewhere between my whimper and melting, he pulled away and apologised. I could never get him to try anything like that again.' I don't mention how wrong he made me feel for bringing it up again, or the weeks of guilt that followed—the sense that I'd become some deviant. And how, in a fit of jealousy, he'd told. *I'm not going there. I don't need the misery.*

The room is silent for a beat but for the pitter-patter of rain against the window.

'You really dated a boy named Brad?'

'What's wrong with that?'

'It's just such a cliché, isn't it?'

'And a one-night stand isn't?'

'So we're both clichés. I can live with that. Girl meets boy. Girl wants it a little rough and got exactly what she bargained for.'

'Is that so?' I'm almost certain a smile can be heard. 'And how do you suppose that happened?'

'Perhaps they moved into familiarity much easier than either of them had planned.'

'They did?' I feel a little breathless all of a sudden; not at all surprising considering I feel like my heart just stopped.

'Into an intimacy that could undo them both.' Dan rolls onto his side, moving my body so I'm curled into him.

I fight to keep space between us. 'What do you mean *undo*?'

'You remember the house rules?' He pulls his arm from under me, and I sit straight on the bed, pushing the hair from my eyes.

'The house always wins?' I use a faux sweetness, suddenly full of daring.

'That's a fact, but in this instance, it's more about you doing what I say.'

'Oh, I remember. At the door that night, the whole *my way or the highway,*' I say, mimicking his bass tone. 'Unless I don't want to because then? Well, you're pretty much screwed.'

As I shrug, something shines brightly in his eyes. *Excitement*, I think, as his eyes fall to where my nipples stand taut.

'Freudian slip, love?'

'Hah! You wish.'

'Wishes aren't really a priority for me. I'm more about demands. Roll over, darling.'

'You can't make me.' Shoulder to ear, I shrug. I'm like the girl in the playground, all attitude and chewing gum.

'I'm sure I can.' His voice is quiet, almost chillingly so. He'd definitely had lots of practise. 'But if I have to force you to, then mark my words, you'll be sorry.'

'Mark my skin, and I might smile.'

'Maybe. Maybe not. Time will tell.'

In that instant, I'm up from the bed. Sweet baby Jesus, I hadn't planned on running around the house naked, had I? I really ought to take the time to think these sorts of things through.

Especially recalling now who lived next door . . .

'I don't have to do what you say,' I counter, coasting along the edge of the bed. 'You're not the boss of me.'

His smile was slow and sinister as it rose. 'You're going to regret this.' His smile flashes teeth. 'But I'm going to have so much fun.'

'You think?'

He lunges for me as I step away from the bed. 'Nowhere to run, love. Give up now and I might go easy on you.'

'What makes you think that's an incentive?' On his feet now, as naked as myself, my heart beats wildly, and I can't quite tell where my bravado is coming from. Eager, excited, and more than a little bit scared, I laugh as I nimbly dodge his arms again.

Unashamedly naked, he stalks me like prey. 'I'll get you, you know,' he counters with a dangerous gleam in his eye.

'And my little dog, too?'

'Dog?' he questions. 'All I can see is pussy.'

I laugh loudly, my hand flying to my mouth in an attempt to smother it. A mistake, it turns out, as he catches me by my shoulder, pulling my flailing body until we're skin to skin.

'Lions and tigers and . . . you're bare,' he whispers, sliding a hand across my belly and down between my thighs. I clamped them together—as much to keep his hand there as to keep up the pretence.

'Oh, my.'

Just a breath of words as he pulls me to him, my back flush to his chest. Wrapping an arm around my waist, Dan brushes the hair from my face.

'What I want to know is, are you a good witch, or just a bad little girl?' The whisper rasps against my ear, but I can't help being impressed. And by more than his film references.

'I'm whatever you need me to be.'

'See, you're learning already.' Walking backwards toward the bed, he pulls my reluctant form over his knee. It might be a state of shock that allows him to place me there, though it's more likely that he didn't give me time to protest. Perhaps, it's more likely that I knew what was coming. Likelier still, that I hoped it would be me.

'New house rule: you enter the house, you hand over control.'

He punctuates this with his hand on my ass, the sound reverberating around the room. Truthfully, the noise is worse than the impact, though it was definitely a little more painful than the kitchen spatula. That had been a dull thud, this a sharp sting.

Arching my back, I turn my head over my shoulder to glare at him. If looks could kill, he'd be pushing up daisies, as the saying goes. But I don't ask him to stop, just inhaling a deep breath on the next slap. Despite my position and his obvious intent, the second slap still comes as a shock. I lower my head over his knee, trying hard not to part with the sounds, pushing my fingertips to the floor as he slaps me again.

Slapping and stroking, my cheeks are stung and soothed in equal measure. This isn't like in the kitchen. This was so much more. Through the soundtrack of my indignity—breath after breath, slap after slap—through the mixture of my anger and embarrassment, the pain blurs my resistance.

A stroke, a caress, a whispered word, then the meeting of flesh, hard and fast. My belly tenses against his thighs, my back and shoulders shuddering with small, stifled cries. Cries I have no intention of offering him as I instead try to bite them back.

Time blurs, the pain turning to pleasure, each slap taking on the guise of a caress. And as Dan slides his hand under the front of my thighs, I allow him to manoeuvre me onto the bed. On my front, my ass in the air, I whimper as he kneads my smarting skin, then in response to his fingers, my whimpers turn to moans as he pushes two inside. When he twists his wrist, the sensation takes on a whole new meaning. My moans become desperate, his positioning so accurate.

Pushing an arm under my hips, he pulls me back into position from my collapse.

'I'm not finished yet.'

I raise my head to tell him no more—to tell him to hurry—all of that, but at a pink blur flashes across the floor, I whisper hoarsely. 'Twat.'

'You'll get extra that way,' Dan says, laughing almost devilishly.

'No,' I reply, holding out a limp hand to point. 'It's your cat.'

He hadn't been wrong about the colour; its fur a kind of salmon pink. The thing sits on the floor, just out of the line of Dan's sight, staring up at me with a malevolent eye as Dan leans over the bed.

'Shit!'

Jumping up, he grabs his jeans from the floor, stabbing his legs into them.

'I thought we were in the middle of something,' I demand, rolling onto my back. 'You're going to neglect me in case you offend the cat?'

'It's not the cat that bothers me,' he explains. His hair falls across his forehead not quite concealing his deepening frown. 'She's usually one half of a pair.' His words are called over his shoulder as he disappears through the open bedroom door.

'You have two cats?' I sit bolt straight. Surely not . . . the cat can't be accompanied by his ex-wife? *Did they both have visiting rights?*

'No.' Dan's head appears around the door, his expression contrite. 'I'm sorry, but the furry fucker is usually accompanied by my son.'

Chapter Eight

LOUISE

Sitting on the bed, my mind is blank. I've no idea what to make of this turn of events. Sure, this is only our second ... date? Assignation? But aren't parents supposed to be inordinately proud of their offspring? Why wouldn't he have mentioned him?

Because you're just a temporary attraction, my mind whispers. And not around long enough to matter. I pull the duvet up over my legs because what else am I expected to do? Other than my tank top and bra, my clothes are in the kitchen. Along with Dan. And a child of indeterminate age. One— my clothes—I need in order to leave, the other— namely Dan—deserves a kick in the nuts. But I can't do either draped as I am in a duvet.

'Fuck my life,' I whisper to the empty room.

Pulling the bedding over my head, I fling myself back against the pillows, growling words about fatherless persons having intimate relations with their mothers. Arms and legs straight, I pummel my fists and heels against the mattress, groaning from anger and frustration.

Something lands on my legs; maybe I hear a murmured apology? By the time I'm once again upright and free of the sheet, the door is ajar, but Dan has already gone.

'Why is your friend asleep in the daytime? Who tucked her in? Is she a very fun friend? Did you play any games when she was awake?' A solid stream of consciousness spews from the kitchen as I approach the door.

'Which question do I answer first?' Dan's tone is wry and amused. 'And grown-ups don't play games. Mostly.'

Oh, Dan. That isn't true.

'When Tom sleeps over, we stay awake almost all night,' the higher voice admits. From my position in the hallway, I inch closer, wondering what the child knows.

'Does Mummy know?' asks Dan in a calm tone.

'Mummy said you had someone over to play,' the child chides. 'She told Charles you'd be doing a new friend. I think she meant making, though.'

'Did she indeed.' It isn't a question. Not really. 'What I meant was, does she know that you stay awake?'

'I don't think so. Her bedroom door is always locked. I think they like to watch grown-up TV alone. Did you play Xbox with your friend?'

Pushing the door fully open, I enter the room, reminding myself that I'm a grown-up, and as such, I should appear calm and confident. I'm not certain I manage much more than tense with a small measure of sheepishness thrown in.

I so don't get kids, and I don't know anyone with them. As the thought arises, I quash it, reminding myself I don't really know Dan.

A small boy in Batman pajamas sits at the table where Dan had fucked me sometime earlier this evening. Thankfully, the child was at the other end, the dinner dishes cleared away. But still, the contrast between the act of our passion and the boy's soap-scented innocence makes me feel a little ill.

Dirty. Illicit. Those thoughts aren't always fun.

Blissfully ignorant of the sordid relationship between the wood and sex, the small boy continues spooning what looks suspiciously like chocolate pebbles into his mouth with a large, plastic spoon. With an inarticulate noise, chocolately lumps spray across the table, joining the half-spilled box and a puddle of milk.

The noise, without the cereal explosion, might've been *hello*. Hedging my bets, I murmur the appropriate response, bending to pick up my shoes.

'Hal, this is Louise, my very special friend.' Daniel stands farther into the kitchen, guarded by the island bench. He holds a phone in his hand as he addresses his son, though surely he can't miss the venomous look I send his way. Turning from him, I slip my feet into my shoes.

'How do you do?' the little boy intones.

Bent forward, I notice his feet dangle in the air, unable to reach the floor. Grass clings to his feet, soil smudging his toes. What kind of parents were they, letting a little boy wander out during the night? I manage to return his greeting as my eyes begin scanning the room for my jacket and purse.

The little boy bursts into a fit of giggles, pointing at my shirt.

'You have your t-shirt on inside out!' He holds his hand across his mouth as he chuckles.

'Oh, so I have,' I answer, twisting and lifting the hem.

'You should let my daddy help you,' he answers very seriously. 'He never lets me get tied up in my clothes.' His voice lowers to a whisper. 'Would you like some of my cereal? I won't tell that you didn't eat your dinner.'

He was right; we hadn't gotten around to eating, though a few select implements lay here and there. Daniel picks up the spatula thing, tapping it absently against the butcher block surfaces as he begins punching numbers into the phone.

'No, thanks.' I cultivate what I hope looks like a smile, watching his father lift the phone to his ear.

'Mummy's in trouble.' I turn back to the child, concern etched on his face. 'I'll be next.' I almost feel sorry for him.

'You're not supposed to sneak out, huh?' Maybe I should ring the authorities; he couldn't be more than maybe seven or eight. 'Your mom must be worried.'

The child taps his heels against the chair leg, looking unconcerned. 'No,' he explains, 'I have my own door in the fence. And I left her a note,' he adds in explanation and, most likely, his defence.

'So what makes you think you're in trouble?'

'Because I'm only six.' He answers slowly, allowing for his father's friend dimwittedness. He returns to his late supper. Or midnight snack, depending on his perspective, I suppose.

'Of course, he's done it again. No, not particularly.' Dan pauses, running a hand through his hair, both voice and mane strained. 'He can stay in his room.' A pause for the other end of the line. "Yes, well, that is none of your business. Really? Well then, I'm sure he'll tell you all about what she's like in the morning. I don't care, Annabelle. Good night.'

With force, he places the phone flat against the bench.

'Finish up, Hal. Teeth time.' His words were for his child, but his gaze was all mine.

The little boy argues he's already brushed them before burping, then giggling, but eventually planting his feet on the floor.

'Will you be here in the morning?' he asks, turning back to face me, almost an afterthought.

I shake my head as the little boy tilts his to the side as though committing my features to memory. He pads from the room as Dan moves towards me.

'Don't,' I spit through gritted teeth, holding up my hand. 'Just tell me where the hell you've put my purse.'

'You'll give me five minutes.'

He rests his hand against my shoulder, his head tilted to the side in an echo of his son. I frown, noting the lack of request. What had earlier pushed all the right buttons now just pisses me off. I'm not in the mood for listening and jerk my shoulder from under his hand. Turning my back to him, I begin lifting seat cushions from chairs. After a beat, he walks from the room.

My body vibrates with emotion I keep suppressed; I can barely see past my anger; the grip on my temper tenuous, at best. I hate that he's the cause of such emotion, hate that I can't project my usual mask of calm.

'Sit down,' Dan directs, re-entering.

'I'm in no mood for your goddamn games,' I retort, brushing past him, intent on moving into the kitchen as his hand grasps my wrist.

'Please,' he murmurs. 'We need to talk. I'd like to apologise.'

'Talk?' I can't help but sneer—can't but fail to see the reflection of it in his eyes. 'Don't you think it's a little too late for that?'

'Verbosity is hardly your forte either, darling. At least this time I got your name.'

Despite their casual delivery, his words sting. He pulls harder on my wrist, and though I resist, the balance of experience is on his side. I stumble, and Dan pulls my body to his chest. My heart begins to pound, and as he twists one hand to the small of my back, the beat moves from my chest to between my legs.

'Don't go.' His whispered breath is hot on the skin of my neck.

I try not to demean myself and attempt, in vain, to resist the resulting shiver. His hand drifts to my ass, his fingers running lightly where he'd marked me earlier. Each touch against the denim elicits a deeper throb. It goes on for a minute. Or an hour. Each thud pulsing and racing straight to my pussy. And I hate him for it. Hate myself even more.

Opening my mouth to protest, to stop this from progressing—for the child, for myself—he silences me, covering my mouth with his.

His kiss is full of regret. A kiss that's slow, one that heeds my goodbye. It's with sadness that I allow myself to go with it until, languidly, his mouth pulls away.

'Bondage comes in all shapes and forms.' His eyes are dark depths and level with mine. 'What holds you down is being tied to the belief that what you enjoy is wrong.' I open my mouth to protest, to tell him his lie of omission was worse than my hiding, whichever way you cut it. Perhaps reading my expression, he places a finger across my lips. 'We need to discuss that.'

For a reason I can't currently fathom, I allow him to pull me to the window seat.

'I didn't tell you I have a son, but try to see it from my point of view. I've met this girl who is fabulous. Smart and gorgeous. But she's also a bit of an enigma. Initially, she didn't even want to know my name.'

'I thought guys found that hot.'

'Until they want more,' he says, scratching his neck. 'Getting information out of this girl is like extracting blood from bricks. Even when she's a little drunk.' He smiles, but I find I can't return the expression, beyond feeling the corners of my mouth twitch. 'Except, that is, when she's full of post-coital bliss. Can't get her to keep quiet then.'

I narrow my gaze and try to cut in as his hands grip mine a little more tightly.

'That's the only time I learn anything about you, apart from when we're fucking, but that's not the same. It doesn't allow me the way in.'

I open my mouth to protest, but no sound comes out. I know he's read me right. Repressed doesn't even cover it. Scared, too.

'Put yourself in my shoes; you're about twenty-three?'

'Six.' I clear my throat, the word hitting the air as a squeak. 'I'm twenty-six.'

'I've got almost ten years on you. You're not from here, and there's every chance you won't be here for long. You don't want to talk, and I didn't want to frighten you off. And, technically speaking, this is our first date. Maybe I was just working up to it.' His attempt at humour falls very flat. He pulls his hands through his hair before resting elbows on knees. 'I'm extremely proud of my son. I wouldn't have chosen for you to meet him tonight nor under these circumstances, but I wasn't hiding him. More like trying not to frighten you off.'

For lots of reasons, none of them about me, I allow him to pull me into his arms.

'Don't go like this, disappointed and angry. I've got what you want. Just give me some time. Let me put things right.'

The fight leaves my body like a puppet with cut strings. I've no idea what the future holds, and nowhere to go from here. But for now, I'm right where I want to be.

Chapter Nine

DAN

I wake shivering from the cold with my back pressed against the cool, damp window. Lying on my side and painfully compressed, my brain is slow to realise I'm curled in the window seat. I stretch the stiffness in my legs but am prevented from moving more than an inch by the wall at my feet, my knees uncomfortably bent but, thankfully, still fitted behind Louise's. I thank God and divine providence that she'd stayed. Unlike last time. And wonder if it has anything to go with the way my arms seemed to have remained wrapped around her all night. Smiling, I breathe deep the scent of her hair, uncomfortable but content with this girl in my arms as the morning stirred, sunlight stealing across the room like a thief.

It's strange how it feels like she belongs here. Like this is right. Can a person fall that quick? And would she want me when she knew all my secrets?

I was wrong not to tell her about Hal in the first instance, but in my defence, we have spent most of our time together playing and fucking. *That's where the interest lies.* I consider the thought, discarding it. I've fucked enough women to know what we have here is the beginnings of something else. *But what if she isn't interested beyond the casual?* Another thought I send on its way, tightening my arms across her waist. Her shoulder rises and falls in a steady rhythm, and I resist the urge to bury my head in her hair. To kiss her neck. To rouse her from sleep, to stir her to consciousness beneath me. But there was Hal, in the back of my mind and in another room. Poor boy had enough issues from the divorce without walking in on his father balls deep in his new "friend". Because, ultimately, I know that's where kissing Louise would lead to. Especially given what we'd left unfinished since Hal interrupted us last night.

My cock twitches at the thought, belying my body's physical discomfort, and I wonder, not for the first time, how anyone would relish being trussed in awkward positions for any length of time. Would the aches make me think twice before tying up Louise, or anyone else, for that matter? Probably not. My thoughts are wry. *Each to their own kink.*

A creaking floorboard sounds from the other side of the kitchen; the French doors. It could only mean one thing.

My former wife and darling. The woman I could quite happily strangle some days. Belle.

I close my eyes, feigning sleep as my ex's footsteps pad lightly against the floor. When they stop quite suddenly, I open one eye. It was absolutely worth being squashed against the damp glass just to see her expression. A taste of her own medicine was only part of what she deserved.

She looks . . . horrified.

Her eyes roam and travel over our entwined bodies, her expression morphing from distaste to distress. Turning swiftly on her toes, she opens a nearby cupboard, realising she'd been caught as her gaze reaches my face. *I wonder what she saw there?* No expression I've worn of late, I'm sure.

I rest the back of my head against the glass, eyes cast to the ceiling, wondering what the tiny but beautiful malevolent devil would do next. Slowly disengaging myself from the warm body beside me, I climb over the warmth of her body, resisting the kiss to her head. But the last thing I want is for her to wake to this awkwardness. Bad enough I'd sprung Hal on her last night. My foot hits the floor with a *thump*, and I thank the heavens she's still asleep.

'What are you doing here, Belle?' I ask wearily. Leaning against the island bench, I rub a hand across my face, sliding them into the pockets of my jeans. Probably to stop them from propelling her through the door. *Play nice*, I remind myself. *It's not worth the grief to be anything else.*

'Would you believe I came to borrow a cup of sugar?' The levity in her voice is as empty as the sugar canister she holds in her hand. 'Besides, you have my son.' She doesn't turn around, one hand clutching the open cupboard door as she begins moving the contents around with her other hand. Seeking, stalling, her hand shaking.

I ignore the lie, the reference to Hal being hers as opposed to ours, and I absolutely ignore the tightness in her shoulders, I add to the list ignorance of how she's arrived dressed. Something from the past . . . A *peignoir par excellence*, the boutique owner had called it. We'd been in Paris on a second honeymoon of sorts. A swan song of sex might be more appropriate, our marriage already ebbing. Silk and embroidery, soft billowing sleeves, and like a starlet of yesteryear, she'd swanned around our hotel room, barely concealing her nakedness underneath. I hope to God she's wearing more under it now. Yet I know if I slid the silk to her hip, I'd find bare skin. Call it instinct. Survival, probably.

'You can't keep coming in whenever you like,' I repeat tiredly, now rubbing a hand across my stubbled chin. 'You don't live here anymore, remember?'

Her hand slowly lowers from the shelf. Pausing, she turns. 'I still have keys.'

'Then maybe you should leave them.'

'What would be the point? The door is always open. You're the only man in London who doesn't batten down for the night.' She uses a chiding tone, toying with a lock of hair that's fallen against her breast. Her eyes slide to the side for a moment, before she looks back, gazing at me from beneath her pale lashes. 'Darling, you just invite trouble in.'

Could she be any more obvious?

'Use the front door next time. Ring the bell. Your kind of trouble I don't need.'

'Rather large, isn't she?' Belle replies, ignoring my demand as her gaze falls to Louise lying in the window still. 'Not really your type.' Her words are light, but I see well enough the tightness around her eyes.

'She's taller than you are, if that's what you mean.' I keep my tone even, but can't help but twist the knife. 'But isn't everyone? And since when have you been an expert on me?'

'Since forever,' she replies simply. 'Since the first day I saw you. Since I began picking girls out for you to fuck in the club.'

'Funny that. They were always some facsimile of you. A little heavier, a little plainer, but always a . . . little . . . bit . . . you.'

'Because I, my sweet, am still what you need.'

Her words are smoky as she steps toward me, loosening the belt on her gown. I can't stop her. Not without touching her. And I don't want to do that unless it's to wrap my hands around her neck. I say nothing and keep my eyes about her mouth as she lets the robe drape open like some porcelain peep show.

I still refuse to look as she steps into me, laying her palms against my chest. 'Don't,' I grate out, grabbing her wrists swiftly as they travelled to my waistband, finding a sliver of naked skin.

I shiver; revulsion, not desire. This woman has put me through so much, I'd happily never set eyes on her again.

'Will if I want to,' she murmurs. 'You're not the boss of me. Not presently.'

'I said *don't*,' I growl, pulling on her wrists hard. 'Not fucking ever.'

Her eyes cloud with want, her knees caving slightly as she pushes herself against me. It's not the reaction I was aiming for, but perhaps one I should have anticipated.

'There's my darling monster,' she exhales libidinously. 'I thought you'd left. Gone all vanilla on me.'

I smile, aiming for malicious intent, but then bend my mouth to her ear.

'I don't *go* anything on you anymore, Annabelle. I don't come in you nor come on you. I don't even think of you anymore.' I slip my fingers around her elbow, gripping tight as I move her towards the door. 'You left *me*. You don't get to do this.' Pushing her out into the cool morning, I almost yell, 'And tie your gown; you look like a wanton slut.' Then I quietly closed the door.

'Unfinished business?' Louise's dry tone catches me off guard, my heart beating as though I'd just sprinted a mile. Fuck.

'You're awake.' My stomach twists. I'd hoped to spare her—us—from this.

'Did I miss anything?'

'Embarrassment of mammoth proportions,' I murmur hopefully, moving towards her, watching her as though she were a skittish animal. Did she hear everything? See?

'Would that be hers or yours?' Double fuck.

I shake my head in some semblance of an answer because what could I say? That I loved her once? That she'd ruined my life? Up until the day I decided she deserved none of my pain?

'She doesn't really mean it. She's greedy, that's all. The cake and eat it kind.'

'*Okay* . . .' There's levity in the word, but she isn't laughing. 'I'm not really sure what that means.' She pulls herself upright, straightening her inside-out t-shirt and refusing to look at me. 'If she's the cake eating kind, what does that make you?'

'Nuts.' I bark out a laugh, not sure of its source. 'An absolute fruitcake. I must've been mad for marrying her. God only knows.' I exhale a heavy sigh, my shoulders moving along with it. 'Still, you live and you learn, apparently.'

'She's tiny,' Louise states, her words brittle, though bright in tone. 'Cute, like a pixie.'

'That sounds right,' I say, frowning. 'Though not the Disney kind. Ruthlessly manipulative and cunning, but I'd rather not discuss her.' I take a seat beside her, our thighs almost touching. This would surely be it. The straw to break the camel's back. Finding out about Hal the way she had was bad enough, but I wasn't going to let her leave without a fight. 'Let's discuss us.' I nudge her playfully with my shoulder, heat radiating with the small touch.

'There's an us?' She cocks a brow; a reflex reaction, I think.

'I'd like to think there is. Perhaps, if you're honest with yourself, you think the same. I want more from you, Louise.'

'You mean more of me?' She doesn't seem impressed by my honesty. Does she fear the sudden weight of my words?

I shake my head a little sadly, glancing around the kitchen as though seeing its condition for the first time. The abandoned dinner dishes. The bottles of wine waiting for recycling.

'It's such a fucking mess.'

'Hey, I'm not slave material,' she says, forcing a laugh. 'I'm not the domestic type.' I cock a brow, grateful for her making light of things. But more than that, she seemed to be testing the waters. Sounding out my needs. Would she ask me outright exactly where my proclivities lie?

'I don't mind helping out, maybe loading the dishwasher from time to time, but beyond that, my limits are hard.'

Good girl. Stop pussyfooting. Ask the questions out loud. But she doesn't, her eyes falling to her lap where her hands rest.

'I'm not looking for someone service orientated,' I reply softly, taking one of her hands in mine. 'I think what you're asking is if I'm in the market for a sub.'

'So maybe we're back to my browsing too many dubious websites then, huh?'

She looks relieved as she stares up at me. The right thing to do at this moment would be to tell her what I actually do for a living. Tell her about the clubs. But then what? Watch the cloud of dust form as she runs? I think there've been enough revelations for one night.

'You've been ruined by porn.' I shake my head disparagingly. 'I don't want a playmate. Or someone to clean my floor in the buff. But I do want to hurt you. Bend you. Twist your mind and your body. I want to do it all while getting to know you. That's what I want.'

For starters, that'd do. Probably still a lot to ask after the past few hours. The rest we'd get to. *Hopefully.*

'That's all?' Sure enough, her reply I almost a rebuke. It's a lot to take in, for sure.

'Along with regularly fucking you into a state of inexplicable bliss, of course.'

'Of course.' Along with her smile, her eyes seem to discover some fascination with the kitchen floor. 'Where do we go from here, then?' she asks quietly.

'Given the choice, today I'd continue where we left off. With you on all fours, my darling.' My fingers find her chin, encouraging her gaze to mine. I push her hair from one shoulder, pulling the strands through my fingers where it shines like the sun. 'Given time and opportunity, I'd place my hand around your neck . . . just to feel your breath under my palm.' She swallows deeply as I lay my palm at the base of her neck to reiterate the point. 'Given your encouragement, I'd peel you out of your clothes, spread you across my knee, and run my fingertips through the slick, pink ribbon between your legs.' My words were meant to entice, but the images brand my brain. 'And when you've given me everything, my darling, and you're wrung wet and shaking, I'd make you come on my tongue.'

'But those plans can't happen today, right?' There's hope in her question, though her expression showed she understood our reality as I shake my head. She swallows audibly, the libidinous lilt in her voice clear as she says, 'So what's the alternative plan?'

'Date night.' I cup her face in my hands and rub my thumb across her bottom lip.

'Wine me, dine me, sixty-nine me, huh?'

'It's like you know me already,' I reply. 'Date night. Next Friday, because I'm all about the anticipation.'

'You mean you're a tease.'

'Darling, you can't possibly know. But you could definitely find out.'

'If I play my cards right?'

'I'd show you my hand any day of the week.'

God, if she didn't like the sound of that. She was probably wet. My hands move to her shoulders, my need burning her skin.

'How much time do we have?'

My smile slips. 'Hal's due to wake any minute.'

Her responding shrug seems to say that's okay.

'Date night,' she says, almost as though trying the phrase out.

And then I remember something, leaving her side for a moment to pull something from a kitchen drawer. Returning, I lay the small silver box on her thigh, taking one of her hands in mine again.

'I'd planned on using these earlier,' I tell her, tapping the silver lid. 'But the best laid plans—'

'Sometimes get fucked?'

'Exactly.' I laugh again. Things could've gone such a different way. 'Last night, you brought me juggling balls because I like games. These,' I say, tapping the lid again, 'are ball games of a very different nature.' I curl her fingers around the gleaming case, grazing her cheek with my lips. 'And I can't wait to play.'

Chapter Ten

LOUISE

I'd heard from Dan only once since the weekend; same afternoon to be precise. Shortly after he'd kicked his wife, *ex-wife*, out the door, I'd returned home and was asleep on the couch when I'd missed his call. Something told me I shouldn't return it. Probably the bizarre events of my visit, despite how much lighter I'd left feeling after we'd talked.

Waking to his message from my much-needed nap, I'd decided I should take a few days to let it all sink in. To make sure I hadn't bitten off more than I could comfortably chew. It's one thing to admit to my stirring sexuality but quite another to find myself irresistibly drawn to him. One was a fantasy, the other a reality. A reality with experiences I can only imagine. No longer a nameless fuck, Dan was all sorts of things. A father, for one. He'd been a husband. Was he also a dominant? Not that I know much about those sorts of things.

Yes, no longer nameless, but he was still a stranger. And out from under his dark and compelling gaze, I begin to wonder of the sanity in continuing to see him. The man had more baggage than the Louis Vuitton store on New Bond Street. My mind slips back to my waking to his ex's seduction attempt. She's the kind of crazy I like to steer clear of. Not to mention he had a kid. Cute, but still, that's a lot of baggage to content with.

I huff a little, and the woman on the other side of the counter frowns, pulling gently on my hand.

'Sorry,' I murmur, forcing it to relax again

The manicurist shrugs as she examines the smudge my huff caused. 'It's fine, all fixed.' Satisfied, she raises her eyes to meet mine. 'Got any plans for the weekend?' she asks amiably.

I find myself for once on the opposite end of my usual reticence—words falling from my mouth in a rush. 'I'm supposed to be going out for dinner.' I may be a little over excited.

'With the girls or a bloke?' she asks, bent over my hand, painting my nail in a precise pink stroke.

'A date. It's date night.' I smile widely. Like an idiot.

'Supposed? You sound like you haven't decided.'

'I missed his call, and he hasn't called back.'

I'm not concerned, not really. I should've been the one to call *him*. Should have. But didn't. And not for the first time. It wasn't right to keep him guessing. *Fuck it*, a little voice in my head said. It wouldn't do any harm to keep him on his toes. After all, he was the one with all the plans.

'Men, eh?' the manicurist mutters in a disparaging tone as she gestures that I should slot my hand under the lamp. 'Probably playing some kind of mind game.'

This time, I can't help but laugh. 'It sounds like you've met him.'

'Babe, I've met them all.'

Something tells me that she's never met a man like Dan.

~*~

I spend the rest of the morning shopping and return home spent, figuratively and literally, having spent a ridiculous amount of cash and energy in the search for something to wear tonight. I'd hesitated at the window of an underwear boutique I'd never entered before, its windows an appealing mixture of kitsch and kink. Polka-dot panties looked cute on the mannequin, but it was the blond ponytail protruding from its plastic butt that had intrigued me the most. I hadn't been so taken by the mannequin wearing the leather horse mask. But still, I'd gone inside.

It was like wandering into a kinky rabbit hole. Silk and leather, paddles and whips. Clothing for all shapes and sizes. Toys for all orifices.

I came out with bulging bags and a dirty high.

Back at the flat, I run a bath, fill a glass, and spend the afternoon in careful preparation. My phone buzzes once, but I ignore it, balanced precariously on the edge of the tub with a razor in my hand. Once wrapped in a fluffy towel, I read,

Seven tonight. I pull the towel tighter as I read the second text. **Wear a skirt or a dress.**

A thrill courses through my body, my fingertips aching to reach for my throbbing clit. Wear a skirt. The images flashing through my mind are vivid. Sordid. A recent fantasy. I'm lost to the imagery of being touched and fucked while others watch on. As my phone rings, I curse.

'Louise, honey. I was beginning to think you were screening your calls,' my mother titters a little nervously, and my stomach twists with guilt. 'It's so good to hear your voice. How are you?'

'I'm fine, Mom. Great.' I inhale deeply, covering the pregnant pause audible on both ends of the line as I wonder how Xanax is treating her today. 'And you—how are you?'

'Oh, I'm just fine. Busy. You know. Same old, same old.'

I know, all right. No time to be anything but busy. My father is a fire and brimstone pastor—one of God's soldiers—who runs his household with military precision. My mother is no more than one of his grunts. Idle hands do the devil's work. I smile as I think about Dan; it seems busy hands still find time to dabble in the dark arts, too.

'And . . . Dad?' Please don't let him be there.

'Daddy's fine. He's here. I'm going to put him on next.' *Hell.* 'How's work?' she adds quickly. 'Is my baby girl running London town yet?'

'Work's fine, Mom, and London is . . . interesting.' In a lot of senses. On the surface, it's cold and wet pavements and crowded buildings, but around every corner is a piece of history, a slice of elegance, and greenery.

'Well.' She pauses, and in the silence, I hear her emotion, tight like a violin string. 'We miss you. I miss you, but I'm so pleased you're having fun.'

'Fun?' My father's bass tones take over the call, no doubt from a line in his home office. 'Hang up, Marion. I'd like to talk to my daughter, now.'

Possession is everything, and power is love in his eyes. Between a hurried, 'I love you', and a whispered, 'Call soon', my mother does as she is told.

'It was my understanding you were there for a promotion, Louise.'

I close my eyes and inhale over a count of three. Holding the breath there, I release it over the same count. Coping mechanisms. Don't internalize. I open my eyes ready to deal with him. Remembering I no longer have to be frightened of him.

'Your understanding isn't wrong, but everyone has to live a little, Daddy.'

Daddy. As long as I live and have sex, I'll never understand those who like daddy games.

'Keep your eye on the prize, Louise,' he commands gruffly. 'You get nothing for second place. Did your mother tell you that Trent has been offered a partnership?' Trent. My brother. The man with whom I'd competed in all things. Grades. Sporting achievements. Possessions. And most of all, our father's approval. For years, he's sat between us, feeding the rivalry.

'I don't know. Maybe I missed that bit. You were listening in; you tell me.' I almost want to bite off my tongue in regret.

'Your insolence is so generalised; I try not to take offence.'

My throat thickens at the reprimand, the fingernails of my free hand digging into my palm.

'I apologise. I spoke out of turn.' It's ridiculous that I can't seem to suppress the urge to bite. Or apologise.

'Trey and Stacey are doing well?' Trey married last year and had a baby on the way. I don't know if that makes him the winner in my father's eyes, but it didn't matter. There's no way I'm ever competing on that score.

Having zoned out, I become aware of my father's voice once again.

' . . . you'll be home in six months, anyway.'

'I have eight months left.' At least. 'Speaking of which, Mom caught me at a bad time. I'm in the middle of preparing for a meeting.'

'Yes, I should let you go,' he replies with a gruff sort of pride; early Saturday evening and his baby girl was still hard at work. Well, I have high hopes of being hard at something in a few hours, that much is true. 'Keep in touch, and I expect to see you at Thanksgiving.' Not an invitation but rather an order.

'Yeah, maybe. Speak soon.'

I hang up following a terse goodbye, releasing my fingers to view a palm full of bright red and stinging half-moons.

~*~

'You're out again tonight?'

Balanced on her forearms, Flo appears to be doing something that looks suspiciously like yoga as I enter the living room. A New Age chakra-fixing chant plays in the background, and the room smells like incense with the underlying hint of weed.

'Yeah, dinner.' I lift my head as I answer, simultaneously fastening my shoe to my foot.

'From the club? The same man?' Not wanting a discussion, I give a noncommittal shrug. Not that it matters; Flo doesn't see it as she has her head on the floor and her butt in the air. I'm sure she'd said before this position was called the downward dog. To me, it looks like it should've been called *come hump my ass*.

'You're like a foster fail.'

'I'm a what?' I ask, not really caring as I concentrate on my tiny shoe strap.

'It's like this,' she says, now sitting cross-legged. 'When people take care of abandoned kittens and end up keeping them. That's called a foster fail.'

'Who do you know that fosters kittens? I'm sure you know girls who'd skin them and wear their fur,' I tease. I couldn't swear to it, but I've met some of her set. The Tabithas and Savannahs who smoke like chimneys and are as thin as rails. 'But open their homes to them?'

'I read it in a magazine article at my gynaecologist's office.' She waves an inconsequential hand. 'The point I'm trying to make is, a foster fail is someone who keeps the creature rather than let it go to a new home.'

I glance at my watch. 'I still don't get your point.'

'You're a one-night stand fail. You were supposed to have shagged him and moved on. Set him free to fill holes elsewhere,' she says, throwing her arms wide.

'I'll bear that in mind,' I reply, picking up my purse.

'That club has a sinister side, you know.' In a change of tone, Flo eyes me gravely.

'What does that matter?' I reply. 'Pretty sure they don't serve dinner there.'

'No,' Flo says, raising her head. 'They serve you your arse.'

As I close the front door behind me, I decide Flo can be so cryptic at times.

Chapter Eleven

DAN

At ten past seven, Louise saunters into the restaurant; her heels the cause of her swaying gait, and the saunter its hypnotizing effect. High, high heels and swaying arse and hips. Peach cheeks and pink lipstick. She looks like a dream.

I stand as she pauses by the hostess, my expression calm.

'You kept me waiting.' My words are a whisper as I hold her to my chest. A moment later, I relinquish her to her chair.

'Only ten minutes,' she says, fussing with her bag. She doesn't return my gaze.

I thread my fingers through hers to focus her attention. 'Try all week. You didn't return my call. You think I might be used to it by now, but I'm not. I don't appreciate it.' I'd fretted. Wanted to call—caving only earlier today. I'd also considered she might need a break to think about things.

'I-I didn't know whether I'd come,' she stammers.

'Liar,' I purr in response, suggesting all sorts of things, though mainly that I'm pleased she's here. Our fingers entwined, I bring the tips to my mouth for a kiss. 'You're only kidding yourself,' I add. And torturing me.

As she shrugs lightly, I make her a small promise. 'I'll go easy on you,' I murmur, my voice low in register. 'While we're in public, at least.'

Her tongue darts out to wet her lip, heat crawling across her cheeks.

'Who says I want you to?' Her tone is blithe, even as she begins fiddling with her napkin.

'Wanting and receiving. One doesn't necessarily follow the other, but I think you know that.'

'You mean you can't always get what you want?'' She almost sings her response. Can a person sing and snigger at the same time?

I school my expression as the waiter approaches our table with the drinks menu in hand.

'The lady would like wet pussy,' I tell him, deadpan, and ignoring Louise's dumbstruck expression, I carry on. 'It's not on the cocktail menu, but if the barman would like an introduction, do let me know.' I add an imported beer to the order, while also requesting the wine menu. And I do it all without acknowledging Louise.

The waiter doesn't know where to look—doesn't take down the order on his tiny pad. He seems to have been struck mute. So I coughed, and the young man nods quickly, seeming to come back to himself before stumbling away.

'What the fuck was that all about?' Louise whispers—no, hisses—narrowing her gaze.

'You didn't want me going easy on you.'

'I don't appreciate being embarrassed—' I chuckled darkly, and she begins to splutter with indignation. '*I do not*! And I don't appreciate having my drinks ordered for me. I'm not a little girl.'

'You aren't? Then stop acting like one,' I reply, straightening my cuffs. 'And while we're airing our grievances, I don't appreciate being made to wait.' The crux of it. The reason my stomach had been in knots since she left last weekend. 'Let's move on now, shall we?'

'Whatever,' she huffs, folding her arms. 'But there's no way I'm drinking that god-awful ick.'

'If you know what's good for you, you will.' My cadence is even, but she couldn't have misheard the steel underlining the words.

'Good for me how?' she asks, sounding more curious than coquette.

'Good girls get rewarded.'

'What do reasonable women get?' she snaps in response. But I don't answer. Don't lift my head from the menu. I don't reward outbursts unless it's for my benefit. 'Maybe if you ask nicely,' she begins, changing her mind and her tone. 'You know what? Fuck you.'

I place the menu down slowly, leaning back in my chair. 'I don't do nice very often; I thought you knew. Thought that's why you liked me?' My smile takes on a brutal edge, one that, if appearances are to be believed, creates a shiver against her spine. She blushes. Fully. Her cheeks as red as her arse cheeks last week. And I want to do it again. Want to hear her cry for me again so beautifully.

'When I offer you a wet pussy, you take it. Otherwise, you're just being impolite.'

She's prevented from answering, prevented from rolling expletives from her tongue, as the waiter returns, placing the gaudy pink drink in front of her. I almost laugh at her expression of distaste, though am intrigued as it morphs into something else.

Dipping her forefinger into her drink, Louise lifts it to her mouth. Devilment is her absolute purpose, and her eyes glint as she lifts them to the waiter, her eyelids and lips closing languidly. The noises she makes as she sucks on it? Pure seduction. A moment later, she withdraws it with a soft pop.

'I've never fingered a pussy in public before,' she purrs, dipping her finger back into her drink. 'It tastes . . . sweet. Here, baby, taste.' She offers me the finger, surprised when I take her hand in mine and play along.

'You do taste sweet. And sticky.' As she withdraws her finger, I catch the end with a long flick of my tongue.

The poor waiter stands unmoving as if he doesn't know where to look—where not to look—frozen stock-still like he's been caught watching porn. *By his mother*.

'And wet, just how you like me.'

'That will be all,' I drawl, curling a brow. I'm not sure if the direction is for Louise, the waiter, or both. 'You're wicked,' I add on the breath of half a laugh as the waiter snaps out of his daze to stumble away. 'The poor boy's going to be wanking to images of that for weeks.'

'What's not nice? I just gave him . . . material. I'm lovely,' she says, laughing.

The heavy atmosphere changes to light in the blink of an eye. I'd been more anxious than annoyed as the minutes had passed by. *What if she wasn't coming? What if she didn't feel the same?* And then she had arrived, sauntering into the restaurant without a care. Or an apology. Anxiety had certainly turned to annoyance. But now? Now I'm just relieved. And a little bit overwhelmed as I lean closer, interrupting her with a sudden kiss. I don't imagine it as she melts at the touch of my lips.

'You've such a beautiful mouth,' I whisper. 'And it talks such a fierce game. But anything you don't see with your own eyes always creates a cloud of doubt, I find.'

It's always easy to redirect the conversation to sex, I find.

She frowns, not quite grasping my meaning. 'You want me to . . .? Is that why you had me wear a dress?' Swallowing audibly, she closes the space between us. 'You want to follow me into the bathrooms?'

'Tempting, but a bathroom stall isn't nearly big enough for me to do all that I want to do to you. Tell me something else.' *Distract me before I drag you from your seat for just that.* She deserves better than being bent over a toilet bowl. And I don't do those kinds of things anymore. 'Tell me something about your week.'

Her teeth graze her lips as she considers her answer. 'Maybe you'd like to hear about what I've been doing to myself while thinking of you?'

'Have you been touching yourself?' She nods, though barely blushes. 'Interesting, I'll agree. But I'm not some horny teenager. I need more material to go on. You can show me later how you do the deed.'

Chapter Twelve

LOUISE

We ordered dinner, but I barely ate, feeling as nervous as the waiter who'd delivered our plates. I hadn't meant to make him feel so uncomfortable, but being around Dan does all kinds of things to me. I replace my dinner with the liquid kind. One cocktail and a *lot* of wine. I'm all about quelling the nerves for tonight, to help me in this corner I've painted myself into.

I can probably bring myself to do that—to masturbate in front of him—but it would certainly be for Dan's pleasure rather than mine. Because I can't imagine masturbation is any kind of pretty when alone and aiming for release. Unlike dirty movies, it was grunting, writhing, and frantic finger work.

But his evening would be different. It has to be. And I'm certain I can manage something a little prettier that the regular two-finger twist, but a porn star performance? And that's where the wine comes in. I think I can do this and do it well if I've had enough to drink.

Damn me and my big talking mouth.

'I like that you wore a dress.' Leaning back in his chair, Dan's gaze seems calculating, though not deceitful. It's more as though he looks at me as if I'm something to solve.

I raise the glass to my mouth as I speak. 'Actually, this is a skirt.' I sip rather than explain the intricacies of the peplum and matching top.

He shrugs, not appearing to care; a kind of *whatever* motion, catching me off guard as he asks, 'Are you wearing stockings or tights?'

His voice is low and tempting, and I lean into him, placing my palm on his thigh under the table. 'You could always find out for yourself.'

Moving closer, he presses soft lips against my cheek. His mouth hovers over my skin for a minute, his breath on my face as he whispers, 'I think we're back to the point where you've been watching too many dirty films. This isn't the kind of establishment with dark corners and play rooms.'

Rather than a reprimand, his words create other things, my mind slipping to the places he's alluded to. What were the kinds of spaces a man could slide his hand under a skirt without causing issue? How many of these did he frequent? Would he take me, too, if I asked?

We leave shortly afterwards, hailing a cab. Climbing into the back, I tremble with desire as I slide my hand to the inside of his thigh, my mouth seeking his. I'll admit I'm a little put out as he grasps my fingers, refusing them passage to travel over him. He kisses my forehead, smiling when I whisper getting to second base in the back of a taxi seems like it could be fun. He doesn't respond, but instead begins outlining, explicitly but quietly, what he'll do to me when we get back to his house.

~*~

Dan's hands reach for his belt before he's even closed the front door. Half unfastened, he kisses me savagely, walking me backwards along the hall. At the base of the stairs, he slides his hand around my waist in his quest for the zipper of my skirt. I giggle, and he curses, so I hold my hands aloft, the only concession I offer him. His eyes shine with triumph as he finds it, pulling on it quickly in his haste. He yanks it down my thighs, wrapping his hands around me to lift me as he slides my legs around his waist. I might squeal a little as he buries his face between my breasts. It might turn into a moan as he bites.

As Dan climbs the stairs, our kisses are hot, wet, and unravelling. I'm so caught up in the moment, I don't realise we've reached the bedroom until the door hits my back and it swings open. We stumble towards the bed, our need to be as close to the other overcoming all civility. Grasping and desperate, Dan growls, his fingers tight on my ass as he rubs me against his shaft as I arch my back to deepen the sensation.

'I might not be able to make you behave, but I will make you beg,' he rasps, almost throwing me to the mattress and slipping the jacket from his arms.

Anticipation balls in my gut, need fanning out and making my limbs weak. I want what he's offering— know he's more than capable of making me beg. He takes my foot in his palm, removing one shoe and then the other, his body an elegant arch as he places them neatly on the floor. It's almost like a warning or a signal that he's controlling this thing and in complete contrast to how he'd removed my skirt.

Hands at my side, he loosens the side zip of my top and we both work to peel me out of the tight-fitting garment. I'm left wearing nothing but my underwear; a black lacy bra and matching thong and lacy-topped hold-up stockings.

As he begins working his cufflinks loose along with the buttons of his shirt, I prop myself on my elbows and watch. Expectant. Excited. Definitely on the edge. His belt and buttons are already undone, his pants now riding low. I can't seem to stop my gaze from flicking to that perfect bulge as Dan's dark eyes watch me watching him. The cotton rustles as he pulls it from his arms, his abdominals flexing as he releases the tip of his cock from his loosened fly.

I lick my lips without thinking, and Dan smiles, the moment free of pretence.

'You want this.' It isn't a question, but I answer anyway with a nod. 'You remember your big talk?' I crease my brow a fraction, not liking where this is going. 'You can't have my cock until you've made yourself come.'

That one sentence, one suggestion, causes my insides to pulse. Who said stuff like that outside of porn? Almost of their own volition, my hands begin trailing over my warm skin. Between the valley of my breasts, I pull my nipples into peaks over the lace. My sigh is natural, and not for him, as my fingers travel down over my hips and my whole body begins to writhe. Turned on by his dark expression and by the way he looks at me as I touch myself, I'm so desperate for relief as I hook my thumbs into the elastic of my panties.

'Keep them on,' his voice rumbles. 'To the side, slide your fingers in.'

It isn't the instruction or the tone that lights my nerve endings; it's his direction. His dominion over me. I do as he says, running one finger against my warmth and dampness, whimpering as I dip it inside, rolling the slick digit across my clit. My eyes fall closed as I stroke once more, my limbs moving suddenly as though poked by hot pins. I find I don't have to pretend as I caresses and touch—I can hear myself moaning and bite my lip to try to stem the flow of half-spoken words and moans. My legs begin to twitch, my hips lifting as the sensations build. Then as Dan moves over me, I remember why I'm doing this. His lashes lowered, his dark head rests against mine as though to feel my climax build. And he whispers encouragements, the sexiest of things.

He tells me how glorious I look.

How sweet smelling this all is.

How he'll lick my fingers.

And when I'm done, he does.

On his knees between my parted legs, he pushes them wider, inhaling deeply as he adjusts my panties. Sliding a finger down my fabric-covered crease, I know he sees that the fabric is damp, but I can't care. I'm just coming down—an aftershock twitching mess. He stands, pulls a condom from his back pocket, and slips it over his length once he's stripped out of his clothes. I don't know how the sight could be so erotic, but it is.

Returning his knees to the bed, Dan places the tip of his cock at my opening, sliding his hands under my ass to raise my hips. And, sliding the lace of my panties to the side, he teases me with the tip.

'Please.' If the word sounds desperate, it's because that's what I feel, the end of one climax tied so tightly to the next. I want it. I *need* it.

Without a word spoken, Dan lifts my ass higher, and with one smooth push, he slides inside. I shudder with delight and frustration, my body clenching in its instinctive embrace, but he doesn't move again. Through my wordless appreciation, his fingers dig into my hip, urging me to repeat.

'Are you ready?' he then asks, moving his hands to my wrists. I nod as he pulls them above my head, clasping them in one hand. He pulls out almost fully then, his fingers tightening, his mouth filling the pause with dirty promises before thrusting back in.

I cry out, my fingernails stinging my palms, my insides gripping his cock.

I beg. I plead. I promise to be good, if he'd only move.

Dan smiles, not exactly sadistically, but maybe with triumph, before kissing me long and sweet. Driving into me so hard and fast as he anchors himself by my wrists. Over and over again, he pounds like he'd crawl inside if he could. Such abuse. Such pleasure. I wrap my legs around him, my fingers grasping the air. I detonate, coming hard while wondering if my wrists can stand the pressure as he throws back his head, undulating above me. He makes a sound of plaintive pleasure—half agony, half release—so strong it echoes through my bones. Through my very existence, I feel him everywhere as his body cries my name.

Chapter Thirteen

DAN

In the blue-dark of the morning, I wake naked and without an inch of bedclothes. Turning to the warmth radiating from the other side of the bed, I can't help but smile. Pale light from the streetlamp outside highlights the chaos of tawny golden strands across the pillows next to me, its shadows half-concealing how Louise appears to be rolled in every item of bedding I own. That my balls seem to have retracted inward and my nose feels numb are of no consequence because I'm quite content just to watch her.

The more time I spend with Louise, the more I need. So I don't move; I just lie watching her, my ridiculous smile deepening. Until it falls. None of this—my thoughts, our fucking—is reality. *Yet also not quite in the realms of fantasy.* My fantasies lean toward the hard; places Louise has no business in. She's real enough and interested enough to dip her toe in this, but did I want to be the one to take her? To corrupt her for my pleasure. Would it turn her into Belle? *Impossible,* my mind whispers, *for Belle's is responsible for dragging you to hell.*

By what method did a night with a no-name girl snowball into this? A craving to be near. A longing to be cradled within. So much for self-preservation. For not getting involved again. Those plans had been obliterated from the minute she'd stepped through my front door. The place I'd kept detached from the rest of my existence.

Maybe Belle was right this time. Maybe I do invite trouble.

The thought of my ex has me groaning and dragging both hands through my hair. Has me swearing under my breath. Belle calls me her monster and, to an extent, she's right, because she made me this way.

How Belle hadn't frightened off Louise was, quite frankly, amazing. Amazing yet strange. Louise seems to keep her thoughts contained. She'd even met Hal, the one thing good from my marriage. But despite the questions, and how well things seem, all I can think about is but how does she feel about me? Like a schoolboy in the first crush, I've spent hours analysing and dissecting everything Louise had said. Scrutinizing and verifying every nuanced breath. We didn't discuss work. She didn't ask me what I did while we're apart. She made no effort to get to know me—not beyond the bedroom. Why wasn't she interested in the information other women sought?

I know I'm attractive, though perhaps a little vain. Interesting. Commanding. Erudite, even; knowledge gained in the pursuit of pleasure. Gestalt, Jeung, a little Freud. Worldly. Charming, when I'd half a mind. Also a father. An ex-husband. And now a liar.

My head falls forward, my eyes shuttering closed, as I remembered how, in the heat of the moment that first night, I might have suggested I was an academic of sorts. Why hadn't I told her I owned a club? Either of them. The one we'd been in or the one I seemed to be hiding her from. *Or was it the other way around?*

Would she forgive me for a suggestion that had grown into a lie? Would we ever even get to that point?

And why wasn't she asking questions?

Perhaps, it was that she didn't intend to hang around.

Something in my chest tightens. I sit abruptly, swinging my legs out of the bed, my back to Louise. It feels wrong lying next to her. *Like I'm some sort of a viper in the nest.* I need to get up—man up—tell her! But as she stirs, and I turn to look at her in all her languid-eyed loveliness, I know it won't happen right now.

Chapter Fourteen

LOUISE

On the edge of the bed wearing little else but one of Dan's shirt and a wide smile, I watch as he pulls himself to sit. Gloriously naked, the morning light makes the hardness of his body seem more marble than real. Leaning closer, he pulls a couple of damp strands of hair from my face.

'Go on,' he coaxes, fully aware of how uncomfortable his suggestion makes me. 'Spill the beans.'

'I-I left them at home. I told you.' I look away and try to quell my nerves by busying myself by towel drying my hair.

'Nervous looks good on you.' His voice is low and sexy, but he's not distracting me this way. 'I love looking at you when you're embarrassed, too.'

My head whips around to him and his admission, which makes me feel a little uncomfortable. At least, the squirming kind. I resist the urge to tell him he's a pervert because that would make me one, too.

'Come on. Tell me,' he whispers.

I shake my head as though to shake off his questions, or maybe the thoughts. 'They . . . they . . . weren't much fun, honestly.'

'So you tried them at least?' He sounds a little titillated. Comically so, for effect.

'Well, yeah.' I shift slightly, the bed creaking beneath me. 'You don't give a gift and then demand a report.'

'Oh, Louise.' He shakes his head, though his smile sneaks through. 'You didn't really expect me not to ask what kind of effect they had on you, did you?'

'Pervert.' *Damn.*

'Stop trying to distract me with compliments. The verdict, love. I bought you a gift. Placed the shiny silver box in your hand. Give me my reward now.'

His words hang in the air like a heated fog. I remember opening the box; the flare of recognition at what was inside. The longing I'd experienced wishing I'd them here, at Dan's place, rather than alone in my bedroom.

I'd unpacked them, dropping each steel ball into my palm where they'd lain heavy and cold. *What would he have done?* Probably had me naked and spread-eagled, or maybe bent over a kitchen stool while he'd pushed them inside with his finger? With his cock?

Coming back to their purpose, a little wet and little flustered, I'd run them under the warm faucet. *For sanitation and comfort,* I'd told myself. Then, in my bedroom, I'd leaned one forearm against the dresser, watching my expression carefully as I'd inserted them, feeling extremely perverted for a Tuesday afternoon. Not that I usually have any problem touching myself, but this instance had taken on another dimension. I'd never watched myself . . . play with myself. And Dan hadn't even been there coaxing or cajoling. Daring me on.

'I'm still waiting.'

His words are quiet, his hand on my bare thigh. I blink heavily; where to start? How to separate the action from the recollection? And where to begin.

Would embarrassment always ball words in my throat?

I recall feeling full . . . not unpleasant in itself but hardly earth-shattering. Despite rinsing them in warm water, the balls had felt cold and moved a little inside me as I'd stood. The feeling was mildly disconcerting, but ultimately, they'd made me feel needy. Horny, as Flo would say. But was it the balls themselves, or the thought of being directed by Dan from a distance. Maybe I should've suggested some kind of communication. Skype, maybe?

I think I might be going insane.

Dan is on me in that instant, over me, his body pressed hard against mine. His kisses hot and wet as he pushes me up against the pillows, his hands roaming everywhere as he feeds his hips between my legs. Rearing onto his knees, he smiles down at me and all I can think is, Oh, shit.

'Are you being a deliberate tease, or are you genuinely embarrassed?'

'Does it matter?'

'Absolutely. I'll punish you for the first.'

'And the second?'

'Delight in it, as I've said. Which is it, love?'

God, his voice. Threats and honeyed promises. My eyes lower to where his shirt lies open, my pussy exposed, then to where his cock hovers, vulgar yet beautiful.

I look up, inhaling shortly for effect. 'Boring.' I add a light shrug, then roll my eyes a little. 'Thanks for thinking of me, but I'm sorry to say, Ben Wa balls are as much fun as a training bra.'

I don't have time for further teasing or insults as he leans over me, slipping his hand into the nightstand. To my shock, and possibly my delight, he pulls a length of rope from the drawer. My breath halts and stutters as he trails it over my shoulder, then down where his shirt gapes, tickling between my breasts.

'Boring? We'll have to improve on that.' He trails the length down one leg and up the other. 'There isn't a girl around who isn't silenced by twine.' As he pulls it tight against the flesh of my thigh, it marks in an instant. The scratchy, criss-crossing dents are apparent only for a second before fading.

'You don't play fair,' I croak, watching him winding it around his fist. Rope. Who'd have expected this would be my reaction. Excitement. A little fear. Did I mention excitement? My nipples stand to attention, gooseflesh stippling my skin.

'You aren't here for fair, sweetheart.' He sounds amused and full of self-satisfaction. It makes me squirm, like I've been called out or something. 'You're here because you want to pretend this isn't really who you are. You're here because you want to be excited and reprimanded in turns. You don't want me to hold you in my arms and make sweet, tender love. You can get that from any Tom or Dick on the street. You're not the same as other girls, love. You're the rare kind. You just need time to find out for yourself.'

The light in his eyes is so mesmerising, I couldn't have formed a denial even if I'd wanted to.

'Because you're exquisite. Any man would be glad to have you in his bed, only most wouldn't know what to do with you once you were there. You're quite unique. It's like the children's game; opposite's day. Are you familiar?' I nod again, his tone hypnotic and as sexy as anything I've ever known. 'I'm coming to find that for you, every fuck should be like opposite day. Because to you, cruelty is more like a kindness. It's better to be tied and tortured, don't you think?'

I don't trust myself to answer as he slides the rope around my wrists.

Chapter Fifteen

LOUISE

Lying on my side, the rope chafes the skin of my arms in several places. I know my expression registers discomfort, but it seems to fall short of Dan's notice. Whether by accident or on purpose, I'm not sure.

'I think you're the devil.'

I keep my tone light—it's not his fault I'm trussed. He gave me the opportunity, and I was greedy for it. Now I'm not so sure. I try to remain still to prevent any rope burns. It's hard enough to hide the thumb-sized bruises he leaves on my wrists. So I keep still. Isn't that what submission means? Taking without complaining. Can I really want this?

From the other side of the room, Dan chuckles. 'I might have guessed you'd make me the villain. If it makes it easier, I aim to please.'

Stepping closer, his eyes flick to my collarbone made prominent by my position and the intricate tying of rope. *Wrists tied to elbows behind my back—an elegant not-quite bra making my nipples hard.* Despite the initial feeling, and despite his beautiful handiwork, maybe I'm not quite ready for this.

This isn't pretty silk tying my wrists to the headboard. This was . . . real in the rawest sense.

'How are you doing?' he asks amiably. We'd discussed how he'd untie me immediately. All I had to do was say the word. True, the first twinges of discomfort have turned to aches, most tellingly in my shoulders. I exhale a rush of air. Yes, I'm a little uncomfortable, but I want to see where he'll take this. And I hate giving in. Hate losing. Hate being second best. 'Ready to tap out?'

'Not yet,' I reply. Forgetting the rope for a moment, I relax my elbows, causing the rope to chafe. I wince, my body tightening again.

'My poor darling, does it hurt very much?' His mouth makes a teasing moue, not that I'm buying his sympathy. His eyes burn too bright for one thing.

'Would it matter if I said yes?'

'You with your pained expression and such wide, innocent eyes. Anyone would believe you didn't want to be strapped down.'

'I don't think I want to be. Not like this.'

'No? I hardly forced you to comply. You could— can say—stop at any time.'

This much was true, but I'd been up for the experience. Truthfully, I still was. I wanted to know where he was going with this. If he'd just get to the point of my release—yes, that kind of release. Before untying me, that is.

'Remember, this is a punishment. I bought you a gift and not only did you forget to bring it along, but you also rubbished it.' His jeans are back on, though barely. Buttons popped, they ride dangerously low on his hips. It was hard not to see his bulge. Any other time, I'd have a quip at the ready, but presently, my mind is filled with other things.

'How was I supposed to know you'd want to use them tonight? And just so you know, this fucking rope burns.'

'It isn't a fucking rope, silly. It's a tying one. If only you could've seen your expression when I'd pulled it from the drawer. It was like Christmas, right there in your eyes. That wasn't shock. More like delight.' His hand reaches out to touch my right knee, drifting farther to mid-thigh. 'I know you like the cuffs, but rope brings another dimension; rope hurts to resist. Twine makes you more mine.'

'You're a poet—' Would never know it? I don't get to finish as he pinches my inner thigh.

'*Ouch!*'

'I can be the devil, the villain of this piece—of your piece. So long as when it hurts, you remember I am so, that I *do so* at your behest.' His eyes glitter dark and sexy, his voice hoarse and strained. 'It's ironic, isn't it?'

I frown, familiar fears sprouting at the truth in his words. No one normal wanted their sex like this. Who wanted to be tied like a partly trussed pig? Pain and embarrassment and sex hardly go hand in hand. Which means I'm an aberration, not normal. I'm—

'And there it is; the first flickering of doubt.' Hands on either side of my waist, he pushes me onto my back, leaning forward and kissing me full on the mouth. 'The flame that blisters. The blaze that bites.' Then he does the same, taking my bottom lip into his mouth.

My sigh is libidinous, and softened by his attentions, I become almost malleable, sinking into his biting touch. What was the use of overthinking when he knows the inside of my head better? Stiffening at the sudden realisation, my arms ache as my knuckles press further into my back.

'Every little movement, each tiny twist of rope against your flesh, reminds you how helpless you are.' Coming closer, Dan's whispered words touch my skin, his body an elegant arc over mine. I close my eyes to the intensity in his tone, anticipating the weight of a body that doesn't come.

'Every hint of discomfort, every degree of disquiet, pushes you closer to that edge. The rope may secure you, may keep you in place, but it's the questions that keep you hanging there.' His lips hover over mine as though to remind me of his point. 'It's not what I've done that excites you. It's the thoughts running through your head. The endless possibilities. The scenarios your mind creates. Now that I'm helpless, what . . . will . . . he . . . do . . . next? He punctuates each word with a kiss. My forehead. My cheek. My mouth. And then, as an encore, he presses his teeth into my bottom lip.

A sigh stutters from me, my thighs widening and opening as though this is enough to bring him to me. I want him—crave his body and touch.

'This *is* a pretty invitation.'

I moan loudly as his fingers sweep along the slick seam between my legs. I push my hips from the bed to get closer, and in an instant, he slips his hands under my shoulders, edging my head to the side of the bed. Strands of hair cover my face, and Dan tilts my chin, brushing the strands away. I smile up at him and, for some silly reason, wink. But then he sighs in that protracted, long-suffering way. It's a sigh that says *it pains me to do this* or *this will hurt me as much as you*. Whatever the idiom of his choosing, I don't have to wait long to see what he's up to.

My smile falters as his sadistic one grows as his hand tightens at the nape of my neck, rolling me unceremoniously onto my front. My chin hanging over the bed, I can't see much for my hair again, though this position is way easier on my arms. As I contemplate the sisal carpeting, my heart jolts at the distinct descent of his fly. My heart rate dances a tango, the beat seeming to match the solid pulse between my thighs. But then my hair in his fist at the base of my skull as he whispers, 'Could have been worse, you know. I could've used the cable ties instead of a bit of limp hemp.' Then he tilts my head up and back. It's then that his plan makes sense.

'That's right, my lovely Louise. Open wide.'

Suddenly, discomfort doesn't seem such an issue anymore as I widen my jaw to comply.

Chapter Sixteen

DAN

Has there ever been a sight more perfect than this?

The rope compliments her golden skin, her hair is wild and her expression dangerous. The usual flecks of green in her eyes seems to have been extinguished by a tawny gold. She's like a lion tamed. A lioness tied. And for all the beauty of the situation, I'm still half surprised she let me use the rope. Half surprised but so bloody grateful. Despite her inexperience and her playful complaints, her tendencies in the bedroom are submissive. *Especially when she leaves her attitude at the door*.

I need to remember I didn't do this to her. She came to me this way. I might have unwrapped the package, but she stepped from the confines of the wrappings all by herself.

I smile to myself, settling the elastic of my boxer briefs under my balls, and once pulled free of the constraints of the material, I place the tip to her mouth, running the smooth head along her full bottom lip. We both groan at how this looks; her lying trussed on the bed, itching to touch herself. Me towering over her, cock in my hand, the head balanced on her lush pink lip. The pearl of liquid at my very tip as she harvests it with her tongue.

'Where did I find you?' My words feel scratchy in my throat, the need to drive myself into her mouth great.

'You didn't find me. You made me,' she whispers in response. Her compliment like pure lust to my veins, but before I can answer, she seeks to remind me of just how wild she is, bringing down her top teeth like a trap. I instinctively jump, but she's just playing, though my heart still thunders like hooves.

'And you call me the villain.' I tighten my hand in her hair as I pull back with a hiss. The delicate graze of her teeth and lips are like a shot of vodka downed too fast.

'You are the devil. For tying me like this.'

'Say the word and I'll set you free, my lioness.'

Her expression lights up as I return the compliment. She twists her mouth to one side as though considering. 'I don't think I will. I'll wait and see what you have in store.'

I chuckle low and soft. 'This isn't painting a picture for you, love?' The human mind is so fascinating. In her position, she still finds the strength to goad.

'Well, yes,' she replies. 'But it's more than just me. I want to see what kind of effect this has on you when you come.' I shake my head. I'll come like a freight train, and she wants to see? She'll more than see it—she'll feel it hitting the back of her throat so fast she'll gag. 'I only hope it's worth the discomfort,' she says.

'It will be. At least for me.'

'Have you ever been tied?' She tries to contain her smile, trapping her lip between her teeth. 'Physically, I mean.'

'We each have our quirks and foibles, my lioness. Mine prefer this side of the rope.'

'You didn't answer my question.'

Nor do I intend to.

As her eyes flick to my cock, they seem to burn with wicked thoughts.

'Given your position, I'd suggest caution.' My warning is clear. Teeth may be her only weapon, but they're fucking dangerous.

'Smug much?' she replies. 'Do your worst.'

'Darling, don't tempt me. My worst won't be best for you. I'm not sure you're ready for the ugly side of this relationship.' I shake off her words. It was her inexperience talking, but I still shoot her a warning. 'You're taking quite a risk.'

'You're the one thinking about putting your money maker where my mouth is,' she teases.

Instinct tightens my grip on her hair, and in response, she makes a small noise of annoyance.

'You talk a good game,' I say, instinct tightening my grip on her hair. 'But how about you stop talking now and suck my cock.'

Is it possible to smile *and* keep your mouth wide? Well, she fucking tries. She looks so delicious. All pink lips and eagerness.

My bare toes curl into the rug as I slide in because she's warm and wet and fucking divine. And so tight as I enter the channel of her throat. The muscles of my abdominals tighten as I ease in a little deeper, feeding my hand under her chin as I fight the instinct to ram myself in. Her anterior neck muscles contract as I slide in slowly—deeply—tightening around my hard cock.

'That's it, sweetheart. Take me. Take all of me.'

Was it always this wonderful?

As I slide back, tears teeter on her lids, her clear and guileless eyes staring up into my face. Grim satisfaction grabs me viscerally . . . right before she flicks her tongue over my sensitive head again. My body bows, caught by surprise, and she actually giggles. I can't hold back my own smile. I don't even try. Though I'm certain it takes on a different slant as I feed her my cock again.

God, she's gorgeous. So beautifully used.

Mascara stains, running in uneven lines down her face as my hips begin to flex. She's a messy kind of gorgeous now. Not so golden. A little more red. I bring my other hand to her hair. Not for control, but a way to be closer. To draw her to me. To get under her skin.

No greater honour exists than being offered control. And there's no greater pleasure for me than taking it from her. With this final thought, white hot power shoots down my spine. Knees bent and my heart bursting, my climax begins to pulse into her throat.

Chapter Seventeen

LOUISE

Rain still falls softly against the window as I wake with the duvet covering me and tucked under my chin. I'm alone as I stretch the sleep from my body, pushing the duvet to my waist. I felt light. Like a load lifted as the cool morning air kisses my skin. I smile imagining Dan slipping from the bed earlier and quietly tucking me in. Feeling all sorts of warm and fuzzy, I nestle my head further into the pillows, stretching my legs out along the bed.

I startle as a hand grasps my foot which peeks from the sheets, relaxing again as the hand reaches my calf. I sigh, pointing my toes in a horizontal *en pointe*, not yet ready to speak.

'You can tell a lot about a woman by the condition of her toes.' His voice is husky and like a tongue flicking between my legs.

'You just like them because they're painted blue,' I say, my voice sleep filled.

'Your assumption being?' He sounds amused as if he knows where this is heading.

'Because they look like they're bruised.'

He chuckles as he begins crawling the length of my legs, growling words against my skin. 'Not exactly the kind of marks I like to leave.'

'Not your preferred calling card, huh?'

His lips reach my neck, neck bone being connected to my clit, or so it seems. 'I don't need bruises to tell where I've been.' His words are barely a whisper as he draws my hands up and over my head. 'Unless I decide to leave one like this.' His teeth graze my neck, lips sucking the flesh just a touch.

I sigh, turning my head in invitation. *Fuck the marks*, I decide. *I'll wear a turtleneck for work.*

'I aim to please,' I drawl, turning my face into the pillow to camouflage my smile.

'Oh, you do.'

His praise blooms in my chest, warming me through.

'Did you go for coffee?' A girl can hope for lots of things.

The answer to my question is no, it seems. He halts, his head hitting the pillow next to me. He drapes his arm over my waist, pulling me closer, bringing the scent of soap and cologne and the faint smell of coffee.

'There's coffee downstairs. Don't pout.'

'Where've you been, then?'

'Answering emails, browsing Sunday supplements, eating copious amounts of cereal with my son.'

My body tenses, my eyes flicking to the door. 'He's here?'

'No.' Dan laughs, his arm tightening in its hold. 'He just popped in to say good morning. And eat. And talk my ears off. He's gone back next door, then off for a play date.' His gaze lowers unashamedly from my face then. 'He wasn't invited to ours.'

Pulling on the quilt for modesty, I cover what I can. 'You might've warned me, at least.'

'You were asleep. I didn't want to wake you.' His stronger grip holds the bedding, restricting my plan. 'You looked far too beautiful, my sleeping lioness.'

'I might've walked in on you both, naked. Did you think about that?'

His eyes close slowly, sliding those slender, refined hands beneath his head. 'I hadn't.' He sighs. 'But I am now.'

'Kid would need therapy,' I say, laughing and pushing him hard with my knee.

'Exhibitionism isn't your thing,' Dan replies, opening one eye and matching it with a sly smile. It almost sounds as though he's trying to goad me into the opposite.

If only he knew.

'You don't know everything about me,' I respond, something hot and sweet flaring deep in my gut. An image rises like smoke in front of me, tiny whispers of sensations, of people's eyes on me as I writhe in ecstasy. The full effect of the desire is just beyond my reach. Unexperienced. 'Have you never heard the saying *there's a first time for everything*?' So many firsts with Dan recently, but this one? This one is staying as a fantasy.

'First times are fantastic,' he rasps, suddenly pushing me flat and himself over me. The cool metal of his belt buckle prods my hip. 'Virgins, as a rule, are overrated. But first times and you are something else.'

My heart jumps ever so slightly at his powerful words, though I manage to shrug off the compliment. 'I so don't want to hear tales of your deflowering exploits.'

'Not to worry. The only recent deflowering I've been guilty of is joining Hal in knocking off the heads of his mother's roses.'

'The poor kid's already in therapy then?'

'We were playing Power Rangers.' Dan shrugs. 'Not acting out. Well, he wasn't. He's fine; she's the one who needs a shrink.' He seems to shake himself as though to eradicate the thought. 'But that is a tale you don't need to hear.'

'Agreed.' It's too soon. Not to mention, he clearly doesn't want to share.

How are you faring this morning?' Pulling himself onto his elbow, he peers down at me with a cryptic smile.

My eyes slide away quickly, my cheeks starting to heat as I recall last night. The way he'd looked as he'd come. His whispered praises and his ecstasy. The marks of the rope on my skin for hours afterwards, a map telling the tale of our evening. His exquisite aftercare.

'I'm fine, thanks,' I manage. *Booboos all kissed better, thanks.*

'Positively verbose,' his clipped tone announces. 'You don't want to talk? Discuss last night? Go for a review?'

'God, no!' This comes out more like a laugh.

'How very un-American. Perhaps you don't like first times with me?'

'I just don't need a dissection,' I say with a shrug.

'But it's part of the fun.'

'Anyone ever tell you you've got a sadistic streak a mile wide?'

Lying back against the bed, he slides an arm under my head. 'Sweetheart, I've been a pussycat. You haven't the capacity to like being truly hurt.'

'That sounds like a slight; should I be offended?'

'No slight implied,' he says, before asking suddenly, 'What would you like to do next?'

'I . . . I . . .' Images danced behind my eyelids as though shown on screen; cuffs, hands, teeth. Hot, heavy kisses. Discomfort. The chaffing of rope. An avid audience. 'Can I j-just get over last night first?'

Dan laughs, drawing me closer and kissing the crown of my head. 'You never get over ropes, but I was referring to the rest of the day. How about brunch?'

'Oh.' My cheeks burn immediately. Seems this spiral is all of my own making.

'Not that I don't have a million nefarious plans rattling around in here.' He taps his head. 'If I can persuade you to stay.'

'Oh, I don't know. I've got things to do. If you want me to stay, you might have to tie me to the bed . . . '

'If you ask nicely,' he answers, leaning over me to glance at the bedside clock. 'I might just do that.'

As he moves, I get an inadvertent glimpse of his tattoo. The words in swirling script make me feel quite sick. *Belle.*

'But I thought we might go for brunch first.' When I don't answer, Dan turns to me. 'What is it?'

'What does this say?' I ask carefully, reaching around him to draw a finger across the ink.

'*Sois belle et tais-toi.*' His French accent sounds perfect, but what would I know.

'What are the chances,' I ask carefully, 'it translates to *I used to be married to a cunt*?'

His smile is almost sad. The reasons behind I don't want to think about.

'I had stuff added to the original one. It more or less now says; *Look pretty and shut up.*'

'That's . . . not great.'

'It was either that or some trite comment about beauty. Written above my arse, I might add.'

His ass is worthy of the title, but I don't tell him that. All this talk of his past? It seems a little too much. And why does it make me sad? Could it be because the woman looks like a china doll? Or that she bore him a son?

'Why?' I whisper, not quite daring to look him in the eye.

He tilts his chin to his chest and looks down at me in confusion. 'The tattoo? Because laser surgery wasn't appealing.' When I don't answer, he adds, 'Why brunch? Sustenance—a social ritual?'

'No, I . . .' *Tell me why I'm like this.* I can't make sense of my thoughts, suddenly feeling overwhelmed. Instead, I hear myself asking, 'What is it you like about me?'

'You mean apart from *your* arse?' He folds his body over mine, his hands sliding around my hips.

'Be serious. What is it that—'

'Drew me in? What's not to like?' he asks, incredulously.

'Past experiences tell me kind of a lot.' I don't do relationships and can't remember the last time I felt invested or involved. As for the rest, I'm passably pretty, I think, plucking at the sheet by my hips. I have a pretty good track record at attracting the opposite sex. *For a little time, at least.* But I'm not beautiful, not like Belle.

Breathing out, long and hard, I can almost feel Dan's displeasure. But I'm not trawling for compliments. I really just need to hear it from him.

'Darling, you are beautiful, but in a very unapproachable way.'

'That's not right. I'm not—'

'You're prickly. And I like that.'

'Like a hedgehog?' My words are incredulous.

'No,' he scoffs, trying not to laugh. 'Hedgehogs are cute.'

'You'd better qualify that statement. I'm ready to push you off this bed.'

'You're cold—'

'Not helping!'

'On the outside, at least. But, by Christ, I've never known a woman burn so hot in my arms.' Breath literally leaves my chest in a soft *whoosh*. 'Most people probably don't realise that *stay away* veneer you wear is because you're not comfortable in your own skin. I think drunk Louise drowned all that out.'

'Maybe drunk Louise was just out to get laid.'

'Drunk Louise was unafraid and full of truth.'

'Drunk Louise left your house with a smile on her face.'

We both try to bite back our smiles. We both lose.

'This Louise in my bed is all new. Full of challenge and daring, she's burrowed under my skin.'

'So now I'm a parasite. Prickly *and* a rash? I could be something you're allergic to.'

'I said under my skin, though I do like you naked and over my skin.' His words come out in a rush as Dan sits up, swinging his legs out of the bed. 'Come on, lazy daisy. Stop fishing for compliments and get dressed.'

And with that, he bends and kisses me on my forehead, then bounces from the bed.

Chapter Eighteen

LOUISE

What if he breaks my heart?

'Isn't it called the British disease?' We sit outside a café on a quintessential English spring day. The pale sun hangs low in the sky, providing just enough light to give the appearance of warmth.

'Since when has spanking been considered a disease?' One fine brow rises as Dan taps the article I've spread out on the table. '*Le vice Anglais.* I think I prefer that.'

The article is in a Sunday supplement left behind by the previous table occupants. An article discussing the rise of kink and, more specifically, spanking clubs. It's strange Sunday morning reading, for sure.

What if he breaks my heart? What if he can't make room for me?

My heart beats louder, so much so that I can hear it pounding in my ears.

'Vice, disease. Same diff,' I say, flicking my hand with inconsequence. *Inconsequence I don't feel.* The closeness of a couple seated at the next table makes me uncomfortable as thoughts run through my head like a pack of wild, rabid dogs.

'I prefer vice to disease,' he replies evenly. 'Disease implies there's something to cure.' Dan places down his cup, folding his arms across his solid chest and stretching his legs under the table in satisfaction. 'It's a lifestyle choice, not an affliction.' His voice, a touch loud, carries in the air.

What if he hurts me in a way I can't stand?

'I'm not sure about that,' I murmur, turning the page. My eyes flick to the suddenly quiet couple, gliding past them in an effort to seem unconcerned. It's as if I can see their ears straining, not appreciating being part of their morning entertainment. Like a freak in a side show.

What if he breaks my heart? Shatters my soul?

'No one forces you, Louise.' His eyes rise slowly, full of knowledge and filth, causing my belly to fizz. 'More than you want me to. True?'

'True. No hypothetical person or persons force me against my will. Much . . . much more than I can stand.' *So far.*

He turns his head to the couple, perhaps sensing their ears, too. He flashes the pair a dazzling smile before stating, 'Safe, sane, and consensual; all the cool kids are doing it now.'

The woman of the pair turns quite pink—by his attentions or words, it's hard to tell. They're effusive in the return to their own conversation, anyway.

Dan's chest moves in some semblance of a laugh as he turns to me again. His voice quieter now, he asks, 'What's bothering you?'

Under the weight of his gaze, I sit very still, fighting the instinct to spit an unfriendly response. When I don't answer, he slides a foot between mine as I decide it was a good idea to pack an overnight bag; skinny jeans, a long-sleeved tee, and her leather biker-esque jacket.

Another nudge to my foot brings me back to his gaze. 'Well?'

'It comes easier to you guys . . . the British thing. You just have to watch a little TV to see how different your outlook is.' Deflecting. I could at least try, though it might've helped if I'd thought things through rather than just babbling words.

'You mean beyond the stiff upper lip, we're all rampantly free? You're elevating a bit of nudity and swearing on the idiot box to something that isn't.'

'You mean you're as repressed as the next nation?' My disbelieving brow lifts. He's obviously never watched anything recently on HBO.

'If you're a representative of a particular nation, then perhaps not,' he says, chuckling. 'But I do believe we're getting there. Getting you there. Fuck, I'm getting hard.' His eyes slide from mine as he discreetly adjusts himself under the tabletop.

'The journey isn't the issue. It's the destination that frightens the hell out of me.' My words are mumbled as I screw my paper napkin into a tourniquet around my finger.

'The destination is wherever you *get off.*'

If I had a dick, I'd be joining him in some discreet beneath-the-table rumbling. His cut-glass accent and honeyed purr. The double meanings. The suggestion of reprimand.

What if he hurts me?

'Torture's in your blood,' I whisper. 'It's easier for you to accept; it's in your history.' Fire, brimstone, and the wrath of hell is in mine. 'The English vice, the Victorian vice. Everyone knows you Brits are a kinky lot.'

More than I can stand.

'You keep arguing the point like it's academic, like you have no participation. I'm beginning to become quite offended.' His tone holds a note of seriousness as he slides his hands towards mine. 'Yes, I like hurting pretty girls, but you're a pretty girl who likes to be hurt. I also like taking pretty girls—that would be you in this instance—out to dinner and the cinema, given the opportunity. I'd also like pretty girls— that's you again, by the way—to be curled on my sofa with a book while I cook. We aren't a nation of deviants any more than Americans are a nation of Bible-thumping extremists. Just because I like you over my knee doesn't mean I resent my mother or that I secretly craved being buggered at school by the upper sixth.'

This isn't working. This isn't talking either of us out of it.

'Nature versus nurture.' He snorts, raking long fingers through his dark hair. 'It's such bullshit.

We are what we are just because we are.' But his eyes slide from mine in an uncharacteristically reticent moment. 'And I like who you are more than anything else. I like you and want to be with you. Can't you just accept that?'

My heart lifts as I swallow audibly. Not that it takes much to lift, malnourished and perhaps underdeveloped as it probably is. This isn't the first time Dan had alluded to actual feelings, though it was the first time he'd done so outside the bedroom. But that he mirrors my own growing sentiments doesn't help. Not one bit.

What if I can't do this? What if I hurt him?

Without answering him, I reach for my coffee cup, hoping its bitter contents could dissolve the ache.

'Not quite what you expected?' His words are quiet, and there's an almost rueful twist to his mouth. 'An escape from the subconscious. Very much conscious, I'm afraid now. Becoming more so by the day.' He clears his throat, straightening on his chair, his hand retracting slowly across the table.

Are we falling in love?

'I don't even know what you do for a living,' I say, hoping to change the direction of the conversation. How was it possible we haven't discussed this kind of stuff? *For the same reason you didn't want to tell him your name,* my mind whispers. Because you didn't want this to be real.

'Because you've never asked,' he said, standing and holding out his hand.

I thread my fingers through his; holding hands no longer foreign territory between us but feeling as natural as when he pins them to the bed. Things are changing. Maybe it's time I stop lying to myself because casual isn't the ache you feel when you're home alone and wanting to be near him. It isn't the clawing need to feel him between your legs. And it isn't placing your teeth over his scar, desperate to overcome the brand with one of your own.

We trace our path back to his home but barely speak. At the garden gate, ever the gentleman, Dan gestures me ahead, giving rise to a sudden thought. My mother would think him ideal. She'd approve of his looks and his beautiful manners. And his accent, of course. My father, though . . . he doesn't believe in divorce. But then, he doesn't rule my life anymore. It's strange how I can hear my mother's voice asking me, *Honey, what's the problem?*

Then I realise one of the problems stares at me from the door. A note in an immature hand.

Pulling it from the door, Dan reads, 'Gone to Benjamin's house. Mummy says you'll pick me up. Can we have pizza for supper?' Pausing, Dan looks to be thinking twice about folding it into his pocket. 'What in God's name did he use to stick it to the wood?' he mutters, his fingers rubbing through the sticky brown residue on the paint.

'Looks like Nutella,' I murmur as he pushes the door wide. 'You should buy the boy a cell phone.'

Closing the door with his heel, Dan wraps an arm around my waist. I feel him sigh against my back as he rests his chin on my shoulder.

'Is it Hal that worries you?'

I make to pull away, murmuring my denials as his arms tighten.

'The idea of Hal? My responsibilities?' I shake my head; it wasn't really, was it? 'Tell me what it is.'

I set my jaw and tilt my head, turning swiftly to look at him. 'This wasn't supposed to get real.' If it sounds like an accusation, it's because it is.

He sighs, this time with frustration. 'You really are the most infuriating woman. This may have begun in the realms of fantasy—an unlikely scenario, absolutely—for the start of a relationship. But at some point between our first fuck and the last, things have become very real. For both of us.'

My teeth feel the strain of biting back tears, my brow creases and my gaze not on him. *What if? What if? What if?*

'Look at me.' Harsh, his command leaks disapproval but not scorn.

Aiming for defiance, I raise my head slowly, chin rising high and haughty. My battle armour. My push to his shove. My silent *go fuck yourself* hanging in the air.

'We've spent more hours together than most people do through months of dating,' he says, stepping into me. 'What started out as you exploring what you like to think of as your ugly side turned out to be quite beautiful in the end.' His dark gaze bores into mine. 'Admit it, Louise. You like me.'

Options, wants, and needs run
quicksilver through my mind as his fingers tighten,
his expression becoming fierce.

'You'll give me an answer,' he grates out, 'even if
I have to take it out of your hide.' He smiles almost
cruelly. 'But that's right up your alley, as they say.
And not how this is playing out today.'

He spins me in his arms, pushing me along the
hall to the base of the stairs.

Chapter Nineteen

LOUISE

Sitting on the chair in the bedroom, Dan draws one shod foot on top of his knee. A large hairbrush dangles from the fingers of his right hand. It's a very utilitarian kind of piece with a wide wooden paddle and a mass of metal spines. It's the kind of brush suited to a Rapunzel mane, the kind requiring a hundred strokes at night.

I frown, disturbed by the brush but not for the reasons you might think. It isn't the kind of hairbrush a man uses, but as he swishes the bristles back and forth along his thigh, the motion is mesmerising.

'It has possibilities,' he drawls, 'but not much imagination, I'm afraid.'

'I don't know what you mean.' My voice is soft, the quiver in it audible as he taps the wooden back absently against his knee.

'I was thinking I'd beat it from you.' Angling the brush upwards, he shakes it a little in the air. 'Extract an answer by means of this,' he says, bringing it down to his thigh sharp and swift. 'Smack your arse until it's red and smarting and you're just dying to tell me why you insist on shutting me out.'

'For a minute, I thought you were going to threaten to take it out on my hair,' I reply, pulling a distasteful face. 'A brush is your answer? Surely, the metal spatula would've been worse.' Excited? Nervous? More than a little scared? None of these cover how I feel right now, despite my flippant response.

Flippant or not, Dan smiles indulgently before throwing the thing onto the mattress where it lands with a soft *thunk*.

'It's not the weapon, but the arm that wields it. And the intent.'

Reaching for the threatening item, I turn it in my hands. 'It's a very feminine piece,' I state evenly, trying not to show my hand.

'What's feminine about it?' Rising, Dan takes it from my hand as he lowers himself next to me on the bed. 'I rather thought hairbrushes were unisex,' he says, weighing the item in his palm. 'It's a solid piece of apparatus, this.'

As though to prove a point, he slaps the pale wood against the palm of his left hand. My body jumps at the point of impact, my telling gaze sliding away. I don't need to tell him how exciting I found that.

'Long hair, that is . . . i-it's a brush for long hair,' I stutter, sliding a chunk of hair behind my ear, my tongue darting out to wet my dry lips.

At the action, Dan's fingers reach out, pushing the curl across my shoulder where he twists it

around his finger. 'No, it isn't Belle's brush.
Nothing in this room belongs to her now. Actually,
I bought this thinking of you.'

As my brow creases, he begins to touch it to the
very ends of my hair, toying with them at first
before gathering the strands. I half expect him to
fist it at the nape of my neck, but instead, he lets
the weight of my hair fall over his palm as he
begins running the brush from nape to ends. After
a moment, my head falls back at the unexpected
action. I don't remember when someone last
brushed my hair for me.

Silence follows. I'm aware of nothing but the
sound of the bristles slowly sliding through my
hair. With each stroke, my spine liquefies until
Dan's chest is the only thing supporting me.
Placing the brush down, Dan folds me in his arms,
pulling my back flat against him.

As we sit, I become aware of the differing layers
of noises in the distance. A car passing, children
playing in a nearby garden. My body and mind
absorb the stillness, recognising it for what it was.
Peace. I'm not thinking or overthinking. No
fretting about what might be. I don't need to as
reality crystallises in my mind.

This thing between us may have begun as pure
escapism, but now was somehow real. Dan was
probably the only person I'd ever known who
could anticipate what I need to feel . . . just right.

'Am I so unappealing?' Dan's voice cuts through
my thoughts, a hint of sad humour tainting his
words.

'You know that's not it,' I reply softly

'Do I? You think my ego doesn't wound?'

'Your ego is impenetrable,' I reply, hoping to make him laugh.

'How little you know,' he responds, pulling me closer still. 'Maybe you should tell me what you need.'

There haven't yet been words created to describe what was between us, had there? I turn my head over my shoulder, peering at him as best I can.

'The moon on a stick?'

'Sorry?'

Embarrassed at my verbal slip, I shake my head, but know this isn't going to cut it for him. 'Sometimes,' I say sighing, 'I think the only thing you could add to improve this would be the moon on a stick.'

'The moon? Are you implying you feel this is pretty much perfect?' he asks incredulously. 'Why are we here again? Oh yes, I remember, because the lady doth protest to a little affection, to a little depth.'

I shrug tightly, trying to pull from his embrace 'You wish for more, and it all goes wrong. Nobody gets the moon on a stick. You can't have it all.'

'I don't think I've ever heard such fatalistic bullshit.' I try harder to pull away now. 'No, not so fast,' he says in response to my wriggling. 'You mean to tell me that superstition is the only thing holding you back?'

'No, not superstition. Knowledge. You can't have a connection where one partner gets to bully the other. Hurt the other.' This can't be a component of a healthy relationship, and I should know. Look at my parents—look at my mother, for God's sake.

'Come off it. You're not afraid of becoming a battered partner. Enough with the smoke and mirrors act. Tell me what this is about.'

With my hands on his forearms, I dig my nails into his skin through his shirt, holding back my snigger as he grunts, drawing parallels between the noise and his *come* grunt. My triumph at pulling free is short lived as, hands behind me now, he pushes his palm between my shoulder blades, forcing me down against the bed.

'I don't believe you,' he growls in my ear, pinning me down with his own body. 'Stop struggling. I won't let you up until you tell me what's going on.'

Frustration tightens every fibre inside me as his weight pushes me into the mattress. My last lucidly angry, hot thought before he moves was at least he wasn't enjoying this; his cock isn't hard. Isn't pressing into me from behind.

One firm hand against my spine pins me down while the other snakes under my body, pulling at the button of my jeans.

'Damned fucking jeans,' Dan snarls, fighting to drag them off while, hands at my waistband, I try to keep them on. 'Maybe I should insist on you always wearing skirts.'

'Fuck you,' I growl, scratching his hand. My heart is racing, but it's not fight or flight because I want this. I'm wet for him.

'Ouch! Not tonight, my darling,' Dan responds laughingly.

He's much stronger than I am. Plus, my fight is partly fake, so it isn't long before my dark denim and white panties are hanging below my butt cheeks. He slides two fingers between my legs, and we both groan at the wet sound, at how obviously turned on I am.

I place my forehead against the bed, giving in. Only, what I submit to is not what I receive. Yes, Dan's fingers work me deliciously, but unseen, he drags the spines of the brush cruelly across my hip. My voice fills the room; is there such thing a as a squeal of ecstasy? The action is sadistic, the sensation sublime, as the bristled brush carries on down to the cheeks of ass.

'Fight me all you like, darling. Fight me as your wet cunt contradicts you.'

My answer is just garbled sound as I begin to ride his hand, pushing back, my fists curled under my chest. I want the thorns and his fingers, and I want him to make me scream.

My mind hazy around the edges as my orgasm builds. Two fingers become three? Four? As I chant for him to do it—for him to fuck me like this. And all the while, I won't look at him, won't give him the satisfaction of my reddened face. My sick pleasure.

'I was wrong,' he rasps in my ear. 'It does take a bit of imagination to make you properly submissive.' His fingers are as rough as his voice. My answer is only to bite back a whimper as his fingers move away, sliding wetly down my legs.

'There's nothing like a bit of old school,' he grunts, the paddle of the brush swiftly following his words. I hear it in the air before I feel the impact. It isn't enough time to prepare.

My cry is like an expletive in the air, my insides pulsing emptily along with the bloom of pain.

Again. Two swift whacks. As hard as the first.

And this time, I do swear because it *really* fucking hurts. But I don't move. And I could. I could roll away. I could tell him no. As though reading my thoughts, he asks me this time, a note of something quite sweet in his voice.

'Are you ready?' I nod a little eagerly. 'Silly girl,' he answers, raining down a torrent of blows until my cheeks are painfully warm. Smarting. Hurting. I cry, sob, but not for him to stop. Especially not as his fingers return, filling me. Rubbing my clit. Filling me again with something entirely else. Unfamiliar and unyielding, I realise at once what he held in his hand, I now hold inside.

The handle of the brush.

'Necessity is the mother of all invention,' he whispers hoarsely, twisting the handle. Moaning, I press my forehead to the bed as Dan pulls it out.

The following moments happen in a blur of sensory overload, from my burning skin to the heavy weight of him. The phrase *brooked no argument* seems appropriate as he drives himself inside, covering me as if his own body is my skin. His hands at my shoulders, grabbing and pulling in a frenzy, fucking me so hard I don't know where I end and he begins. The knot inside me from earlier—my loathing and fear—is replaced by the aching sensation. This need of him.

I want to pull away, the sensation too much, but he anchors me there by the sound of his voice. By his touch.

'That's it,' Dan rasps, pulling me back onto his cock again and again. 'Fucking come. Come like this, now!'

And I do. The feeling builds and builds, and at his word, the sensation bursts like fireworks. I'm aflame. My whole body a blaze of sensation. Electrified. Sent heavenward. Behind me, Dan's movements turn jerky as he slams into me one more time. I ache instantly with the loss of him as he pulls away, before his climax lashes my back in hot, wet bursts.

Moments later, we're collapsed on the mattress, a tangle of creased clothing and sweat-shining skin. I shiver in the cooling air as Dan pulls the edge of the duvet over my bared skin.

'Tell me that wasn't hard on both of us,' he says, still breathing heavily as he slides a tangled lock of hair from my face.

'You're a sadistic asshole,' I murmur happily, allowing him to slide an arm underneath my waist.

'But you love me for it,' he growls in my ear, rolling me closer.

'And therein lies the problem,' I whisper, 'because I think I actually do.'

What if, what if, what if?

Chapter Twenty

DAN

'Hello, stranger!' Kit's hand claps me on the back, pulling my attention from the business article I'm currently reading. I place the newspaper down and stand to shake his hand.

'A bit of an overstatement. I only saw you, what? Two weeks ago?' I gesture in the vague direction of club Mede.

'Try nearly four,' he says disapprovingly. 'Next door. We had a drink.' *The night I met Louise.* 'You haven't been around The Den very much,' he adds, adjusting the knife-sharp pleats on his suit pants, taking the seat across from me. 'What gives?'

'New suit?' I goad, ignoring what seems like a slight.

Kit runs a chain of boutique hotels and works as hard has he plays. He's also such a natty fucking dresser—tailor made all the way from his eight-hundred-pound shoes to his silk Windsor knotted tie—that his sense of dress makes him an easy target for piss taking. It's all good-natured banter, of course, as we also happen to be friends.

'Fuck off,' he retorts immediately, removing a piece of invisible lint from his cuff. 'And stop tryin' to change the subject.' Crossing one leg over the other, his brow furrows, his Scottish accent kicking in. Ordinarily, the brogue is barely discernible. Unless he's annoyed. Or talking about his twin brother. Or playing football. Or fucking. *Guess which it is now?* 'Haven't seen hide nor hair of you in the club for weeks.' His words are as heavy as his brow.

'I've been coming in during the day,' I reply with a light shrug. 'I get more done when it's quiet.'

He makes a very Scottish sounding noise from the back of his throat. 'You're either avoiding pussy or gettin' it someplace else.'

'And that would be none of your business.'

'Indeed!'

He sends me a lewd wink. Kit is bisexual, though the word really doesn't encompass everything he is. *Fucking filthy might.* And coming from me, that's a compliment. Though I'm pleased to say I've never had the pleasure. Threesomes no longer hold any interest for me, though there was a time in my marriage that . . . I brush the thought away immediately because Belle is a head fuck all of her own.

'And that's the way I like it. I can't be doin' with becoming friends with the people I fuck.'

'And how's it going with Simone and Greg? Still seeing them?'

'Still fucking them. Well, her. He just likes to be manhandled a bit. And demeaned. But we all have our own little foibles.'

I burst out laughing, having said something similar to Louise myself.

'That was funny?'

'Inside joke,' I answer dismissively.

'What I want to know is, who's taking care of your little foibles now? And by that, I mean your little cock.'

'Christopher,' I drawl using his full name. 'You know better than to start with those kinds of insults. How many times must I tell you, it's what you do with it that counts.'

'One time,' he says laughing and referring to a particularly embarrassing incident he'd had on the main floor. 'It was the first time I'd been licked from both ends—'

I hold my hand up, warring off his words. And he stops, before returning to his previous line of questioning.

'Which is it, then? You're either avoiding pussy— though I don't know how as I haven't seen you with anyone at The Den lately—or else you're getting it somewhere else. Come on, Master Daniel. Whose arse are you spankin' these days?'

'Not that it's any of your business, but I have met someone.' I gesture for the waitress and order us both a coffee, doing my best to ignore his delighted expression. I hadn't meant to get into this. We're here to talk business. *Business in a sex club is still sex, though, I suppose.*

'Thank Christ for that. I was beginning to think you'd returned to your campanologist days.' His words and expression are both heavy with meaning, but what that meaning is? No bloody idea. 'Campanologist. You know, the study of bells? One in particular . . .'

'Someone showed you the benefits of Google, then? I thought I'd heard screams last week,' I say. 'Was that you getting dragged into this century?' Kit looks over at me, unimpressed. 'And Belle, for fuck's sake! If I even show the *remotest* signs of interest in my ex-wife, you have permission to book me a bed in Broadmoor hospital.'

'Good. Glad to hear it. Also that your needs are being met.'

My needs. Why must it always come back to kink?

'And if you bump into me on the street, do me a favour? Don't call me that.'

'What? Master Dan?'

'That's not who I am. I don't need a *nom de guerre.*'

'I was only taking the piss. But name or not, you are what you are. You can't hide from it.'

'I was only ever that person with Belle.'

'So you're done with kink? With holding your lover's heartbeat in your hand? Done with pretty red arses and girls tied up with string?'

'All right, Julie Andrews,' I say as the waitress returns. 'You've made your point.' I take the proffered cup, inhaling the dark cloud of bitterness.

'They'd definitely be on the list of *my* favourite things. Anyway, who is she?'

'A woman I met.'

'Here?'

'No.'

'While you were looking for new premises?'

'Finally, the reason we're here! Work shit. Let's discuss the place in Manchester you mentioned last.'

'No, it doesn't suit your needs. I've already told you. Too close to residential land. And the parking is shite. Did you meet her at one of the parties you were gonna give a try? Kill Kitty? Torture Terrace?'

'No.' I'd planned on attending some very specific kinds of parties. Call them competition. I hadn't. Because Louise had happened.

'It's like getting blood out of fucking stone,' Kit complains in a frustrated undertone. 'So you met her at the supermarket, then? Because Christ knows you do nothing outside this club. Unless it involves looking after Hal. Was there that spark of electricity when your hands touched over the last microwave meal? Was it love at frozen carbonara?'

'You're a nasty fucker, you know.'

'Aye, I do know.' As though struck by divine inspiration, he slaps a sudden hand to his head. 'It's not one of the divorced yummy mummies from Hal's school, is it?' Such a ridiculous sentence to come out of this man's mouth. 'If it is, Belle will probably end you both!'

'She's American,' I say quite suddenly. 'A little younger. And she knows nothing about any of this.' I open my palms, indicating the space around us. The Den, the lifestyle, anything.

'How can that be?' His expression then morphs to one of knowing. 'Too busy fucking?'

'It's not like that. I like her,' I begin tentatively. 'I really like her.'

'So what's the problem?' he asks, not without frustration.

'Honestly? I've no idea what she thinks of me, beyond how I fuck her.'

'I'm guessing that's hard and often,' he deadpans. 'Which says she might not be opposed to all this.' He mirrors my earlier action, opening his hands to indicate the space around us. 'You're a complete bellend. What happened to the immortal line, *spare the rod, spoil the sub*?'

'She's not my sub.'

'Sounds like she isn't your anything at the minute.'

'Fuck you.' There's no malice in the words, though his assertions stings.

'Take a ticket and get in line. I'll see if I can fit you in. Look,' he adds, seriously, 'The longer you leave it—'

'Don't you fucking think I know that already? But it's more than that. It's like she doesn't want to know. What kind of woman doesn't even ask what the man they're screwing does for a living? She's closed off and new to all this. I just don't know. Maybe she's only in it for sex.'

'I didn't know you were such a fatalist. When did that happen?' I shake my head, too weary to even defend myself. 'Ask her—you bring it up. It's not like you to be such a pussy, is all I'm saying.'

'Yeah, well, this is where divorce leaves you.'

'No, this is where Belle left you. Move the fuck on, man!'

Easier said than done though.

'And there's one thing for sure. If she's not asking those kinds of questions, it's because she's hiding shit of her own.'

And truthfully, that's what scares me the most.

Chapter Twenty-One

DAN

Weekends seem to be our thing. Dinner Friday night. Saturday morning in bed. Sunday Brunch, if I'm lucky, before she leaves on Sunday night. And that's where we are right now. On the brink of another week we're in bed. Her body is a soft weight against me, knees fitted behind knees with my possessive arm slung across her waist. We're not sleeping. In fact, we've barely spoken since we'd fucked. It's strange, but it's not an uncomfortable silence. It feels as natural as breathing having her in my arms. She'd said she loved me last time we fucked, but I don't think that heavy a declaration can be valid at that point. I don't know how it is for women, but I can be pretty effusive in my love for all kinds of things right after I've come.

As Louise begins to fidget in my arms, I can't help but think she's building up to something that's weighing on her mind. I decide to help her along.

'Spit it out,' I drawl, tightening my grip on her. 'My brain's never at its best for a while after I've woken up. Or after I've come.' I draw a languid finger down her arm, making her shiver. 'Words of small syllables,' I now whisper. 'Make it easy for me.' I keep my words as unhurried as my movements as I stretch out along the bed.

'This can't be normal, can it? Do you think I'm . . . normal?'

'It's a relative term, darling, and—'

She pushes my arms away, sitting upright, the look in her eye one of combat. 'This can't be normal,' she spits, daring me to deny her words. 'Being spanked, being fucked with a brush. Who enjoys that?'

She's not looking for an answer. Just an argument, for some reason. 'You're a pussycat.' Rolling onto my back, I slide a hand beneath my head. I close my eyes with a sigh before speaking again. 'There's nothing wrong with you. Besides, you haven't the capacity to be truly hurt.' I'm thinking of canes, especially. That she isn't truly a pain whore is more than fine by me. These are thoughts I'll keep to myself today.

'I shouldn't *want* to be hurt. I shouldn't want this.'

I can't be sure if her words are aimed at me, but they cut all the same. *She shouldn't want me? Us? This?*

'And if I'd been born without a dick, you'd be sleeping with a lesbian.'

'Well, there's no need to be so . . . crass.'

'And there's no need for you to keep beating yourself. Not when you have me nearby.' My smile is feral. I mean it to be—for distraction, if nothing else. 'You've got to be the biggest masochist out there.' In a certain sense.

'That's not helpful.' I can see she's struggling not to cry as she pulls the bedding up to her chin.

I want to pull her into my arms, but something tells me it's the wrong thing to do. Instead, I place my hand on her hers, stilling her. 'Are you going to tell me what this is about? Why now?'

'I don't know,' she replies, her words bubbling. 'It's just every now and then, I know I shouldn't. Not like this.'

'Shouldn't fuck?'

'It's not that. It's the bits between.'

'When we have dinner? Eat brunch? When I eat you out?' I keep my voice light, trying to make her laugh. To no avail.

'How? How can I like it?'

'Because I'm very good at it and, well, just look at me. I'm what your friend would call a bit of a sort.'

'You're what my therapist would call an abuser.'

Slowly, I sit up straight, my voice taking on a cold edge. 'I suggest you tread carefully. Think very clearly about what you say next.' Is she trying to offend me? Lashing out? Whatever her reason, I take this very seriously.

'I'm sorry,' she replies quietly. 'That wasn't fair. Truthfully, I don't know how she'd label you.'

'How would you define me?' I keep emotion out of my tone and my body very still. Tension—fight— whatever this is, seems to drain from her immediately.

'How would you define us?' This is dangerous territory.

'I don't think there's a label big enough to define that.'

'This therapist. This is someone you're seeing currently?'

'No. Before. At home.' She inhales, air expanding her lungs until they could accept no more. When she exhaled, it's all words. 'I have issues with intimacy and control. I expect she'd say I've gone from one extreme to another this time.'

'Meaning what?'

'I never commit, and I like to hold the relationship strings. Do what I want, unlike now. Although you do kinda do what I want you to,' she adds sheepishly, trying not to smile.

'Not quite true. I do to you what I want.' This is ridiculous; the chicken and the egg argument. 'You're a little uncomfortable in your own skin, I know. I've no issue warming it up for you.'

'I've spent my whole adult life trying to maintain some sense of control. According to the good doctor, it's to take back what was lost during my childhood. To recover what my father took from me.' Beside her, my body becomes taut. 'No, not like that,' she adds quickly. 'My dad is a control freak. Obsessive, overbearing, with rules like the military. One of God's fucking soldiers!' She doesn't often swear and looks on the verge of tears again. 'He's controlled my mom and his family our whole lives; what to wear, what to study, how to conduct ourselves. The opposite to how you are with Hal. His dirty feet, the puddle of milk and cereal.'

'When you first met him?' When he'd brought himself over to meet Daddy's play date? Or rather, when Belle sent him.

'Never in my whole life have I been anything but pristine. Except when I'm with you, when you fuck me messily.'

It's like even the words are difficult for her. I begin to wonder if a little homemade aversion therapy might help, restraining an inappropriate smile at the thoughts of Louise splodging. *Jelly and ice cream. Cake and cream.*

'I never got to make mud pies or be covered in paint,' she continues. 'As a teenager, I swapped out wild, awkward, and funny for worried and sedate. I got out of that house as soon as I could, and now I'm the living, breathing mockery of my suffering. He belittled me to control me. You demean me because I want you to. I'm sick; can't you see?'

Underplaying her reactions, I stretch out my limbs like an overindulged cat. 'If the hair shirt fits . . .'

'I knew you wouldn't understand.'

'So tell me.'

'My father. He . . . he's a religious man. He found out. About me. From Brad.'

'Brad?' The boyfriend I teased her about? 'I'm not sure I understand.'

'Brad dumped me,' she says on a cry. 'He said I was broken. Disgusting. That I'd never be right.'

'But you've had therapy—you said he was your first boyfriend? While feeling blindsided, I also feel something is off.

'No, you're right,' she says, swiping her hand under her eyes. 'But that's only half of it. He told my father and he—he sent me to camp—to pray the gay away I didn't have.'

'A what?'

'A camp, you know, like a church camp or summer camp? Only this wasn't just for homosexual kids. No, this one was for all kinds of sinners and sexual deviants. All those needing to be led back to "God's path". There was no path leading to God in that forest.'

I've heard of such things. Of course, I have. But truly, they seem like something off TV, and unprepared, I have no idea what to say.

'What did they do to you?'

'Nothing too horrendous,' she admits, her eyes falling to the bed. 'Pray. Sing. Trust exercises. How to repent. But I wasn't their usual type of sinner; I didn't meet their remit. I was too much of a freak for even them.'

'Darling, you're not sounding very sane. This is the first I'm hearing of this. You've loved what we've experienced together. You're an adult, and what happened was misguided and disgusting and wrong, but—'

Louise springs from the bed angrily, bending to retrieve her discarded jeans. 'I knew you wouldn't understand,' she growls at the floor, yanking the fabric up her legs.

My movements are as swift as hers, my hands landing on her hips. I pull her into me, my mouth at her ear. 'There's no correlation here. No need for further therapy as far as I can see. Liking a bit of kink doesn't make you sick. What you are is a double masochist. You want me to demean you so you can beat yourself up about it later. You want me to hurt you while I love you, so you can hate yourself a little more.'

As I tighten my arms, Louise lets her body go slack.

'We can even play daddy if you like.' I pitch my voice as like a growl. Probably despite herself, she laughs.

Nothing more needs to be said, so I pull her back to the bed.

Later in the kitchen, we make tea. I stand behind her, my hands splaying her stomach before she turns to face me.

'I can only guess at your experiences growing up with a father like yours. And a camp to cure you? That's fucked up beyond my comprehension. But, darling, whatever happened during that time should have no bearing on how you live. You let me do these things because you need me to, and because you trust that I'll keep you safe. But these feelings you have—these convictions—are keeping you tied down tighter than any binding I could fasten to your wrists. Darling, it's time to trust yourself.' I kiss soft and slow before pulling away as the kettle begins to sing.

I know I need to tell her, but that day isn't now. She needs to make peace with how she feels first.

LOUISE

For all have sinned and fall short of the glory of God.

I'd put those experiences behind me so long ago and at great expense. I'm shocked they came out this way. I'd tried to hold back the deluge, thinking I'd maybe find a new therapist. Work some things through again. Try a reboot? But to no avail; my tide of insecurity has come in anyway. *And I almost drowned him in it.*

Dan's reaction, though maybe not typical, was perfect. It was good to decompress that way, almost like flipping the bird to my experiences. And then his kind words in the kitchen . . . this man is so much more than I ever expected. I'm thinking he's pretty damn near perfect until he insists I come along to collect Hal from his play date, and I feel like a teenager again. I don't wanna! I go, but stay in the car as he walks to the door. No way I want to be introduced as the new girlfriend.

I also don't want to be *not* introduced that way. Go figure.

Our trio go for pizza afterwards, his little boy happily smearing himself in tomato sauce as I begin, ridiculously, to panic again. I can see weekends mounting before me; Saturday and Sunday spent as a pseudo family, the next weekend spent fucking in bed. Could I do that? Would I be able to walk away from Dan, from his son, at the end? And it had to end. Visas only last so long.

'Mummy always has a salad when we come for pizza,' the little boy states, eying my plate of spaghetti. 'She says pizza and Pilates, never the t-train shall meet.' He swallows a mouthful of orange juice, asking, 'What's Pilates, Daddy?'

Dan tries not to laugh, responding with the explanation that it's a sort of exercise session. Torturous, he says.

'That's what Mummy said yesterday to Charles using her very loud angry whisper. Why don't grown-ups use proper voices when they're angry?' I can almost see Hal's eyes cast into the back of his head as he tries to recall the exact words. 'She said his bed was tor . . . torturously boring, and that she might have to use yours instead. Are you getting a new one, Daddy, so Mummy can have your old one?'

Dan kept his eyes trained on his pasta as he prods it around the plate. While his hooded expression mightn't have hidden his thoughts, he can't quite conceal his growing smirk. 'I think Mummy was probably just having a bad day, H.'

'I think Mummy has a lot of those lately.' The little boy sighs. 'Maybe that's why she tells Charles she has too many headaches. She says it's all his fault.'

Dan laughs then; one loud bark from the depths of his chest. I suppose this is divine payback for screwing around.

No longer concerned by his mother's frame of mind, Hal springs into a conversation about the family cat. Half listening, my thoughts turn down Jealousy Street. From debating a vague future and contemplating his domestic scene to a growing realisation that Dan is mine as much as the other way around.

Later, once Hal returns next door and is presumably tucked up in bed, I find myself snapping and snarling at Dan's every suggestion, yelling at one point I'd fuck off home if he didn't stop asking what was wrong.

When did I become such a fickle fuck?

'Would you mind giving me back my head? What has gotten in to you tonight?'

'What? You're concerned we're going to turn out like boring Charles and the missus next door?'

His eyebrows rise to the top of his head. And he utters nothing, save for a telling, 'Ah.'

'Ah? Ah? What's that supposed to mean?' I snarl, poking him in the chest with a pink-painted finger.

As a flicker of amusement ripples across his face, I lift my hand with the intention of wiping that smirk off his face. In my life I've never struck anyone, other than my brother, and I can't quite believe my reaction once my hand is in the air. I'm not sure if it's my shock or if he catches my raised hand, but we stand locked in the moment endlessly.

When Dan eventually speaks, his tone is even but steel-filled.

'Don't.'

'Then don't you mention her ever again!'

It's a ridiculous demand—we can both hear it.

'I didn't,' he replies calmly. 'Hal did, but I'm pleased it's provoked some kind of emotion. Jealousy definitely suits you, darling.'

'It's an emotion I could do without,' I growl, unsuccessfully trying to pull free of him. I move the hair that has fallen across my cheek with a savage gesture of my free hand. 'I don't want to feel like this. I didn't want to get involved!'

'What are you shouting at me for? That's not my fault,' he replies, no less amused.

'I didn't say it was your fault, but I am blaming you!' With that, I cut off any answer. Curling my fingers around the back of his neck, I seal my mouth over his. I kiss him hard, our joined hands still absurdly in the air. After a stunned moment, Dan responds in kind. Teeth clash and lips bruise as our hearts pound against the other's skin.

'I blame you,' I say finally, my breath laboured and raspy. As my gaze levels on his, his eyes flare like a lit flame. And at that very moment, I want nothing more than to throw myself onto the pyre of him.

As Dan's grip loosens, I rest my hand flat on his chest, the other still knotted in his hair. I push my body against him, walking him backwards until the sofa hits his calves, as I kiss and tease his lips with every stumbled step. Pushing him down hard, I climb onto his lap, my legs straddling his. Fingers pull at clothing, each of us frantically wrestling for control and possession, though neither of us quite manages it, and neither of us keeps score this time.

My back arches as I feel the length of him through his jeans. I exhale a ragged breath, pressing my hand over his mouth as he begins to speak. Grinding myself against him, I'm desperate to get closer, to climb under his skin. We stay like that—Dan beneath me, covered by my fingerprints and need. I rub shamelessly against him until the point I come when my movements become as jagged as my breath.

We end in a tangled heap on the floor, breathless though eventually sated. Grazed and definitely sore. Wordlessly, Dan carries me into the bedroom, placing me on the bed as though I'm someone to be worshiped. Someone he adores.

Streetlamps light the room, playing shadows of trees against the walls. Dan climbs on the bed pulling me closer—pulling my hands above my head. With his mouth against my ear, he whispers softly, 'Darling, come blame me some more.'

Chapter Twenty-Two

DAN

Breakfast was a quiet affair, the holiday Monday meant Louise didn't have to be at work. The radio plays quietly in the background, a station she'd never have chosen. One I hadn't chosen, either, come to think of it.

'Can I expect The Archers anytime soon?' she asks, gesturing to the radio with her head.

Pulling a mock indignant face, I shook out the newspaper in an exaggerated motion before covering my expression with the sports section.

'The Archers and Earl Grey. You certainly know how to show a girl a good time.'

I don't answer, instead collapsing the paper and reaching for my cup. I sip, then hesitate before placing the cup down, all the while studying her, making her feel the weight of my gaze.

'You object to the station?' I ask eventually.

'Part of the pipe and slipper brigade?' she responds sugar-sweet. 'Whatever gave you that idea?'

My eyes slide to the Bose system from where the classical music emanated. I rarely have the radio on, the current channel either random or one of

Belle's choosing. 'It's just background noise,' I reply. 'Turn it off if it offends you. It's just a station. Not my choice.'

I probably should've qualified that. Though for shits and giggles, I don't.

Louise sighs and begins destroying her toast with her fingers, crumbs mounting on the plate.

'Don't play with your food,' I say without menace, though my tone may have been a little hard.

I turn back to the sports section when a sizable crumb bounces off my shirt. She wants my attention. So I give it to her by way of the lift of an indolent brow.

'Sorry,' she murmurs, lowering her gaze. 'Promise I'll be good . . . *sir*.'

My cock twitches, and my response is in the air without thought.

'Don't play with your food, and don't play with me. Not unless you mean it.' I tilt my head to the side, considering. 'If I didn't know any better, I'd say you were trying to goad me into action.' Given how she felt yesterday, I'm relieved to see she's all play. *And that she appears to mean it.*

Louise's brow furrows, eyes falling to the plate in front in an unsuccessful attempt to hide her growing smile.

'And if I were, hypothetically speaking, trying to goad a reaction,' she asks, dusting the crumbs from her fingers before raising her head. 'How would that . . . what's the expression? Go down?'

'Going down is always welcome.' I smirk, folding the crushed newspaper in half. Leaning back in my chair, I fold my arms. 'At the risk of sounding trite, are you trying to be a naughty girl?'

Hers is an instinctive response. 'No, not at all.'

'I'm mildly disappointed,' I purr.

Hands knotted in her lap, her secret smile is back. 'Then maybe I am. Just a little,' she admits, pinching her forefinger and thumb together in a sign of tiny measurement.

'How naughty?'

'Whatever level constitutes a punishment where you take me back to bed.'

I watch her, my expression one of consideration with the intent to put her on edge. I stand quite suddenly, the chair grating against the floor, and hold out my hand, my smile disarmingly wide.

'You dislike my taste in music. I'm going to punish you for that first.'

Throwing a hand to her cheek, she adds fluttering lashes for further effect. A distressed damsel she is not.

'Oh, no! Whatever will I do? Stop!' She might invoke a little Penelope Pitstop, but excitement added to her breathlessness, I can tell. I begin to stalk to her side of the kitchen table.

'Shall we start the bargaining, then?

'Bargaining?' She looks suspicious. Not really surprising; she's already called me a devil from time to time.

'The desired punishment,' I reply as though this is perfectly apparent. 'My expectations might not meet yours. Where shall we start the bidding, love?'

'Bidding on what?' She sounds bewildered. It's hard not to laugh.

'Bids are not on, but rather for. You're not that gullible. Come on, you've got your desired reaction. I'm going to punish you.
What's your master plan?'

'I haven't got one. I just thought I'd, you know, get you to take me back to bed.'

'I don't need goading into that.' I shrug for effect. 'Oh well, too late to go back on it now, but we can get to fucking later. For now, what will it be?'

'I have no clue. No idea what you're talking about,' she replies, looking a little perturbed now.

'Come now,' I purr, sliding my hand to the metal buckle of my belt. 'Don't pretend not to know. What happens if I want to, say, smack you with my belt?' I shrug again as though this is a reasonable request. She obviously hadn't thought of this as a consequence.

I watch her gaze sink down to the Italian leather wrapping my waist. What was in her eyes? Was it anticipation or fear? It's hard to tell.

'I suppose that'd be okay,' she replies quietly, though she doesn't sound convinced. 'Let's just go to the bedroom. Fool around a little first?' It almost sounds as though she was building up to the belt. Excited. A little scared.

'A fine plan, but it's not really a punishment then, is it? And I doubt we'd get to the belt in the end.'

'Good.' Her eyes flick southward again. 'Looks like it'd hurt.'

I laugh. 'Maybe, but isn't that the point of punishment?'

'Doesn't sound fun. Or warranted.'

'But you know you'd enjoy it; that delicious sting right there at the end.'

Her expression seemed to say, *not as much as you, by the look on your face.*

'How about I whack you first, just to be sure. You can tell me how it feels?' God loves a trier, so they say. Not that her attempts are working here.

Ignoring her bravado, I push my hand under her arm, helping her to stand.

'You'll endure it,' I whisper. 'Of course, you will. For me.'

Sitting on her vacated chair, I pull her between my open knees, splaying my hand across her collarbone and moving it steadily south until it's insinuated between her legs.

'Pick a number,' I say softly, watching her face as I rock my palm against her clit. As I rub my fingers along the denim seam between her legs.

Her legs begin to tremble, her response little more than a needy rasp.

'Five.' Her hips jerked, reckless and vulnerable.

'Higher,' I demand. 'And you can do the maths. Add your misdemeanours up.'

'The math,' she corrects. 'Not plural.' Her forehead creases as she prepares her answer. 'Five for throwing toast and five for insulting your choice in radio.'

'And five for making my breakfast go cold. And another five for using the word *math* wrong.' She opens her mouth to protest, closing it again as I cut her off. 'And a forfeit. You'll make breakfast again, afterwards. Entirely naked.' As I stand, I remove my hand, sliding it to her hip to turn her around. 'And because you want this too much, I won't use my belt, I'll use my hand instead.'

My arms around her waist, I begin loosening her jeans from behind. She trembles so hard, I worry her legs might give way. Jeans and underwear at her knees, I place a hand between her shoulders, bending her body down across the table as I sweep the breakfast dishes away.

Her head on her hands, she stares out of the window as I slap her arse. We'll call it a warm-up.

'Don't forget to keep count.'

Chapter Twenty-Three

LOUISE

'Louise, those projections are in. I dropped them off upstairs, and I can tell you they're none too happy about the figures.'

'They need to take off those rose-tinted glasses.'

I hadn't meant to answer her, other than to offer the blandest of deflections. Barbara has to be the most indiscreet PA I've ever known. But she'd caught me off guard, lost to my thoughts. Okay, dirty thoughts. I was busy replaying the highlights of yesterday through my mind.

My core flares as I recall my hipbones grating against the table with each thud of his hand. They're still a little sore today, to be honest. The sting in my cheeks eased when he placed both palms against me as he'd bent to kiss my ass. The sensation of his fingers trailing my ear as he'd gathered the hair draping my face. The flare of absolute need as he'd knotted it hard at the base of my skull. The deliciousness as he'd pushed inside slowly, push against pull as he held my hips and my hair.

He'd taken me slowly—he'd had to. There hadn't been much leverage due to my position and clothes. Somehow, this had added to my desperation and the taint of hurried dirtiness sitting at the edge. Recalling the slow sensation of him behind me—filling me, taking me—sent waves of remembrance between my legs.

Taken. What a cliché, but taken me he had, further and further down into the seductive rabbit hole until I'd come hard. Bent across the table with my jeans and panties pulled tight and digging into my open legs.

And afterwards, as Dan helped me stand, I'd taken his face in my hands and kissed him. We'd never reached the bedroom, fighting each other through our kisses and falling hard against the sofa. Fierce kisses turned to tenderness, and we'd fallen asleep, almost curled around each other like a pair of cats. For a little while, at least.

Back in the office, I come back to my senses, wet, my ears hurting due to Barb's excited squeal.

'You're thinking about a man, aren't you?' The delight in her voice is obvious even without the screech.

'What? No!' I begin immediately. 'I was thinking about the projections.' And I was, but not the work kind.

'Oh, have you a beau? Will we meet him at the McCartney opening? Just wait till I tell the girls! We thought . . . well, you know . . .' Her words trail off as she caught herself.

'No, I don't think that I do know.' Fleetingly, I wonder why I was even asking. Who cares what they thought? But all of a sudden I'm determined to discover what Barb meant.

'Well, you've no man. A powerful job . . .' Barb moves her hands in a weighing motion. 'No interest in the lovely single men working here. And, well, you're just so . . . *masculine.*'

'Masculine?' I repeat, shock colouring my tone. Fucking hell. Barb is right. As in, hers is a name that fits perfectly. Why am I surprised? I've heard her barbed gossip before.

'Well, not exactly masculine,' she wheedles. 'But not exactly feminine, either. Dominant!' she exclaims as though she'd only just located the word.

I almost laugh . . . almost. 'It's called professionalism.' My voice matches how I suddenly feel. *Ice-cold.* I know my reputation precedes me unfairly. I'm considered a bit of a cold fish, perhaps even a little unfriendly because of how I've chosen to conduct myself. I'd also been labelled the Ice Queen, but that had to be sour grapes and bruised egos, because the gibe had come from a man.

It seemed my own sex had now joined in the fun.

'So,' I begin, 'are you going to tell me what people think or do I have to run a poll?'

'Well, it only . . . see, people assumed you were, you know, batting for the other side?'

This time I do laugh, not sure about batting, but I was battered, all right. For pleasure. But gay?

'No. Not gay, Barb. Just choosy. And yes, I do have a man.' My words are overtly careless but pink rises in my cheeks anyway. 'And I might just bring him along to the opening. I'll get back to you on that.'

But even as the words left my mouth, I was mentally talking myself out of them.

Chapter Twenty-Four

DAN

'But darling, you're just so good.' Belle sucks in her lower lip for a second, releasing it pink and wet. As I turn, I can feel her eyes on my arse.

I pause for a beat but don't halt my task, the top rack of the dishwasher almost empty now.

'Go home, Belle.'

'Do you remember when—'

I glance down at the wooden spoon in my hand, remembering how the shape of it had stayed on her pale skin for almost a week that first time.

'No.' Not if I can help it, I don't.

Sliding the offending item into the drawer, I frown as I also remember reassuring Louise that I'd purged the house after Belle.

It's just a spoon, for fuck's sakes, I think, slamming the drawer closed.

'Not even for old times?' Not a question I can answer. 'Where did it all go so wrong, Danny?' Not an answer I would know where to begin.

Straightening, I run a distracted hand through my hair. 'There are no good memories, Annabelle.' I chuckle humourlessly. It feels alien. 'All were obliterated the moment I found you fucking someone else in our bed. But if you're looking for a reason, perhaps you could start there.'

'Maybe if I'd known you'd feel so passionately about it—damn it! Did you ever stop to think why?'

'A million times!' I yell back, finding her fragile shoulders in my hand. 'A million fucking times.'

I push a lock of hair behind her ear, bending my face towards hers. Tiny any day of the week, she wasn't wearing shoes. But I'm not a fool. Not these days, anyway. She's obviously hoping to remind me of how small she is. How malleable she could be in my hands. *Like old times.* Easy to fuck against the wall, her whole weight balanced on my hips or forearms. Easy to bend into all kinds of shapes.

I sense rather than hear her sharp intake of breath as my mouth came down on the crown of her head. I place my lips there. Hardly a kiss. More something to stop me from shouting again.

'A million times,' I repeat softly as I pull away. 'But not anymore.'

My phone skitters suddenly across the butcher block, Belle reaching it before I can get to it. She prods the screen.

'The code is still our anniversary.' Her voice sounds like triumph, eyes gleaming with, could it be, unshed tears?

'Give it to me.' I hold out my hand, my words not a request, my molars feeling the brunt of this.

'Why? What are you going to do about it?' Belle purrs, sliding along the row of cupboards, hands trailing the worktops as I follow suit. 'You'll have to catch me if you want it back.' She feints left and slides under my arm, her pealing laughter following her along the hallway.

I move to follow her, muttering a hard *'fuck'* as I recognised the light pitter-pat of her feet on the stairs.

In the bedroom, Belle prowls along the far side of the bed, sunlight catching the highlights on her expensively coloured head.

'The text says she wants you to help prove to her colleagues that she's not gay. I wouldn't have thought desk fucking with an audience was your thing, darling. What happened to *there's a time and a place for everything*?' She mimics me with a bass tone. 'But maybe you've changed. Maybe you've learned to accept some people just desire being the centre of everyone's attention.' Despite her nervous giggles, there's an edge of accusation there.

'Give me the phone, Belle.'

'Why don't you make me?' comes her sultry return.

So I did. Reaching for her as she allowed me to. I throw her against the mattress, a breast heaving, eye-shining mess. Her dress wraps her waist, deep pink silk lingerie on view.

'They're new.' There was an almost breathless quality to her words, her fingers dancing tantalisingly across the soft material.

Frozen to the spot, my eyes seem glued to where her fingers touch. I come awake to my actions with a snap, taking one, deep breath before my knees made a dent in the mattress next to her.

'A bit like those,' Belle whispers, her gaze sliding to the cuffs dangling from the wrought-iron headboard. I imagine it's not that she's surprised to find them there, just that they aren't, well, ours. Her eyes return to me as I straddle her legs. 'You know, I cried when you destroyed our bed,' she says more candidly than anything she's said today.

She said she'd watched from next door, watched from an upstairs window as I'd taken an axe to the expensive wooden frame of our marital bed less than a week after she'd moved out. My anger she'd seen as a sign of hope, a sign that all wasn't lost. She wasn't close enough to see my expression. If she had, she wouldn't have such delusions.

'Darling, let's start afresh.' Words spill from her lips, raw and hopeful.

I don't answer, just leaned towards her, drawing a finger up between her legs, not quite touching where she needs it, though my touch does resonate as she shivers. With an ease borne of experience, I flick her dress loose against her chest. Tilting my head to one side, I examine her pale, pale skin.

Belle stretches languidly for my view, arms reaching above her head in a silent plea. I follow the invitation, supporting myself with one hand against the mattress, the other sliding along the side of her body, trailing the sensitive but exposed underside of her arm, drawing the tips of my fingers . . . to the phone she still holds in her hand.

Anger, betrayal, and shame wash through Belle's face as the bed creaks when I stand. At the bedroom door, I pause but don't look back.

'Pull yourself together, Belle. Get out of my house and don't come back, not without an invitation. Understand I think of you only as a fucking slut.'

I didn't look back, her screamed response following me down the hall.

'I used to be your fucking slut!'

I grab my jacket from the hallway and car keys from the bowl on the hallstand, leaving the door unlocked as I take off on the garden path at a jog. My need to get away from her malice is great. The need to clear the scent of her skin bigger still. Belle stirs up too many memories. The good along with the bad.

As I drive, I recall images of parties with like-minded couples, the air filled with a sense of need and superiority, bodies fuelled by egos and drugs. We were professionals, she and I. Tied together by marriage. A mortgage. A child. But like so many of our contemporaries, we'd decided society's expectations wouldn't define us. Such middle class lives we'd lead in other ways. We often spent Fridays in the office before hitting the club, waking Saturday morning with someone else's wife's juices plastered to one or both of our mouths.

Now we have only a history, one I'd gladly ignore. And Hal. Sweet, funny, and by the grace of God, a well-balanced child, despite our fucked-up parenting.

It isn't long before I find myself on the banks of the Thames, phone in my hand.

'I'm outside your building. You wanted me to come and bend you over your desk?'

Louise laughs, hanging up without speaking a word. I begin to worry she hadn't believed me at all when the glass revolving door produced her. She beckons me inside with a wave of her hand.

'You're too late. It's gone six. Everyone's gone home.'

I turned, gesturing to the glass door I'd just walked through. 'Come back tomorrow, shall I? Just be sure to clear the surface of your desk. Save us both some time.'

'Wasn't quite what I had in mind,' she said smiling. 'But I'm glad you're here.'

I pause, my gaze on the space beyond her shoulder. She's never mentioned this part of her life; no talk of colleagues during dinner, no mentions of the stress of her day. I only know where she works because of that fateful business card.

Now what? She'd thrown me a line, and I'd found myself taking the bait. Should it offend my dominant sensibilities? The ones I have on pause these days? The truth, though I don't care to examine it at length, is probably Belle. I'm frightened by how easy it would've been. Rattled that she can still tempt me after all she has done. I wouldn't have. Not really. I just hate that I loved her at one time.

'Hey, you okay?' Louise's hand touches my arm, seeking to catch my attention.

'It's nothing. Just a ghost. Walking over my grave, you know?' Thoughts snake down my spine, curling in my gut, and I shiver under Louise's touch.

Turning, she waves at the security guard. I wonder if I look like a terrorist or just a little mad.

At the bank of elevators, pausing with a key card in her hand, she mentions it probably wasn't strictly professional for me to be here. It seems like an admission; something she hasn't done before. But then, she does prefer to think of herself as a good girl.

She seems distracted when she suddenly adds, 'Hey, what says dyke about me today?'

I return her look, though confused. As the doors chime open, Louise seems to be examining her clothes.

'I'm not sure I understand, love.'

'Someone said . . .' She shakes her head, stepping inside the glass box. 'It doesn't matter.'

'It obviously does,' I reply, holding out my hands in not quite a shrug. 'Because here I am.' I make a slow perusal of her clothing—her body, fingers at my chin. My eyes flick over her, almost critically. 'So, lesbian, you say? Butch or fem?' She looks slightly dubious as I blunder on. 'It's a difficult one,' I say, now cupping my chin. My eyes travel over her grey shirt dress and linger on her heels. 'If you were gay, straight men everywhere would be devastated.'

As the lift rises, the sound of her laughter fills it.

Chapter Twenty-Five

DAN

Her office could've belonged to anyone. Bar the certificates on the wall bearing her name, nothing denoted that she spent most of her week there. No photos from home, no potted plants, not even tennis shoes for the commute.

We sit on compact leather sofas almost at right angles to the other, chatting with inconsequence. As we do so, I realise I hadn't kissed her in greeting. Hadn't taken her in my arms. Crowded her space. In fact, I hadn't laid a finger on her. And that was wrong.

As our small talk petered to an end, an awkward silence begins to grow. Then lengthen. And consume. Louise excuses herself to go to the bathroom.

While Louise was up to whatever in the bathroom, I walk to the window, enjoying the view over the Thames. The sun is setting, though from the grey, dreary skies, it's almost hard to tell. I have a sudden urge—a longing—to feel the heat on my skin. Maybe I need a holiday, a break from everything. Fleeting images filter through my head; Louise draped across a monstrous bed, swathed in white linen, the bottom half of her bikini discarded on the floor as I push the other half up over her chest. She'd be sun warmed, sweat glistening, and sugar-sand coated. Only, as my eyes rise along her body, I can't picture her face. I can only see Belle.

Collapsing back into a chair in front of the desk, I run a hand down my face as my mind slips unbidden to our very first holiday. It had been a few months after our relationship had begun. *Was it Tenerife or Ibiza?* The crux of my thoughts don't so much centre on the country, but the destination we'd reached in that very bed. It has been a defining moment—crystalline, if you will. We were already fucking—her legs wrapped around my waist as I'd pounded her into the mattress—when she'd opened her eyes and whispered something I couldn't quite comprehend.

'Hit me.'

The bed had moved away from the wall because we'd been fucking so hard, but I did as I thought I should. One hand on the headboard, I'd snaked the other under her arse, bringing my hips into her harder still.

She'd moaned, hands balled into fists full of pillow at her head. But this time, she'd closed her eyes and turned her head to one side. 'Hit me,' she'd repeated through gritted teeth. 'Properly. Do it now.'

I'd pulled out a little, drawing back and trying to understand, to will her words to make sense. She'd opened her eyes and looked at me then, honesty and truth spilling, along with one salty tear.

'I want you to hit me.' She lifted my hand to her cheek. 'I want you to *make me hurt.*'

I couldn't be sure if I'd drawn back my arm, or if Belle had pushed it for me. Drawing it back further without the presence of my brain, I'd brought it back down and across her face with reasonable haste.

Her moan amplified through the room, her torso twisting and rising from the bed. I felt conflicted. Captivated by her writhing.

Pulled under by the pulsing motion gripping my cock.

Undone by her hot intake of breath.

Fascinated and revolted by the instant red bloom on her face.

You don't hit girls. The phrase had echoed through my head even as my hips had driven hard, making her cry out again.

And so it had begun—an incline? A decline?—to debauchery. Hard and fast fucks in restaurant bathrooms. Belle on her knees in grim alleyways with a mouthful of my dick. Ours became a gradual slide into depravity until that kind of sex became our default mode. Sex and violence went hand in hand, and it was a very slippery slope.

Belle is the daughter of someone quite famous, her father an actor who'd turned to politics the year she was born. She'd grown up in the limelight, a nation's darling. It's undoubtedly one of the reasons she is so spoiled. She'd been a dancer once, too—a good one. Though lacking in height to be truly successful, she'd always kept a dancer's poise, which was fun. I'd contort her body while she'd twisted my mind because it had taken me years of munches and parties to realise I was the principal in a ballet she'd almost solely choreographed. A ballet for one.

I'd bought the club at her encouragement, branching out from property development. Times were good. The front house already brought in enough to make it a sound investment, adding the members-only area in the back made it even more so. The days before Grey and his red room were heady ones, and we were trailblazers of sorts. It had seemed only natural for us to begin playing there. Natural and certainly much more practical after one of the tabloids had threatened to print pictures of a somewhat compromised Belle. I'd never found out how much it'd cost her dear old dad to buy those images. A close call, though privately, I've always thought Belle believed it as some great adventure.

So the club provided security, if not anonymity. A place to screw with an audience if one at all cared.

The membership list quickly filled, and Friday parties became all the rage. Members paid highly for the privilege—some came for the cabaret and some purely to play. Some wore elaborate outfits while others walked around naked with collared slaves. But by the end of each Friday evening, the great social equaliser of nakedness became king, and most took part in some kind of fucking. Minds, orifices; that kind of thing.

It was the perfect setup for us, or so it had seemed, and we'd agreed to play exclusively within the realms of the club. As time wore on, I saw fit to implement a couple of rules.

Firstly, no fucking without the knowledge of the other. Or to put it into words Belle understood, if she wanted to fuck someone, my permission had to be sought. She wanted to be dominated, and I liked to think I alone fulfilled that role. In that vein, she had to ask. *Usually on her knees.* I'm not at all sure how we'd strayed from monogamy, and it would no doubt sound strange to others, but for me, trust was the central spoke from which our marriage spun.

My second rule was to protect Belle from herself. God knows she needed the help. I've known the thrill of having sex in public spaces, the kick of excitement. The thrill and tension rooted deep in your belly. Will you be caught? Will you be heard? Exposed? That thrill for me had waned shortly after we had been exposed. *Those damned photographs.* But I'd done it for Belle—fucked her in spaces not made for sex, though the theory and the reality were different for me. It was never about an audience, or so I'd thought. In fact, an audience, I'd later found, put me off. But Belle was so impulsive. And spoiled. She had to be watched out for.

Following the clubs fit out, the flat above had been tailored for that very use. Private parties above a members-only club? An exclusivity to beat all. Those invited often looked like they'd died and were headed for sadistic heaven. A night with either Dan or Belle. *Sometimes both.*

Am I old fashioned? Belle, at least, began to think so. Perhaps that was when things started to go wrong.

Small transgressions at first, those I forced myself to believe I could live with. Swallowing the bitter pill and trying for adjustments in attitude. Following her punishment, of course. Difficult when I'd walked into the club unexpectedly some time following our honeymoon. She'd been naked and the centre of attention in a little bukkake. It had been more difficult still when she'd stepped from that same centre covered in cum.

At this point, I believed she was attention seeking. Perhaps on a punishment quest. It was true, she's always been a pain whore, and I never disappointed her on that score.

But by the time Hal was six months old, Belle had begun popping pills recreationally. Only pill popping didn't do her habit justice because she was open to most substances. *Coke. Liquid G.*

It did nothing for her restraint.

It did nothing for our marriage.

I spent countless Saturdays wandering London with a tiny Hal strapped to my chest while Belle stayed home, sullen as she dealt with a dopamine come down.

She was on a downward spiral all her own, one day encouraging me to screw the au pair as an apology for one transgression or another. *What was it she'd done?* Ah, I remember; she'd gone down on someone at the club while I'd been at home. It was a dark corner, she'd argued, and no one saw. Tit for tat, she'd said as I'd baulked at her suggestion. We were standing in Hal's nursery, for fuck's sakes, talking about infidelity as though discussing the weather while our son slept.

And then I'd found her with the neighbour in our marital bed.

By the time she'd said she was moving in with Charles, I'd felt almost sorry for the man.

And now there was Louise, game but inexperienced. Could we be treading the same spiralling descent? By keeping her out of the club, was I trying to protect her, or was I being greedy? Those flashes of daring—if she were truly serious, I'd take her up on them. Deconstruct her fully, in due course. But for now, I'd keep the kid gloves on.

The handle of the door sounded, and my head rose from the filth. Fuck Belle and her mind twisting and conniving, for I realised at that moment I was in love.

Chapter Twenty-Six

LOUISE

The lining of my skirt rubs against my bare skin, somehow affecting my gait. I sashayed and swayed as I pass Dan, perching my bottom on the desk in the front of the chair he sits in. Full of nerves and fright, I raise one foot, placing my toes on the seat between Dan's splayed legs, using the position to push myself up and back onto the desk.

'What's up?'

My voice sounds a little tight. I've never had sex anywhere other than the usual places. *A house. A bed. A sofa. In the back seat of a Chevy truck.* Well, almost. But being bent over a desk at the office is definitely one of my go-to scenarios. A handsome boss—not my boss. He's nearing sixty and bald with a sizable paunch. In my mind, I'd be dressed in stockings, heels, a gossamer blouse, and a grey pencil skirt. A few minutes alone with those images and my fingers, and the job is done. But spank bank material isn't meant to become real. I'm excited and nervous, and well, Dan can play my dominant boss any day of the week.

'Up? The roof. The upper floors.' Dan rests back in the chair, slipping his hands behind his head, sliding into his role. 'The heavens, some would say.'

Tipping my chin, I peer at him from beneath my lowered lashes. The coquette comes quite naturally when you're not wearing any underwear. Struck by instinct rather than thought, I'd hiked up my skirt while in the bathroom and wriggled my panties to the floor.

'Nothing else?' My voice turns unconsciously coy. 'Up?'

Laughter rumbles in Dan's chest, stopping abruptly as my shoe drops to the floor, the toes of my right foot curling around his pant-covered cock.

'Not quite *up*.' I raise my head from the action. 'But it has potential.'

From outside the room, a vacuum cleaner barks to life. My body jumps, and I'm ready to shove this scenario back into the fantasy box, but find I'm unable to move, my heel captured in Dan's hand.

'Are they likely to come in?' His voice is low and seductive and makes my pulse pound.

'No, not usually.' Worried, I bite my lip as my gaze drifts to the door as though I'm able to devine the direction of its path. 'Maybe. I don't know.'

As I look back at him, he's smiling—a smile of decidedly wicked thoughts.

'Why am I here?' Dan asks, his hand moving to massage my calf.

'I don't know,' I whisper, suddenly unsure. Or maybe not so uncertain as his hand moves to my knee, his other curling around the hem of my skirt.

'I . . . I have a question,' I begin. 'Do you want to go to a thing? Together, for work. You don't have to or anything—'

'You're asking me to be plus one?' His eyebrow quirks like a sudden question mark.

'Forget I asked,' I begin.

'Ask me properly, love,' he responds, obviously enjoying my reaction. *The absolute shit.*

'Would you like to be my date?' I ask as though it were no big thing.

His only answer is to push my skirt higher, revealing my thighs. He doesn't speak again, and I'm not sure if it's my invitation that garners silence or what he finds beneath my skirt.

'You're incorrigible.' He chuckles darkly. 'I'm very impressed.' The remains of his laughter hovers at the corners of his mouth, his gaze gleaming as he adds, 'Now, be a good girl and spread your legs.'

'But the cleaning crew? Let me lock the door.'

His hands retract to my knees, keeping me in place. 'We'll hear them. Besides, we're both fully clothed.' His gaze flicks again to my bare pussy, and he smirks. 'Sort of.' Hands sliding a little higher, he massages my thighs. 'You're so beautiful, my lioness. And so brave.'

'But what if they come in?' I'm not feeling particularly brave. Maybe breezy. But between my hurried words, my pussy aches.

In answer, his hands drift to my knees where he parts me farther, the backs of his fingertips trailing up my inner thighs. I tremble as his thumb presses painfully against the bones of my hips, and I sigh another protest as two fingers slide between my lips.

'Because this isn't turning you on one bit,' he murmurs as we both hear how wet I am. His smile turns to determination as he grunts, thrusting those two fingers deep inside.

His fingers plunge and curl as my own grip the edge of the desk. I might've felt powerful in my position above Dan, but his dark eyes undo me, and at this moment, I am owned by him.

With his free hand, he begins loosening the buttons of my blouse, pulling it from my shoulders. I gasp, conflicted, as the noise of the vacuum draws closer, catching my breath.

'Relax, it'll be fine,' he whispers as he lowers his head to my lap. 'But maybe keep the noise down. You don't want the cleaner bursting in as you come.'

Fingers still inside me, his thumb parts me, his tongue brushing my clit. My insides clench around his fingers, and with his other hand, he returns the favour, squeezing one nipple tight.

I arch my back into his hand with a stifled moan, my arms sliding across the desk as I submit myself to his hands and his actions and, almost silently, come undone.

Chapter Twenty-Seven

DAN

'Close your eyes.'

'No way!' Louise giggles, twisting out of my hands. 'Experience tells me I need to keep an eye on you at all times.'

My gaze is solemn as I stop her from pulling away, my fingers drifting across her wrist to her palm. 'Please.'

As she relaxes, I take the opportunity to pull her down onto the sofa, pushing a lock of hair behind her ear before considering it might've been placed strategically there. She'd spent the afternoon at the salon in preparation for her dreaded work party. Hair. Mani. Pedi. She'd even considered topping up her tan in the spray booth, but I'd requested she draw the line there. Her skin is too beautiful to cover in orange dust.

'Who can find a virtuous woman?' I murmur, lost in how beautiful she is.

'You need to advertise. Try Craig's List or Gumtree over here?' I smile at her attempt at levity, but I'm in a much more sombre mood. 'You're worryingly quiet,' she adds. 'If you don't want to come tonight . . .'

'That's not it at all,' I answer. 'I sometimes think I want to place you on a pedestal just to stare at you. Have I told you how beautiful you are today?'

'Just today? Thank the salon, then.'

'Every day, love.'

'Besides, I don't want to be on a pedestal. I've heard they're not very comfortable.'

'Take the piss all you like, minx, so long as you know you're breathtakingly lovely. And very important to me.'

Her gaze slide from mine like silk as she struggles with my compliments. I can't be the only man in the world who's ever made her blush? I push the thought to the back of my mind. Those blushes are mine now, and I love that.

'Darling, close your eyes,' I whisper. 'You can trust me.' She raises a brow in disbelief. 'You can trust me this once,' I qualify.

She laughs as her lashes flutter closed, and I release her hand for a moment before slipping on her gift in the place of my fingers.

'Who can find a virtuous woman for her price is beyond rubies.' My words are a warm whisper as I place her hand on top of the other and back in her lap. 'You can open your eyes now.'

'Oh, Dan . . .' Her words trail off, tears glistening like gold. 'It's the most . . . beautiful thing.' Louise holds out her arm to admire the Art Deco style cuff I bought last week. It was antique. Almost a hundred years old. Silver and studded with red stones the shape of pomegranate seeds.

'Not actually rubies.' I take her hand in mine. 'Garnets, I'm told. Stones of love.'

She places a finger across my lips, her mouth soon following, both palms at my cheeks.

'It really is the sweetest thing,' she whispers, brushing her lips against mine.

I place my hand over hers, kissing her just once more, my lips gentle even as hers sought depth. That I'd taken control of the kiss didn't surprise her. That I'd slowed them down did.

'I'll take thanks on account,' I whisper. 'You've an engagement to attend.'

'I can't believe I've gotten myself into this.' Her shoulders sag as she pulls away, a sudden thought seeming to hit her gaze. 'We could stay home. I could thank you properly.'

'Gotten *us* into this, darling. Why else am I wearing this monkey suit? And come to that, why are you in such a hurry for me to take it off again?'

'You don't look like a primate. And for the record, no clothes is always a favourite of mine.'

I pull back, almost lounging across the sofa as her eyes take their fill. She looks at me as though, given half a chance, she'd devour me. And I'd let her.

Above this pristine white shirt, I'm all clean-shaven and stylish hair. Her favourite cologne, clean and cool, fills the air around me. Midnight-coloured pants hug my thighs, not leaving much to the imagination as they cup the bulge between my legs.

'You're less primate. More . . . primal. More . . . man.' Her appraising gaze travels over me again. 'On the surface, you're the epitome of a gentleman.'

'On the surface? Is there a compliment in there?' I laugh.

'Definitely. You're a gentleman.' She tilts her head as though considering. 'Of sorts. And as for the other, I like my meat'—her hand slips to the bulge in my pants—'with intelligence. Smart gets me off more than anything else.'

I tilt my hips, encouraging her massaging fingers. 'Being outsmarted, that's what you really enjoy.' And that she can't deny. 'We've a cab due in ten minutes.'

'We could cancel,' she whispers. 'I wouldn't mind.'

'And spoil all my fun? Don't you know how much I'm looking forward to being paraded on your arm?'

She pulls away with something between a whine and a groan, shoulders rounded and hands in her lap. 'I suppose I'd better go get my purse.' She shoots me a look that clearly says *please don't make me.* And I've no doubt she'd make it worth my while.

'That's the spirit,' I reply. She rises then, sticking out her tongue.

As she moves away, her black dress clings to her thighs. Falling slightly above her knee and cinched at the waist, it somehow manages both sexy and demure. I stretch out my legs, releasing the tightness between my thighs. I'm looking forward to an evening of bland smiles. *Ridiculously so.* They'll most certainly cover my intentions of whispering filthy words all night long. Verbal foreplay in public is always fun, and I foresee the need for creativity, rising in response to her blush.

The door to the lounge swings open suddenly, hitting the adjoining wall with a bang. I sit up abruptly, and if a stare could do such a thing, I'd surely be able to feel the holes Louise was burning into my soul.

'What's wrong—?'

Something silk and pink lands in my lap.

'Care to explain?' Louise stands on the far side of the coffee table, one hand held on a cocked hip, her gaze venomous.

Pink and silk turns out to be knickers—La Perla—which I move to the table sitting between us with a flick of my wrist.

LOUISE

'You know whose they are.' His words were flat; his face, expressionless.

'Do I fucking ever,' I growl in response. 'Do you want to tell me why they were under your pillow because none of the scenarios that spring to my mind are fucking healthy!' That one last word echoes through the room.

'Give me some credit,' he drawls, sprawling back against the sofa and crossing his legs at his ankles. To outward appearances he seems calm. But for the pulse hammering in his throat. 'Do I look that careless to you?'

'Have you fucked her?' I demand, ignoring his question.

'Of course.' Pain flares viscerally, and I suddenly feel sick. 'We have a son; you've met him. But fucked her recently? No.'

'Define *not recently*,' I demand, pressing my hands on the table to stop me from pummelling him. 'Last month. Last week? Yesterday?' I yell.

My grip on my temper feels non-existent. My head swims, and my heart aches. I suddenly understand what the word turmoil means. He wouldn't—couldn't—would he? Not like this? Yet the pair have a history, and history is apt to repeat itself.

Dan's eyes slide to the darkened window, and the suggestion of light from the streetlamp beyond.

'Last year,' he murmurs quietly. 'In a very weak moment that I regret.' His head turns back to me then. 'But that was the last time.'

Unfolding his legs, he rubs a hand against his smooth cheek.

'She was in the house on Wednesday. Uninvited,' he adds quickly. 'The day I came to your office.' My heart sinks to the soles of my feet, precisely where his eyes had descended to. 'Nothing happened,' he repeats. 'But it shook me up. I wanted to hurt her. I was cold and indifferent.' His eyes rise to mine, pain shining there. 'It seemed to have the wrong effect.'

'But you didn't fuck her?'

'No. Not for the lack of trying. Hers, not mine.'

'But you wanted to fuck her.' It wasn't a question.

'I wanted to fuck her up,' he replies, staring at his hands.

And that isn't an answer, at least, not one with any satisfaction for either of us.

My knees suddenly give way as I sink forward, my hands against the table's surface the only thing stopping my collapse.

Chapter Twenty-Eight

DAN

I stare at her bowed head, powerless. Is it strange that I can't even bring myself to be angry with Belle? Not yet anyway, though it would undoubtedly come. I blame myself; how could I have been so stupid? This was exactly the sort of thing she's capable of. I know her well enough, have known her long enough, yet I'd still managed to let her fuck up my life.

And not for the first time.

As she speaks, my attention is turned inward. Elsewhere. Cursing myself and wondering how I could make Louise believe me. She would leave me now, and there was nothing—*fuck all*—I could do about it. Because dominance doesn't extend to kidnap.

'Are you listening to me?'

'I wasn't,' I admit, immediately regretting the response as Louise levels me with another evil glare. *A look that I deserve.* It's the kind of look I enjoy treating as a transgression. That point, I suddenly realise, would never come now. I rub a hand through my hair, feeling wretched.

'I'm sorry. I was too busy sitting here being shit scared. I don't know what to say, other than I'm sorry, for every—'

She cuts me off again.

'Do you want to know what I think?' Of course, I do. And I want her to recite the alphabet in every language of the world—for her to talk forever. For her to stay and forget that this is the end. But I don't voice those thoughts, and she doesn't wait for my answer, anyway.

'I think she's a fucking cunt, and naturally, someone who's used to getting their own way. She's like a small, spoilt child in need of a good slap.' Her mouth firms with distaste, her hand open in the air. 'And you, well, you're just the man for the job, aren't you?' Her tone is uncomplimentary, but no less than I deserve. 'I expect you've always been that for her.'

I don't reply. It doesn't seem needed as she stands. I didn't say how I longed to wrap my hands around Belle's throat. And not in a good way. I didn't ask what I could do to prove my fidelity.

'But don't flatter yourself. You're just a toy she's discarded.' Her expression is more sneer than smile as she stands above me, indignation swirling about her like a cloak. 'She doesn't want you back, not really. She just doesn't want anyone else playing with you. I know—at least, I can guess— I'm not the first woman since she left. But maybe I'm the first to hang around. To be invited to stay.'

Her arms fell to her sides as I stand, reaching out for her. Fists balled, she snatches them away.

'Don't touch me, just . . . don't.'

LOUISE

I leave the room and the front door open, more due to a lack of thought than any notion of a return. The evening is warm—not warm like home could be, but I welcome the pleasant breeze on my skin. *God knows I could do with cooling down.* When I'd begun this thing with Dan, it had been late spring. On the verge of summer now, I'd felt myself bloom along with it. Thanks to Dan, I'd been learning how to be comfortable in my own skin. Comfortable with its welts, bites, and bruises—the badge of honour I wear but not for him.

Autumn was next on the calendar; could I bear for our relationship to grow brittle and brown along with it? Or would I end it now? Our lives parting at this spot?

I'm still conflicted as I reach the garden gate.

To the left stands a confrontation, a fight that could be a constant in the coming months. To my right stands an escape from it all; a return to my previous life. A boring norm. And behind me is Dan. Would he be my past or where my future stood?

I hear him on the garden path, the soles of his highly polished shoes rough against the stones. He pauses halfway down; is he unsure of his approach or giving me space? I can almost see him without turning, hands in his pockets, feet planted firmly apart.

My hands tighten on the cold metal of the gate as he begins to move again.

'Don't go.'

It's almost as though he were speaking to himself, his voice is so quiet. Emotion strangled those words, his lungs tight and without the capacity for breath. I hadn't meant to allow him to touch me, but the need for this was so ingrained.

It begins to rain—not in earnest, but one of those summer showers lasting mere seconds before moving on with the clouds. Drops glisten like tears on the skin of my bare arms as Dan's fingers wipes them away. I don't watch, unable to stand the sight.

'Stay,' he whispers.

'But she'll always be there, won't she?'

'I'll move. Buy another house—our house.'

'You would move from Hal?' My laugh is rueful, and I feel him still. He wouldn't. Shouldn't. Not for me, at least. No, it was time to put up or shut up. Or get in the car and leave. It never would've lasted, anyway.

I open the gate, his shoes scuffing behind me, his arms falling away.

'I can't live like this. It's hard enough coming to terms with who I am, hard enough sharing my life with you, without some fucked-up bitch playing games with my head.'

Yet my feet turn instinctively left.

The door, painted pillar-box red, is solid under my fist. It opens to a hallway almost identical to Dan's. The décor is different, a heavy brocade covering the walls, and was that an umbrella stand? It takes me a moment to move my gaze down.

'Hal, honey, is your mom at home?' The boy nods solemnly, his gaze, so like his father's, seems to pierce my façade. But I won't cry. Not now. 'Could you ask her to come speak with me, then go see your dad? Tell him to look in my big bag upstairs. There's a package in there with your name on front.'

I thank divine providence for the arrival of the Legos I'd ordered, apparently released in the States a month before the UK. Hal had stared at the website covetously, complaining the piece wouldn't be available here until the new school term had begun. I'd meant it as a surprise. I wished I could've delighted at the light in his eyes.

Haste and excitement hurls the little boy down the hall where he disappears through a door. A moment later, he bounds back, shooting me a shy smile. Belle followed the boy, gliding along the hall rather languidly.

'Can I help you?' she drawls as Hal dashes down the garden path.

'You sure as fuck can't help yourself,' I spit against my better judgment. I hadn't planned on this. Any of it. Working on instinct seemed the only way.

The bitch actually smiles, and for a moment, I almost forget I'm the non-violent kind.

'*Darling*, I don't know what my husband—'

'Don't even try. I know what this is, and I can read you like a smutty little book.' Belle's eyes glitter at my disdainful look. 'The locks will be changed this week, and you'd better damn sure believe if I so much as get a whiff of your perfume in there, you'll be feeling my right hook.'

'You think you're special? How sweet.' Belle's hand flutters in the air, and I long, suddenly, to snap it from the wrist. 'Darling, the man is a whore—insatiable. He truly can't help himself. He'd fuck you then fuck me without coming up for breath in between.'

She looks like she'd actually enjoy that. Without so much as a ripple in my expression, I carry on.

'You fucking wish. Step one foot in that house without an invitation and I'm fucking up your life. Do you really want copies of all those photographs sent to your family?' The box on the top shelf of Dan's closet. If he didn't want me looking, he shouldn't have left it there. 'Your friends? Your colleagues?' I let my eyes travel over her with contempt. 'Pretty pink Belle . . . who'd imagine she'd like it rough and messy?'

Belle's face pales under her peach-coloured blush, no doubt recalling a nakedness covered in rope. Writhing against the bed, skin adorned by lipsticked insults, spittle, and cum. Bruised by anonymous fingertips and teeth.

I'd seen the photographs. I'd looked at them all. Conflicted and jealous—a hundred more emotions that day.

Gratified by her pained expression, I don't wait for her response, but what happens next does so in a blur of motion as I step forward with an open palm. Gratified further, the colour back on at least one side of Belle's face, I turn and head down the path, glad of the shrubbery shielding the houses in this very upper middle class neighbourhood.

Dan steps into the street as I turn a right out of Charles's garden gate. He stands back, expression guarded, almost surprised as I take another right, making my way along the garden path of his house.

'Never underestimate a woman,' I murmur as I pass. 'You of all people should know we're way more devious than we appear.' As I reach the front door, I turn my head and ask, 'How long do we have to wait for the cab?'

Chapter Twenty-Nine

DAN

I'm not sure what had been said at Charles's door, but I'm pretty sure Louise had benefitted from some kind of satisfaction on its threshold. There was something about her posture as she stepped into the well-timed arrival of our cab, her back— always straight—was just a touch more so, and her chin a fraction higher held. I guess Louise's response had been more than Belle bargained for. And at least a little, I hope, of what she deserved.

From feeling as though I watched my future walk away, I'd held my breath as she'd reached the end of the garden path. Anything had to be better than watching her climb into her car. I'd been intrigued and hopeful as Hal had almost shot past me as I stood not moving yet feeling adrift. Almost catching the boy's shoulder as he hopped onto the grass to avoid crashing into my legs, I'd asked in a voice that sounded almost calm, 'Where did Louise go, son?'

'*TalkingtoMummy*,' Hal called in his haste as he tried to dodge my grasp. 'She bought me Legos from America. She says I can go get the box from her bag.' Hal halted at the open front door, his expression suddenly solemn. 'Can we take her to Legoland when we go next month? She's so cool.'

Taken aback, I'd nodded dully. Legoland was supposed to be boys only; *no women allowed.* Two days of rides, burgers, and questionable hygiene practises at the behest of one six-year-old. No girls allowed for our days out. That had been the rule, even when I'd still been married to Belle.

Hal had disappeared through the front door, almost tripping over the cat who seemed to glare balefully back at me. Could it be he wasn't the only one smitten with this girl? *Not girl, woman,* I'd reminded myself. Intelligent, beautiful, and incredibly brave. Yet I'd remained paralysed in my indecision and progress, frozen to the gravel of the path.

To follow Louise to her undoubted confrontation with Belle could only add oil to the incendiary situation. This, I felt, was absolute. I was screwed either way. Defend Louise and my ex would react in ways I didn't care to think about. To encourage Louise to be the bigger person, to rise above Belle's fucked-up ways would surely have the same effect, the parties reversed. A delighted ex, a pissed-off Louise. A leaving Louise, my fuck-up absolute.

Her finger grazes mine, and I'm suddenly back in the cab. All had turned out well. For now. And I'm thankful. I have no idea what had been said, but a definite air of triumph exists in the darkened vehicle, even if it's accompanied by my underlying sense of unease. I know from experince Belle will be far from done. But Louise had called it astutely:

I'm the toy Belle didn't want anyone else playing with.

The irony was far from fucking lost on me.

The cab pulled to a stop.

'Are you all set?' Her voice sounds almost too loud, too exuberant, yet her gaze falls short of mine, her free hand nervously twisting the garnet-studded cuff. Smiling, I hope, I tighten my grip on her other hand.

'To meet the masses?' I murmur, relieved for the distraction. 'Don't worry, I'll behave.'

'Oh, I know you will.' Louise tilts her head, narrowing her eyes at me.

'Or else?' I ask, raising an enquiring brow.

'You'd just better,' she responds with a frown.

My smile falls, but I try to salvage the situation, directing her back. 'Sounds promising. In fact, that sounds decidedly like the promise of a spanking.'

Perhaps, against her better judgment, she laughs.

'Yeah, any shenanigans from you, and I'll totally put you over my knee.'

I watch her eyes flick rapidly to the mirror, further catching the cabbie's gaze. I sense more than see her disconcertion then delightedly watched the resulting blush crawl across her chest.

'I like bare hands best as far as implements go,' I state a little loudly, hoping to keep her focus on something else. She opens her mouth to stutter an answer when I tilt my head and add, 'Though the hairbrush was quite successful that time.'

Her eyes dart around the cab—anywhere other than look at me or the mirror again. As she clears her throat, it brings my attention to the vein throbbing there. A tattoo of discomfort, and yes, lust, too.

'Yes, w-well, enough of that,' she stutters, adding unnecessarily, 'look, we're here.

~*~

The hotel is some way out of the city in a country park that seems vaguely familiar. Louise straightens her dress, smoothing her hair with her free hand, her other still tightly held in mine.

'Louise.' I pull her back from the entrance, threading both hands around her waist. 'Thank you. For not leaving. For believing me.' She nods once but doesn't answer, her eyes studying me carefully.

'She's a piece of work,' she says frowning, her gaze sliding from mine. 'I don't know where this is going, but—'

I smile, placing my finger against her lips. 'Darling, if it's up to me, this is going all the way.' Her lips curve beneath my finger, but as I lower my hand, her smile falters.

'Just don't . . . do anything in there tonight. The people—'

I slide her my best sardonic look before answering, 'I am perfectly house trained.' Threading her arm through mine, I lead her up the sandstone steps with a short laugh. 'I'm hardly going to demand you kneel and give me head.'

The party is dull, as Louise expected, and would probably remain so, at least until the alcohol began to take effect, though we'd determined we'd leave long before this stage. Clients and staff mill around the space as waiters in black aprons served morsels on china spoons. On her third glass of champagne, Louise's eyes catch mine from across the room. Like a good beau, I'd engaged in conversation with a couple of department heads.

As she watches me over the shoulder of her companion, I hold out my hand as though to slide it into my pocket, curling my fingers in an innocuous come here motion, one that only someone watching would see. Even from where she stands, I'm sure she can read the thoughts sliding behind my eyes. And the way my fingers curl as though between her legs. To anyone looking on, they'd be oblivious to the silent signals between us, unconcerned as Louise excuses herself from pleasantries, making her way to the grand entrance of the hotel.

LOUISE

Heated, as though lit by an internal furnace, my skin prickles all over, and I know exactly what I need to dampen the itch. I glance at my watch, wondering how much longer we'd have to endure the evening. How much longer it would be until Dan had fistfuls of my hair and was sinking himself into me, rasping his wicked compliments.

Lost in the memories, I start as a hand rests against my hip, though relax at the scent of Dan's cologne.

'You seemed to be getting along well,' I murmur, leaning back and into him.

'Years of practise. The key is to seem like you're interested while inwardly imagining what you'd like to do to their wife.'

As soon as the words hit air, he curses, murmuring his idiocy. But as I instinctively laugh, he seems once more able to breathe.

'And in my boss's case?' I bring my glass to my lips and hide my smile behind the rim. 'What would you care to do to *his* wife?'

'Introduce her to a dentist,' Dan replies seriously. 'The woman has more teeth than a horse.'

Laughing again, I tell him how bad he is when he spins me to face him and tells me exactly how bad he wants to be. His face is serious, his hands at the small of my back pressing me against his body, where he's hard and all kinds of desperate.

'I need you,' he growls in my ear.

Surprised at his words, I find myself blushing and answer in one whispered word. My safe word for the evening, it seems.

Discreet.

We agree on a two-minute head start, and I watch him walk away, counting the minutes until I can follow.

'Fancy finding you in here,' he murmurs as I lock the bathroom door behind me with a *click*.

'I don't . . .' I place my glass down, my words faltering as he presses himself against my back.

'Remember when I said there's a time and a place for everything?' I nod, trembling as Dan's lips find my neck. Such a small touch, but one that elicits so much. 'How do you feel about getting caught?'

'I-I don't want to.'

'No? Then why are you here?' It was a numbers game, Dan had once said. Everyone got caught eventually. Everyone that got a thrill from public sex.

'Because I need you here,' I whisper, placing his hand over my heart. I move it down between my legs, curling my fingers over his. 'And here.'

'Do you have any idea what you've done to my restraint?' Dan's words come out in a pained rush. 'I'd never thought to find myself in this position again.'

He doesn't speak again as he takes me by the waist, lifting me onto the marble vanity and insinuating himself between my legs. I moan as he presses his mouth over mine, fire crawling my circulatory system, our clothes a barrier too much.

'Say yes.' His words are a breathless sibilance, his hands hot on my open thighs.

'I want,' I moan into his mouth as I fumble wit his zip, eventually threading my hand into his pants. The hard, heavy drag of him against my palm sparks waves of desire, the grating sound of his breath igniting my insides.

I can do this.

I want this.

But, fuck, I don't want people to find out.

Dan's hand pulls on the elastic of my panties, rubbing the fabric along the dampness gathered between my legs.

'Tell me what do you want, darling,' he whispers, threading his hands under the gossamer fabric, teasing and taunting me with deft flicks. 'Shall I fuck you while your work friends talk shop outside? Fuck you so hard that you'll limp from this bathroom, letting everyone know what we've done?'

'Yes,' I moan as his knuckle works its way inside, this thumb following to circle my clit. My nreath hitches as my legs begin to shake. 'Fuck me, Dan. Hard.'

'Then you have to say please. Nice manners are, after all, everything.'

I close my eyes to hide my reaction, hating myself just a little, even as I open my mouth.

'Please, Dan. Do it now,' I pant. 'Do me now.'

He smiles sinfully, his free hand finding the hem of my dress and almost tearing it from my thighs to my waist. His belt clashes with the marble as he loosens it, slipping my panties aside. I'm so wet, one thrust and he glides inside. Once, twice, moaning and gasping, our mouths meet only on the up-thrust.

'You can't leave me,' he mutters into my neck. 'Can't leave me.' His hands suddenly find my knees, lifting them further to the side as he slams slickly into me again and again.

'Then stay away from that slut,' I whisper almost breathlessly, limbs loosened with pleasure, the dig of his hips rubbing my clit with every thrust.

'I've all I need right here,' he growls, pushing his hands under my ass to lift me and push me up against the mirrored wall. One hand flat, he pins me roughly, his hips working like pistons as he ploughs his possession inside. The mirror shakes, a silver-coloured tissue box hitting the floor, and all the while, my cries became louder until he slips his hand to our joined wetness, coating his thumb before pushing it inside my mouth.

'Show me how much you want me on your tongue. Show me what you'll do for me when we get home.'

The images rise like a wisp of breath: on my knees and naked while Dan sits almost fully clothed, legs splayed wide. The wave begins in my stomach, my climax clawing at my insides. I come hard, pushed over the edge, sucking his thumb and writhing, finally biting it at the end as he breaks himself.

Sated and lifeless, Dan leans against me, his breathing regulating as he speaks.

'I'm having second thoughts about the blow job. I'd prefer you not to bite off the end of my knob, if you don't mind.'

He holds up his thumb between us, my teeth marks a vivid red. As I laugh, Dan twitches reflexively, slipping out from my body with a groan.

'I-I love you, Dan. You do know that, don't you?'

He halts from zipping his fly, raising his head and flashing a small smile. 'Not your usual romantic surroundings for declarations. But then, that's what I love about you.'

'What?' I try not to allow my smile to falter. Try, anyway.

'There's nothing typical about you.' In an instant, I'm forced against him again. 'I love you, Louise. You are exquisite, and this is fucking real.'

Our eyes meet and for the briefest of moments, something recognisable shared. Something that isn't just about sex or dominance, misunderstandings or hurt. It's like meeting one half of the other. It's finding your safe place.

I should've known it wouldn't last.

Chapter Thirty

DAN

'As I live and breathe.' We both turn to the somewhat derisive catcall. 'Who'd have thought it? The Master himself.'

Louise murmurs that she can place the man's face but not his name. They'd apparently sat in on some of the same meetings, but he wasn't someone she's completely familiar with. I listen as she speaks, watching the man make his way over. What I don't say is that I know him. Unfortunately.

'Scott.' I address the man with my customary blank mask.

'Master,' he replies, even offering an unsteady half-bow. *The prick*. He's drunk, and therefore, dangerous. And out of order as he begins to leer at Louise. 'You look a bit flushed, love.'

Beside me, her face burns red, her posture stiffening, as though our bathroom activities are obvious to all. Rather, I expect they're only obvious to him. By way of my past.

'Scott,' I repeat, this time in a restrained growl. 'I haven't seen you for a while.' I fuel the words with all the authority I can muster. Unfortunately, the soak is too drunk to care.

'No? Well, that would be on the account of being kicked out of your club, mate.'

My posture is ramrod straight as another of my mistakes prepares to take a chunk out of my arse. 'Darling,' I say, turning to Louise. 'Would you get me a glass of champagne?' She doesn't move, the pieces of this puzzle not fitting yet for her yet. If I can't get her to leave, it won't be long before this ridiculous *tête-à-tête* hurts.

'How'd you melt the arse off that one?' Scot continues, digging his own grave. 'The ice queen, ain't she? Least that's what they say in the office.'

The fickle finger of fate drags down my perspiring spine as I attempt to compose myself, to stop myself from shoving Scott's glass down his throat. Synapses fire, filling my head with deceptions and scenarios; ways to extricate Louise from this fuck up. To not cause a scene.

Whatever, I know I'm right royally fucked.

Louise places her fingers on my forearm, bringing my gaze back from boring holes in this fuck. She can probably hear my molars disintegrating under the pressure of staying calm.

'Not here, please,' she says softly, reading my expression and stunning me.

My face feels numb, though my temples pound. 'Darling, I need to talk to Scott,' I say as calmly as possible. 'Would you mind?' It isn't a question I want the answer to, lifting her hand from my arm. I kiss her fingertips in a promise of calm.

Louise opens her mouth, and sensing it filling with questions, I cut her off, kissing her long and hard. I could be a mistake and fuel for the weapon Scott seems intent on swinging my way, but I can't help it. She's like a cool relief to a starving man. As she pulls back, her eyes are questioning.

'I won't be long,' I repeat—a dismissal I hate. I pull myself away from her side feeling like the biggest, lying twat that ever lived. Her expression causes my chest to ache, but the worst of it is the realisation that I might hurt her so much more by the evening's end.

Should've told her. Should've explained.

LOUISE

As Dan leads the drunk away, I catch him leering at me over his shoulder as he mumbles something about *the quiet ones always being the worst.* Then, much clearer he says, 'She been in The Lion's Den yet?'

By then, they're too far away for me to hear Dan's response. And he doesn't turn back.

My head swims, filled with half-formed ideas and notions as I wave away the waiter and his tray of champagne flutes. I need a clear head—and some explanations. But for now, I'll make do with an escape from this room.

Outside, cars still arrive via the gravelled driveway, the front of the house lantern lit. I have no intention of talking to anyone, so head down the sandstone steps, and skirt around the front of the building using the shadows as a shield.

'Lord! You scared the life out of me!' Flo exclaims. I'd nearly walk into her as she makes her way in the opposite direction; obviously on her way back from a clandestine cigarette. 'What are you doing skulking about?'

'Same thing as you,' I answer distractedly. Much like myself, Flo abhors these kinds of affairs.

'But you don't smoke.'

For the first time in my life, I wish I did. I can't answer, my head full of other things.

'I feel like I haven't seen you in ages,' Flo intones, pulling my stiff form in for a one-armed hug. 'I almost feel bad charging you rent.' She smiles at the absurdity of the statement: *almost*.

'I've been busy. Spending a lot of time with Dan.' I look over my shoulder, still trying to make sense of what could be going on. Why hasn't he followed me out?

Flo frowns and mumbles something along the lines of, 'I thought as much.'

'Aren't you going to ask how we are?' Or about my sex life?' It's not like her to miss an opportunity of questioning.

'None of my business, Lou.' She shrugs one nonchalant shoulder, her gaze on the darkened lawns.

'Because you know, don't you? You know him.' Somehow. Someway.

'It's the guy from the club.' Her response is so flat, so emotionless.

'You know him,' I say fishing. Fishing with an empty net. 'But what else do you know?'

Flo's head shots up, her expression changing in an instant. 'Sweets, whatever are you talking about?'

Something about the delivery of her words makes me uneasy. Her demeanour is almost the same as that of Belle. Standing in the doorway earlier, the woman had tried so hard to project superiority. Deflecting. Truth avoidance. Call it what you will. I know a lie when I hear one, I'd like to think.

I suddenly remember the reason I'm outside; my strange encounter with Scott, and the pieces that don't quite fit into place. And as Flo makes some excuse to return, I grab her arm before she can pass.

'Cut the crap, Flo. Just tell me.' My fingers grip her elbow; I've no intention of letting go. 'What am I missing?'

'Come on, Lou, it's freezing out here. Let's go in, yeah?' She sighs huffily, not enjoying being put on the spot. Flo's upbringing betrays her, the final word sounding more like yar. She only ever reverts to her social class when under pressure. It's her armour.

'No. I can't go back in.' Not yet.

'He's in there, isn't he?' Flo suddenly sounds titillated. Awestruck? 'My God, only you would bring the sex king to a do like this!'

'What do you mean?' I whisper, my hand falling away.

'Look,' Flo replies, her gaze sliding to the dark lawn. 'You must know who he is.' When I don't answer, her attention swings back to me. 'Don't you?' she repeats, cautiously.

'Not really,' I admit, gooseflesh stippling my skin. 'I know his name is Daniel. I know where he lives, and I've met his son.' I know I love him, I might well have said, but hold off from doing so. God, I feel so ridiculous.

'You didn't Google him?' I have to bite my lip from admitting I'd barely paid attention to his surname, preferring instead to try talking myself out of being with him for the longest of times.

'That's it? That's really all you know? Good Lord, Louise, why haven't you asked him about this kind of thing yourself?'

I inhale a deep breath and plunge right in. I tell Flo how, at the beginning, I hadn't wanted to know his name. Told of my desire to keep it casual, of how I'd resisted the usual enquiries and platitudes in that same vein. Then I tell her that, by the time these things are usually discussed, it didn't matter. It was already too late. Too late to ask if he hated small dogs or if he was a serial killer, because I was already in love.

'Oh, God.' Flo's exclamation sounds more like a lament. 'I suppose we'd better get a cab. We can't do this out here.'

~*~

Back at the flat, Flo pours us both a measure of brandy. A bad sign, I think, as she takes us back to the night it all began.

'When you left with him, I knew who he was before you went back to his place.'

'You saw his driving license, you said.'

'I did, though that's not the reason I spoke to him. I thought I'd warn him, you know, make sure his intentions were decent. His reputation precedes him, you see,' Flo carries on. 'He roughs them up a bit. Well, I hear both he and the girls he usually screws like that sort of thing. Anyway, about the time you climbed into his lap and started kissing him, it was clear you were only going one place. I thought that place was upstairs—that's where they say he takes them. Girls, I mean. He doesn't fuck in the club himself.' I look on, perplexed, as Flo adds, 'He has an apartment up there, so I've heard.'

'You know him?' My stomach grips tight; maybe Flo had been invited upstairs at some point? Maybe she knows Dan better than she's saying.

'I know *of* him. He's a bit of a big deal.'

'I'm not sure I understand.' Anything. Anything at all.

'That club we were in? It's his. As well as the private member's area. The one we couldn't get into.'

'Couldn't we?'

'It was totes off limits. Think, Lou . . . when we headed there, what did Luke from accounts say about the place?' Placing her glass down, Flo picks up her iPad, gliding her index finger across the screen.

'That it . . . it was some sort of S and M club?' Was that what he had said?

'Well, it's something like that. I believe those tastes are catered for, too.'

'What does that even signify? You were there; everything was pretty tame. Did you see anything going on? Because I didn't.' At that point in the evening, I'd been underwhelmed and unimpressed. Of course, as the evening had passed in Dan's company, I couldn't say the same. I resist doing so now.

'Where we were, there wasn't anything going on. Only members get in,' Flo says again.

'Get in where?' I'm really not sure of the point she's trying to make.

'The VIP area. Members pay a rather large monthly membership fee, and only they get to use the . . . facilities. And each other. Possibly. Anyway,' she says, shaking off her speculation, 'big money. Very few rules, so I've heard. Here.' Her words come out haltingly as she passes over her iPad.

I'm bewildered. Shocked. Fast follows the clench of betrayal. It's all there in high definition, the club's elegantly designed website proving such a place exists, albeit discreetly. Flo's Google search yields media articles ranging from the broadsheets to online magazines: Daniel Masters. Former property developer and wealthy owner of Mede, and the exclusive members only and—allegedly— anything goes sex club, rumoured to be called The Lion's Den.

'This can't be him.' Am I in denial? Then Scott's words began to slot the puzzle pieces into place. 'He's not even wealthy,' I whisper, hanging on to

the hope that none of this is true.' Well off, yeah.
But I've been to his home. It's hardly Somerset
House.

'In the borough, it's in? Darling, he's minted.
Even if it's a tiny place, that's prime real estate.
And so are the clubs.'

'His home is beautiful.' And the opposite of
small. Three floors. Maybe four? My gaze returns
to the iPad and the club's latest media release.

'How come you haven't discussed any of this?'
Flo's question is hesitant. I shake my head. 'What
the hell have you been doing all this time?' My
cheeks start to heat again, though I can't find any
words. 'I knew he'd be a seriously good shag,' she
adds, a smile colouring her words.

'Can we not discuss that now?' I feel suddenly
angry. If sex is his business, then what does that
make me? 'Why didn't you tell me? All this time
you've never once mentioned this?'

Flo's gaze lowers, and I considered that we aren't
really friends. A least not in the BFF sense. Flo is
someone I work and live with. Occasionally, we go
out. We have nothing in common, and I'd never
made her a confidante. *I don't let anyone in.*

'I didn't know you'd get serious about him.' Flo
makes serious with Dan sound something dirty.
'And I assumed you'd know by now. Christ, Lou, I
was going to ask if you could get me in next
weekend.'

'What's your plan?' she asks when silence falls
again.

'Hmm?'

'When can we expect him to arrive on his rescuing steed or should that be spanking horse?' Flo sniggers a little at her own joke, and even I can't help but smile this time. It's all so surreal.

'It's not likely to happen, considering he doesn't know where I live.'

'My God. Did the pair of you ever talk between fucking?'

Not a great deal. And certainly not enough.

'He knows where I work.'

'Surely, you're not going to leave this until after the weekend? Wait for him to turn up at the office?' Flo sounds incredulous.

I shrug, not quite decided, unsure of how this will play out. Other things I'm certain of. Like how decisions made in haste always bite your ass in the cold light of day. I need time to think, to work this all out in my head. Placing the glass down, I stand and pass the iPad back into Flo's hands.

'I have some thinking to do first.'

In my cold bedroom, I open my phone to a dozen texts.

Where are you?

Please don't leave like this.

Please let me explain.

The final text, sent ten minutes ago, reads, **I'm sorry.**

The strangest thing is, so am I. It's partly my fault things stand as they do. If I hadn't been so closed off, maybe Dan wouldn't have felt the need to hide. He said he loved me, and that was true. I feel it in my bones. But the rest? The things he hadn't told me? What else was fake?

Because a lie of omission is as damning as any untruth.

I feel so sorry for myself. Sorry for a lot of things, but mainly, I'm sorry he isn't here because I ache to be held.

Chapter Thirty-One

LOUISE

'Your office still looks like the Chelsea fucking flower show, by the way.'

On a gloomy Thursday afternoon, Flo collapses into the chair by the window, curling her work-tired legs to the side.

'They're still fresh?'

Scowling, Flo nods. 'And still beautiful. Maybe I should've brought some home. Might've brightened the place up. The atmosphere in here is like a morgue.'

I send her a look that says *what do you expect?*

'Bring some home if you want,' I reply evenly. I don't want his flowers here, but can't help if she does.

Dan's reaction surprised me; I'd expected him to turn up at the building on Monday, and he had. He'd been informed I wouldn't be in for the coming week. The part I hadn't expected were the flowers preceding his arrival. It didn't seem like his style. There were enough flowers to fill a hot house, apparently. Along with lengthy texts I've refused to read. *Except that one time when his words made me cry.*

'Do I look like fucking InterFlora?' she says, interrupting my thoughts. 'I think you're being cruel. Pick him up or set him down for another line if you're through.'

'What? Line?' My mind went immediately to coke for some reason. That's Flo's sometime drug of recreation, not mine. As it happens, I'm no longer talking to my drug of choice.

'It's a fishing metaphor,' Flo says with an apathetic wave of her hand.

'Well, maybe I will.' Returning to my paperwork, I whisper one more word. 'Eventually.'

'And,' Flo continues, pulling herself straighter in the chair. 'When are you coming back in? You can't hide out here forever like some hermit.'

'This isn't a cave, and I'm not hiding. I had vacation to take.' And a plan to create. 'I'll be back in the office tomorrow.'

'On Friday? Hardly worth it. Why not wait until after the weekend?'

'Come in? Stay away?' I tease, smiling. 'Make up your mind. Besides, I've a meeting to attend.'

And I have, but it's not the kind of meeting I care to discuss.

~*~

Dressing for work the next morning, I'm meticulous. If Flora's privileged background is her armour, then mine is my work attire. Tasteful and understated, lots of blacks, buff tones, and muted greys. Pencil skirts and blouses, cashmere sweaters, and occasionally, pants. The only suggestion of vibrancy Monday through Friday are my painted toenails, which nobody ever sees, anyway.

But not today. This morning, my armour is a wrap-dress in ruby red. Nude heels reveal another flash of scarlet from their peep-toe, my legs tanned and bare. I pin up my hair, creating a careless effect, a dozen bobby pins holding together a look that says, *I've fallen out of bed like this*. I keep my makeup light but for opt for lush, red lips.

Today, I'm a siren, and every man I pass will hear my call.

I rarely wear heels for work and find as I do so today, as well as slowing my gait and making me late, they also aid my sense of womanly power.

Mid-morning, I seek out Luke in his office; my heels the cause of my saunter, my swaying hips the effect. Perching my bottom on the edge of a chair next to his, he doesn't acknowledge my presence until I whisper his name.

Looking up from his laptop, Luke's head does an almost comedic double take, though I don't find any humour in it. Instead, I bring his attention to a sliver of thigh peeking from my dress, then back to my face by ghosting my hand from my leg to my chest. I rest it against my collarbone, clasped lightly there as we chat about this and that. As I lean across his desk to grasp a pen, Luke's attention becomes a little lost, falling from the path of our conversation, his attention dropping from my face to my breasts . . . travelling further to the parting at my dress.

I inhale sharply because, believe it or not, the flash of lace between my thighs, though effective, is an accident.

Sitting back, I pull my dress back into place with an oops for propriety's sakes. We speak of work for a while longer while I try to gain the courage to raise the topic of this weekend, eventually asking Luke if he has plans. Before he has a chance to answer, I boldly ask him if he's a member of the Lion's Den. After all, he was the one who'd instigated our trip to the more public side of the club all that time ago. Asking carries a risk, a bit like exposing myself, but these are both risks I'm willing to take today.

Disappointment blooms in my chest as Luke says he doesn't hold a membership. *Effort wasted, more plans to be sought.* It takes me a moment to realise he's still speaking. Not a member, he says, but he has visited, recently expressing an interest in joining their membership ranks. He's confident he can get his hands on a couple of guest passes.

'I can't believe it.' He looks a little astonished as he pushes both hands through his hair. 'You've never shown me any interest before. I even asked you out.'

'Well, that was before,' I say, keeping my eyes on the pen, my stomach twisting as I prepare what to say next. 'Before I knew you were like me.' An abomination. Kinky. Fucked up. Take your pick.

'I-I'll sort my membership today. I really can't believe it,' he repeats, pushing his chair back from his desk. 'The most gorgeous girl in the building likes me, and the way I like to fuck.'

'Slow your roll,' I reply lightly to conceal the wave of fear rolling through me. 'Let's not get ahead of ourselves. At least, not until we're inside.'

'Tell the truth,' he says, a predatory smile growing. 'You wouldn't have mentioned it if you weren't serious about playing.'

'Maybe,' I whisper, my eyes sliding from his again. 'Or maybe I'm just curious.'

He looks at me, and I *just know* he's hoping I mean bi-curious. Some men can be so shallow in their intent. But plan or not, I'm not eating pussy for him. I want to ask what Scott said about last weekend, knowing a man of his ilk would've spouted some shit about the hot, freaky Yank and the things he knows. But I don't ask. It'd just complicate things.

Luke says he'll make a few phone calls, so we set a date for this evening and I move from the chair by his desk with a confident hop. While inside, my heart twists as though tied by Dan's rope.

Chapter Thirty-Two

DAN

Being in the office this week is the only thing that's kept me sane, even if my sanity seems to be hanging by a thread. I'd suffered the week from hell and had even been told by my bar manager that it looked like I'd had a holiday there. A glance in the mirror as I slip on my suit jacket, and I'd have to agree. But I have to pull my shit together. Today, I have meetings to attend and expansion plans to discuss. But all through the day, the networking and the questions, I know all I'll be able to focus on is how I let everything go so wrong.

As Friday evening dawns, I find I can't bear to be alone.

On Monday, I'd gone to her office just to be told she wasn't there and wouldn't be all week. I'd returned home and pretty much stayed put. Waiting. Because she had to come back, didn't she? As the week progressed, my anger had grown. I'm angry with myself, obviously, but also at Louise. Angry that she'd seen fit to reveal parts of her life by drip feed. Devastated that she'd taken me inside her heart and body while avoiding some of the more usual intimacies. I don't even have her address, and that's just fucked up.

I'd resorted to searching for her on the internet, finding no trace. No listings in the phone book, no hints to her address. I'd even briefly considered hiring a detective but hesitated at the level of intrusiveness. No. I had to trust she'd seek me out. Hadn't she invested some part of her heart?

I see her everywhere—in the coffee shop, on the street—even convincing myself twice she'd been in touching distance, my hand on a stranger's shoulder, a face turning to me that wasn't hers. I'm so obsessed, I'd even thought I'd caught a glimpse of her downstairs in the club earlier on. Ridiculous.

Dragging a hand down my face, I return to the one-way window overlooking the bar and the cabaret room. It's still early; couples drinking, mingling, and with the exception of one or two, fully clothed, but all are wearing masks tonight for the evening's theme.

My gaze drifts over the staff, those meant to be seen at least. Two redheads in French maid's outfits serve shots along with a man with slicked-back hair and a handlebar moustache. Later, there'll be a pair of contortionists to titillate, but for now, drinks will be consumed. Later, clothes will be shed. But by then I plan to be long gone. I may be lonely, but only for her company.

LOUISE

After consuming half a bottle of Flora's best viognier, I meet Luke in a bar near the club. It isn't that I plan on getting wasted, but more that I think I'll need lubrication for later. *For what I have planned.* Besides, it isn't like people just kiss then immediately drop their clothes. Usually. There needs to be bits in between, and for me, this means cocktails in an overpriced bar where Luke won't let me go dutch.

It isn't a great sign, but one I haven't fought too much.

'So you were saying?'

I slide into the seat after a moment alone in the bathroom, a moment Flo would call *having a word with myself*, bad decisions being only mine to make. I look on for a blank moment, his question late in making much sense, my thoughts focussed elsewhere.

'I think I was asking how you'd heard about the club.'

'It's not a secret, Lou.' I hate his cockiness and the faux endearment, but I try not to make a point of either as he hooks his elbow around the back of his chair. 'That would be bad for business.' I didn't know where he worked, I'd still be able to tell he sells advertising. He's the epitome of the stereotype. 'Besides,' he carries on, 'it was in all the newspapers last year. Tales of the debauchery for those with plenty of cash. Tales of how the other half lives splashed across the tabloids.'

My stomach lurches quite suddenly. Media? An outing?

'It was mostly guesswork. The journalist didn't get it. The Den's vetting process is first class.'

Of course it was. Members might not be short of cash, but they also had to have other qualities and attributes. Certain commonalities . . . like an interest in kink. Or public fucking. Group sex, in some instances, I'd guess. But mainly, they seemed to want to keep their proclivities secret.

I repress a shiver, the thoughts taking up so much space. Dan had been so against fooling around in public. Other than the bathroom last weekend, all our sex had taken place at his house.

Maybe he keeps all his secrets at the club.

'Have you been on the waiting list long?' I ask, desperate to curtail that thought.

'About six months.'

Luke tells me that once he was promoted, he'd earned enough to meet the application requirements. I don't miss how he slides his hand under the table, adjusting himself, though not quite discreetly enough. I feel nothing but tension, yet he's excited.

I finish my iced tea, the long, alcoholic kind, before adjusting the neck of my blouse. The thing is uncomfortable. High necked and billowing sleeves clasped at the wrists, it offers full coverage but is almost sheer. I know the skin coloured bra I wear underneath gives the impression of nakedness. And that was the whole point of wearing it. Luke's eyes seem unable to hold my gaze, and I hope my outfit has the same effect on Dan. And I want him to hurt.

I've teamed the blouse with a leather skirt I'd found in that underwear-cum-fetish shop. It's knee-length, though anything but demure, with a silver zip running its length at the back, currently fastened from my waist to my knees. It looks the part, though is difficult to walk in. And of course, I've teamed the outfit with heels. Spiked this time.

Noticing Luke's wandering eyes again, I tap the table with my knuckles to get his attention.

'I *am* actually wearing a bra under here.' God. I sound so very *schoolmarm*.

Luke's cheeks pink as he murmurs an apology, very unlike the cocky man who strode into the bar earlier. His change of tone and demeanour is a little startling.

'Anyone looking close enough would see that,' he mumbles. 'But from where I'm sitting, there's some stellar nippleage.'

'Ground rules,' I blurt, immediately folding my arms. 'It seems like a good idea to have, you know, some sort of plan.' Other than the one I have in mind for Dan.

Chapter Thirty-Three

LOUISE

When Flo had said the mysterious den was at the
back of the club where I'd first met Dan, I assumed
that was where the entrance would be; a dark
curtain and burly minders, watching the entry at
the rear somewhere. Not so, it seems, as Luke
leads me into a different street and another
entrance. A huge black door flanked by topiary bay
trees that stand sentry. Tall sash windows sit on
either side of the door, the heavy drapes inside
drawn closed. For the world, it looks like nothing
more than a genteel Edwardian home.

Inside, in the vast hallway, we're encouraged to
hand over our cell phones to a hugely built dark-
suited man. Each is then receipted and locked
away. Relief washes over me, the implications of a
camera phones suddenly obvious. It's true I'm here
to expose myself in some way, but I'd be glad for
footage not to make the internet.

I sign a waiver, my hand shaking, my mind
unable to process the fine print. Next, in the black
and white tiled hall, is a large table adorned with
masks. Some are elaborate, some no more than a
scrap of leather or lace. The attendant mentions
that this isn't standard form, more a theme for the

evening. I find I'm glad of it as she encourages both Luke and I to choose a mask. He opts for one that covers the upper-half of his face, something oddly feline about the thing. I choose something in silver with rhinestones, something completely against my usual tastes. It occurs to me that I'm trying to disassociate myself; a mask, my clothing. And though I'd admit it to no one, anticipation of the evening causes a pulse to beat between my legs. Will I fuck this evening just to spite him? Make myself known, ripping off my mask to let him see that I've moved on?

An arched doorway stands open, and we enter, my heart seeming to try to escape from my throat. The room looks like an elegant drawing room. Lots of tactile fabrics; velvets and brocades. A little Parisian bordello in theme, a small bar situated discreetly at one end. Edwardian style sofas are dotted around the room, maybe two dozen guests already making new acquaintances inside. The lighting is low and intimate. Candelabras stand at intervals, providing the major source of ambience, and a fire burns in the large hearth.

We stand by the fireside, carefully avoiding areas where others stand in small groups. Soft music plays in the background while champagne and oysters are served. I drink but don't eat, my stomach overcome with nerves. At one point, Luke says I look a little pale and laughingly suggests I swallow a little zinc. *It'll help my colour*. Though he hides behind his laughter, it doesn't take much to realise he isn't talking about the salty molluscs being served. The possibility of me fucking him becomes more distant each time he opens his mouth. So I tell him.

Obviously, he protests; he hadn't meant it that way at all. Sure, asshole.

Champagne hits the spot, though doesn't quell my nerves, especially as two couples—no, make that one couple and a *ménage à trois* seem on the verge of making an early start.

'Wanna have a wander?' Luke asks, expectance lightening his tone.

'Why? What will we see in other rooms?' I grip the stem of my glass tighter in anticipation, my eyes avoiding his and scanning the room. I feel a little expectant myself. But not for what, but for who. Maybe it's a little silly to expect Dan to be here on this night of all nights. But I'm resolved now. I'll carry on regardless. And I'm more than a little curious to see what he'd hidden from me. Chalk tonight up to revenge or to moving on. Either would do. Because how dare he expose me— bring to the surface the things I'd tried hard to ignore. Things that would've safely remained theory, if not for him. Some people don't want the moon on a stick. I fear being one of them. Some people prefer the stick alone. And once that knowledge is free, there's no restraining it.

I know with unwavering certainty what I am now, thanks to him.

Deviant. Broken. Abnormal.

Undesirable for my wanting.

Why else would he have hidden all this from me?

I hate myself for letting him in, but right now, I hate him more for proving I'd been this creature all along.

'In the other rooms?' Luke asks, pulling me out of my angry thoughts. 'Just other rooms. Some with beds, some couches. Tables with bowls of flavoured condom and lube. Two rooms upstairs have all the kit—stocks and the cross. Spanking horses.'

Stocks and cross? I feel my eyes going wide. What the hell was he talking about?

'You know, the St Andrew's cross?' he repeats, as though it might help. *Maybe St. Andrew was the patron saint of strange sex.* 'Oh,' he then adds, his gaze sparkling. 'This looks like it could be interesting.'

Once again, I'm pulled from my worrying as Luke tips his head in the direction of one of the large windows. Sat in front is a pale velvet sofa, the kind that used to be called a fainting couch. A moment later, I feel like I could do with my own place to pass out.

The drapes behind are fully drawn, not that the trio sprawled there seems at all concerned by an audience. Almost as though they'd heard Luke's encouragement, the lone girl in the group begins to slide to her knees, her fingers reaching to loosen her partner's pants. A beat later, the larger of the two men joins her on the floor—two pairs of hands working quicker than one until the object of their attentions spring forth.

I don't know where to look—where not to look—because it seems almost impolite to avert my eyes.

The middleman, quite literally, folds his arms across his chest as though he doesn't know what to do with his hands. Pants around his ankles, the juxtaposition between the hot and the ridiculous secures my gaze as the kneeling pair begin to take turns sucking and licking, their own tongues meshing as they reach the tip of a very hard cock.

I begin to wonder about the etiquette for a night like this. Wonder how a person goes about getting someone to suck or lick you. Was it on instinct? A coy look, a secret handshake? A moment later, my thoughts disappear like wisps of smoke. It isn't so much that I don't want to look, more that I can't move my gaze. Heads bob obscenely as the tight sounds of their pleasure fills the room. Candlelight flickers nearby, highlighting one head and sending the other into shadow. One golden, one dark, taking part in something surreal but as sexy as all fuck.

The energy in the room builds like a tension, the sounds of the trio's pleasure stealing air from the space, almost asphyxiating its inhabitants, leaving them to breathe only the trio's whimpers and half-moans. Leaving us all short of breath. The experience intoxicating. Addictive. Like drugs in the bloodstream, or that first shot of hard liquor blooming through your limbs. I feel hot, as if my skin is scorched, every fibre igniting as I watch.

After a moment, or ten, I force my gaze away, turning to an occupied Luke, whose own eyes don't stir.

'What happens if you want to screw in private?' I whisper, fear creeping back in.

I can't stand on the sidelines all night. I'd come to the club with a burning need to punish Dan, though I hadn't quite planned how. But now, now I know. It's hot watching the trio, surprisingly so, though not without a touch of awkwardness.

But Dan had never sought to touch me in public. Well, that was a clue.

'It's not allowed,' Luke replies, placing his glass on the mantle above the fire. Is he distracted? Wanting a better view, as the events in the window come, quite literally, to an end?

'There's a time and a place for public fucking, and apparently, that place is here. Some rooms have doors, but you have to understand you might still attract a crowd.'

His expectant smile is lost on me, the echoes of *a time and a place* gripping me by the throat. And not in the way I like. Did Dan . . . fuck in here? In front of everyone? Why would he ignore my tentative advances outside the four walls of his home? Was he afraid of letting his own deviancy show?

Suddenly, something from the far side of the room snags my gaze, the pull as strong as the sun.

Dan stands in the wide doorway. That he wears a mask makes little difference. I'd know him anywhere.

My heart rises, my hand almost along with it, moving instead to secure my own disguise as I remember that this isn't a social call.

If hope is a thing with feathers, it also has claws sharp enough to tear out a heart.

Chapter Thirty-Four

DAN

I've heard the term incandescent with rage but not with relief. And as I stand at the door to the main salon, I'm certain I must be glowing because the sight of her is pure relief. For at least a minute. Until I take in her clothing, her overtly sexual state of dress. *She looks like a submissive's wet dream. I wonder if she knows?*

If she thinks that ridiculous mask would protect her, she's sorely wrong. She obviously has no idea how much it accentuates her plush, red mouth, a mouth just begging for another's kiss. I wonder how long it will be before someone tries. My thoughts darken as I wonder if she'll let them. And how long they'll retain their arms following. *I'll rip the fuckers off. Beat them to death with the bloody ends.* Behind my own mask, my brow furrows. She's in a sex club and well aware of the fact. She hasn't confused the place, hoping to partake in a spot of afternoon tea. I sigh. The mask doesn't conceal a thing. Not her desirability. Not her desire, ignited by the window scene.

That Louise is here with someone is secondary. But that she's here, in this place I've hidden from her . . . makes my stomach plummet and twist.

Why come at all? Not a reconciliation. That's obvious, especially as I catch the bastard next to her holding out his hand.

Revenge, then.

I curl my fingers around the doorframe, grounding myself, so strong is the urge to storm across the room. Instead, I gesture to one of the staff to follow me out into the hallway. My floor staff are all very discreet, there to oversee while remaining unseen. Jessica, this evening's event manager, happens to be standing close by and follows me out immediately.

'The couple by the fireplace,' I grate out, watching her eyes flare. I don't have the bandwidth for civility today.

She pulls out a small electronic tablet from the pocket of her skirt, anticipating what I want to know. Luke's name and address. How many times he'd visited the club—twice as a guest. His proclivities—mostly submissive. That his application shows he identifies as straight but is open to same sex encounters.

'His companion–'

'Is of no concern to him,' I growl, the cogs in my head beginning to turn.

LOUISE

'It's Dan Masters.'

The whispered statement seems to travel through the room, even though I only truly hear Luke's astonishment.

'So I see.' My tone is a bitter acknowledgment.

'You know him?' Luke's exclamation is paired with wide eyes. I begin to wonder what Scott had actually said in the office last Monday, weighing up how much he'd exaggerated. *Fucking men.* 'When I came as a guest,' Luke continues, his eyes no less wide, 'I watched him use a naked woman as a footstool. Then he caned her for spilling some.'

I swallow pain. I swallow his words. I try not to choke on all the things I don't know about the man I love.

'I've met him.' I try to shrug, my body stiff.

'They say he rarely comes here anymore,' Luke whispers, right about the time it becomes obvious he's making a beeline for me.

'Darling.' One quietly spoken word. And how it makes my heart ache.

'Daniel,' I return, hoping he doesn't notice the waver in my tone. Or the tremble in my hand as I raise the empty glass to my lips to take a sip of nothingness. *Hell.*

'No, darling,' Dan purrs. Taking the glass from my hand, he replaces it with another taken from one of the ridiculously dressed waitress. I wonder if his staff are coached to cater to all Dan's whims? 'That's not how it works here.' His tone is smooth, dark, and dangerous as he turns to Luke. 'Mr. Smith, I believe.'

'No, he—'

I don't get to finish as Luke holds out his hand in confirmation, adding in an all-knowing tone, 'We're all anonymous. Except for the Master here.'

'Within these walls, I'm just Masters, Mr. Smith.'
Dan's words seem deliberately bland as his eyes
slide to me once again. His gaze travels over my
body, as if his eyes alone could remove my clothes.
'But as for anonymous, my darling here never
could be. Even hiding in plain sight. A mask can't
conceal everything, you see.' I take what feels like
a slight, raising my chin. Dan smiles beneath his
mask, all obvious teeth and implied menace.
'What's your pleasure?'

It used to be you, I almost reply. *Until you lied.*
Only, Dan's words aren't directed at me.

'I-I believe I'm a switch,' Luke stutters out.
Which is news to me.

'A switch?' Dan repeats, as though Luke
commented on the time of day using a defective
timepiece. 'I understand this isn't your first . . .
experience here.'

Luke looks to be blushing under his disguise as
begins to stammer a justification for the way he
likes to fuck.

'So you're a submissive,' Dan suggests. Luke
doesn't answer, his gaze swinging between us as
Dan speaks again. 'Come on, man. If you can't own
your sexuality here, you're not ready for our
membership terms. You must understand that my
asking comes from a place of trying to know you
better. A place of offering you some fun.'

My heart hits the pit of my gut. Is he offering
Luke *his* services or mine? And that he can read
me so well, even behind the mask, is frightening as
he leans in to run a finger along my exposed

jawbone as he whispers, 'She's not going to be much fun by herself.'

'Fuck you.' My words hit the air like an impact, conversations all around us stirring to a halt.

'Should I?' Dan replies quietly. *Frighteningly quiet, actually.* 'We both know how good that can be, but perhaps I should fuck him instead?' His gaze turns to Luke dispassionately, gliding like silk back to me again. 'Or we could take turns fucking you?'

His words—his tone—cuts like glass, but I fight to keep my countenance calm.

'I'll play you both for the chance. The decision goes to the winner as to who fucks whom.' His disinterested tone is absolutely belied by the pulse jumping in his throat. 'Darling,' he purrs once again, 'Should we play again? For old times.'

Chapter Thirty-Five

LOUISE

Another red room, I think as I enter, but one very unlike the infamous novel I'd read some time before. No obvious implements or apparatus line the walls. No strange harnesses in the ceiling. *Thank heaven for small mercies*, I tell myself, ignoring a pinprick of disappointment. I fold my arms across my chest, not quite believing I'd been goaded into this. *Provoked. Dared, more specifically.* To make matters worse, as with some of the other rooms we'd passed, there's only a doorway. No discernible door. Nothing to hide behind; anyone could wander in and watch me fall apart.

So much for taking the power back. So much for revenge.

In due time, their foot will slip. Their day of disaster will rush upon them.

I brush away the beginning of the Bible passage forming in my head. Because this is what I get. This is my revenge.

Gilded mirrors of all shapes and sizes covered the walls of the room, glass speckled and cloudy with age. *Debauchery by looking glass and candlelight.*

Is it supposed to make it more tasteful, somehow? I walk around the perimeter of the room on unsteady legs, concentrating on the mirrors, the drapes, the floor; anything but look at Dan. And I don't realise he's behind me until he grasps my wrists. As he grips them tightly, my fragile bones suffer his need.

His touch is like a nostalgia, a sad longing for something I shouldn't want. *Maybe*, I begin to tell myself, *I could be happy with one more time*. One more opportunity to lose myself in him. But before the point I give in—beg him to take me—his fingers loosen, and he turns away.

'We're going to play *Master says*.' Unmoving, I try to make sense of his words. 'And like the redoubtable Simon, I'm in charge.' He pauses, a smile of unpleasant proportions playing across his face. 'And the Master says take it all off.'

Standing almost at opposite points of the room, neither Luke nor I move.

'You have ten seconds to get into the centre of the room and do as I've said. Unless, of course, you care to concede. In which case, I get to choose who fucks whom.'

We draw together as though compelled, mirroring each other's movements, our hands reaching to unmask first.

'No,' Dan calls, his voice ringing through the room. 'The masks stay. The clothes do not.'

I turn towards the smattering of laughter, dismayed to see we've drawn an audience. Dan stands between the entrance and me, the group of voyeurs craning around him to see. Ignoring them all—Dan included—I begin to pull the sheer blouse from the waistband of my skirt.

'In ancient Venice,' Dan says, beginning to move towards me, 'masks were considered a symbol of freedom; a way to behave badly without fear of revealing identity or social class. A way to misbehave without fear of being caught.'

I refuse to look as he draws near, eyes cast downward in mock subservience as I struggle with the button at the back of my neck.

A *swish* of cloth against cloth sounds next to me. Luke stripping his tie from his neck? The *clink* of a belt buckle, the whoosh of it coming loose from the loops. Too fast, I think, my stomach tightening. As I turn my head, Dan is holding the other man's belt in his hand. Luke's eyes are closed, his body practically vibrating as he swallows shallow breaths.

Hands frozen on my button, elbows ridiculously in the air, I watch on as Dan covers Luke's hand with his own, lifting it to his own masked face. As Luke's eyes open slowly, he looks vulnerable. And desperate.

'Do you know anything about the mask you've chosen?' Dan asks softly.

Luke shakes his head, whispering a no that's barely audible.

'My mask,' Dan continues, pressing their joined hands to his own cheek. 'Is *La Bauta. La babau*: I'm the fear lurking in your dark consciousness, the monster beneath your bed. *Se non stai bravo*

viene il babau e ti porta via. As Venetians would
caution their children; if you don't behave, the bad
man will come and take you away.'

Turning his head, Dan's gaze pinions mine.

'I'm the bad man,' he says. 'Just the way you like
it, darling. I do believe Mr. Smith would enjoy the
experience, too.' He steps away leaving Luke's
hand hanging in the air. 'I wonder if your choice of
mask is in any way prophetic, Mr. Smith. *La
Ganga*, your mask this evening, was worn by
cross-dressing prostitutes.'

From those at the doorway comes a collective
sharp intake of breath.

'Shall we continue?' Dan asks neither of us in
particular. 'Of course, we will.'

My hands are still behind my neck as though
shackled there. The button is so tiny and slippery,
I can't seem to work it loose. It doesn't help that I
can now feel the heat of Dan as he stands at my
back.

'Help, darling?' Without waiting for an answer,
he brushes my fingers aside. 'Are you enjoying
this?' As his breath brushes the back of my neck an
electric pulse skitters across my skin. A beat later
than would be appropriate, I shake my head.

'Then let's dismiss the audience. Send the other
players home. Ask me nicely, Louise. We can give
up this charade. You didn't come here to play. You
came here to punish me. Let's hear the truth of it.'

I sense my button loosening, his thumb stroking
the slash of exposed skin. My body begins to quake
from the connection, from missing his touch.

'Ask yourself, is it courage or foolishness that brings you here dressed like this?'

I glance down at the clothing I'd thought bold; and outfit that pushes against my comfort zone.

'What did you see in the mirror this evening?' His words curl around my ear with a softness I find hard to reconcile. 'What was it you were trying to portray? A touch of daring or devil-may-care?'

'Did he . . . the devil, I mean?' I hadn't meant to speak, didn't want to turn my head over my shoulder and look at him. 'Did he ever care?'

He doesn't answer, though a flash of something crosses his gaze. Hurt? Anger? Whatever it was, it doesn't stop him from widening the neck of my blouse to slide it from my shoulders.

'Bravery is more than a skin you don, more than an armour of leather or lace. Courage can be found in the defiant lift of your chin or the catch in your breath.'

If he'd hoped to evoke memories, he has. Memories I choose to ignore. To refute.

'Fuck you.' My voice carries across the room, stern and full of denial.

'You're not an exhibitionist. You just like the idea of being caught. Sex in dark corners, straightening clothes not a moment too soon . . . Looking flushed and deconstructed somehow as we'd walked from that bathroom.'

'No. You don't get to do this,' I answer, my molars gripped tight. Tears teeter on the edge of my lids as I refuse to give in. 'You just get to watch the girl you loved, the girl you lied to, be screwed by another man.'

Shock hits his eyes first, followed by the grip of determination in his jaw.

'Only if the *Master says*,' he returns. 'Your cue, Mr. Smith, I believe.' His voice carries across the room as he steps away. 'The lady requires help with the rest of her clothing.'

Behind him, Luke blinks quickly but doesn't move, his shirt open and his trousers loose.

'The Master says.' Dan's addition is quick, his expression under his mask pained, but maybe I'm the only one here to know him well enough to tell.

At this second direction, Luke makes short work of his clothing, and wearing only black boxer briefs, kneels on one knee behind me, a hand on my hip to balance himself.

'Are you sure you're okay with this?' he asks quietly.

Suddenly crushed by his kindness, I turn my head to look down at him. *Can I really do this?* Hope, expectancy, and desire shine in his gaze as Dan's voice cuts in again.

'Did I say you could touch her, Mr. Smith?' His tone is even, but I can tell he's pissed.

Luke's hand moves as though my skin is suddenly hot to the touch. He returns, touching only the zipper, drawing it from the back of my knees up.

'You do surprise me, darling.' I try to ignore Dan's voice. His amused and satisfied tone. 'Did you visit a fetish shop or buy online?'

Keeping my head down, I refuse to rise to his baiting. As the zip reaches my waist, it parts like the pages of a book, falling stiffly to the floor.

Dan's gaze drops to the triangle of pale lace between my legs, where it stays. Is he shocked by their familiarity? Remembering the times he'd slipped my panties down my legs?

'Mr Smith. The Master requires her underwear.' He holds out his hand with the command.

Near naked, in front of a sea of people, masked faces that cling to one wall as though not daring to enter further for fear of their Master's machinations . . . I feel envied. Desired. My reactions are not at all in keeping with how I probably should feel.

As I glance back at Dan, noticing he now holds a champagne flute by its rim. Seated now, he looks utterly at ease. One ankle crossed over the opposite knee, his posture screams of urbane inconsequence. I shiver as fingers slide between my panties and the skin of my hips, my eyes falling closed at the drag of material between my legs. As I open them again, Luke is in front of Dan. On his knees, arm outstretched. But Dan's not watching him. His dark eyes are too busy burning holes in me.

'Well?' Dan purrs dangerously, his gaze sliding from me.

'May I?' Luke responds, indicating his outstretched hand.

Dan half-nods, and intrigued and half-sickened, I watch as Luke brings the delicate lace to his nose, deeply inhaling. He looks blissful. For a couple of seconds at least, until sitting forward, Dan grabs a fistful of his hair quite suddenly.

'Wrong,' he growls, tilting his head sideward. Luke swallows thickly, screwing his eyes tight. 'You deserve a forfeit. The Master hadn't *said*.' He raises his gaze from the man on his knees. 'Come closer, darling,' he demands.

I shake my head, rousing myself, having watched this play out as though watching a piece of theatre or TV. My stomach is tight as I return to my role like one of Bluebeard's betrotheds. *A lamb to the slaughter might be a better analogy.*

'I believe I told you to strip.'

A slow, predatory smile spreads across his face. I ignore it, glancing down at Luke's tipped back head, the look of desire directed at Dan. I find I don't like it—not one bit—or the jealousy that rises unexpectedly. So much for showing Dan what a fool he'd been, what he'd miss after I'd fucked someone else, leaving one final time. But it's not as though I'd absolutely considered Luke an active participant in my scheme. I look down at him; sandy hair, built, and sort of rugged looking. But no, I hadn't been set on screwing him.

But I also hadn't planned on him wanting Dan.

Dan wasn't into him, was he? He had to be playing with me. Why, then, did his gaze then fall to the man on his knees?

'What do you think I should do to him?' he asks dispassionately. When I don't answer, he directs the question at Luke. 'What do you think I should do to you?' His voice is now slow and sensual, causing my insides to twist.

Licking his parched lips, Luke's mouth moves wordlessly.

'Should I go easy on you?' Dan tilts his head. 'Or not?' He pulls Luke's again making him exhale a soft moan. 'Perhaps I'll meet you halfway,' Dan continues. 'Perhaps, whatever I decide, I'll allow you to choose the hand of its delivery. Who would you choose?'

Luke doesn't answer. He looks a little confused.

'Come now, no one's judging here. You *have* been here before?' Luke agrees, nodding as well as anyone is able in his position. 'And you've played with men in the past?'

'A little,' Luke whispers hoarsely.

'Then perhaps it's still early days?' Dan suggests in an encouraging tone. 'I imagine the men you've been involved with have been part of a group. Always including a woman?' Luke agrees, but Dan isn't done. 'Some soft swinging, paired with a little light dominance? And over time, you've come to realise you'd like to explore . . . more?'

Luke's answer is more a look than an action of confirmation.

A please don't make me answer.

Please just do it—decide for me.

Please just do it already—use me.

'Darling, take my glass.' I reach for it instinctively, pulling my hand away a beat too late. 'A forfeit for you, too, it seems,' he says, his smile taking on a feral edge. 'Then it's decided; we'll start with you both sucking my cock.'

In a moment of naked anger, I hurl the glass at the wall of mirrors.

'You're a sadistic bastard.' My voice quavers, my hands balled into fists by my thighs. I try to control my breathing, try to control my tears—tears of anger and shame—because how can I suddenly see that very thing happening? See it like I want it. Like I need it to happen.

'That's true,' Dan agrees without feeling. 'But if you don't like it, you can always leave.' He inhales, pausing for a moment before adding more earnestly, 'No one's forcing you to stay.'

'No,' I growl from between gritted teeth. 'I'm not leaving.' Not for anything; he's not winning this one. I *will* punish him.

His response is a one of derision, but I still don't believe he'll go through with it. Until he begins to loosen his mask.

'Kiss me,' he demands, but not of me, his fingers making light work of the buttons on his shirt. 'Don't you want to kiss me, Mr. Smith? Kiss my cock? The rules don't matter anymore; I win.'

He pulls Luke closer with one hand, the other reaching out to pull me closer. To pull me down to my knees.

'Let's begin, shall we?' Shirt open, he relaxes once more into the chair, but I can see the tension in his fingers. The tightness in his jaw.

His eyes roll closed as Luke begins to work his zipper. It's just as well my assistance isn't required in the task as my hands shake.

Dan's expression is dark and tight as he's freed from the confines of his pants. His cock stands proud between us, and I'm struck by how oddly erotic it is watching Luke reach out tentatively to touch. His masculine hand against Dan's satin shaft. Luke's head suddenly falls forward greedily, the sight of his sandy head working Dan leaves me wallowing in a pleasurable sort of agony. My perceptions are distorted and muddied—I feel turned on yet needy and confused. But I'm almost surplus to requirements; a third wheel, and more possibly a training wheel, as I hold back, uncertain of my role. Unsure of my place here.

DAN

Under Luke's attentions, my thighs and stomach tighten and flex. This isn't the first time I've been sucked off by a man, but this was the first time not orchestrated by Belle. For Belle. I swallow, wondering how I'll rationalise it this time. Would I tell myself this was Louise's punishment? My revenge? I'd swore to myself long ago I'd never fuck on the members' floor again, yet here I am, beginning that descent again.

Fuck. I can't think clearly, my thoughts hazy and abstract. *I'm certain this isn't Luke's first time at giving head.* I have no interest in the man—no interest in any man. He's just an instrument to bring Louise back to me. *I hope.* On instinct, I bring Louise's hand to my mouth, kissing her fingertips before guiding them down my ribs as Luke sucks down particularly hard.

I pull her closer, kissing her mouth, simultaneously taking her hand and pressing it to the base of my shaft. She's pliant, not hostile, and I need her touch. A moment later, the dual sensations of soft mouth and sharp nails causes me to buck and hiss. Unsure if the action was malicious, or likely to get worse, I'm struck by a sudden thought.

'Tie her hands.' My voice is hoarse, holding a desperate note.

Luke doesn't move, continuing to inhale the bulk of my cock down his throat. In truth, he looks a little dazed as I help him, somewhat forcibly. Dragging the necktie from the depths of my pocket, I almost simultaneously pull Louise onto my lap. Drawing her back against my chest, I hold out her docile wrists for Luke to tie. Once suitably secured, I lift her arms over my head, spreading her legs shamelessly over my thighs.

Luke's gaze zeros in on her bare pussy. Why would it not? The man is clearly bi, and my darling Louise is exquisitely hot.

'You'd like to service us both now, wouldn't you, Mr. Smith?'

'Fuck, yeah,' he answers, his voice thick. He dips his head but then freezes from moving another inch.

'We're not playing now,' I retort, pulling Louise higher against my chest and sliding her slit along the length of my dick. The feel of her hot, wet heat almost drives me to the brink of insanity. 'At least, not in that way.'

Tension coils in Louise's thighs before Luke even moves, uneasy in her position as she watches where Luke's gaze lies. The unholy union. The place where cunt and cock meet.

Is she turned on? Absolutely, but how else she's feeling I can't fathom. Front, centre, and in view of an audience of strange masks, had she imagined these scenes? Saw herself at the centre of things? Small snippets of conversations come back to me, and I wonder if she'd been leaving clues for me all along. Her fantasies of being tied and used were obvious, but this? Will she hate me afterwards . . . or will she love it?

She jerks as the point of Luke's tongue caresses her exposed slit, my fingers gripping her thighs hard enough to bruise. My mouth and teeth work over her neck and shoulder, our joint attentions rendering her short of breath.

'Let go,' I rasp in her ear. 'Let go of all the things you're thinking. All the things you think you should feel. Look around you, darling, look at the people waiting for you, waiting to see you collapse at the finish line.'

Her eyes open languidly, her gaze seeking the sea of masks. 'No,' she whispers tremulously, jolting against me, shuddering against cock and tongue. Doesn't she know that in this type of club, no is often used as an encouragement?

'This is what you want, even if you're afraid to say the words, to articulate. The walls you've built around yourself; they're crowding you, hiding you from yourself.' I know instinctively I'm reading her clearly now; seeing what I'd perhaps chosen to ignore.

'I don't,' she whimpers, writhing against me again. 'I don't want this,' she adds breathlessly. The actions of her body contradicts her lips as she thrusts her breast into my hand, widening her legs and moaning so beautifully.

'Tell me then, darling,' I plead. 'Tell me what you want, and it's yours.'

'I just want you, Dan. And I want you to fuck me.'

Hers is a desire that makes the rest of the world fade away. Unsure quite how it had happened, I find myself behind her as she kneels on the chair. Her trussed hands grip the chairs back, her fingers pale. Fine wisps of her hair lift as my harsh breath brushes the back of her beautifully bowed neck.

In this moment, I agree with the Japanese, never before realising how erotic the nape of a neck could be. God, how I long to consume her. Use her, make her beg well past the point that she should. *Make her beg me to stop.*

I hold my body still, unsure in my control, almost not daring to even rest my hands on her hips. Until I do, pulling her back against me as I thrust into her hot, wet heat.

Louise's body bows on impact as if she's been twisted inside. The muscles in her back are coiled tight as my hands slide along her body, finding a resting place curled around her shoulders. With a roll of my hips, she bows with the impact again, the room around us dropping away. We aren't surrounded by mirrors and people all clamouring to see and be seen. We don't notice Luke on the floor, rubbing himself frantically. The world around us narrows to the scent and presence of the other. And nothing else.

I twist one hand in her hair, bringing her head up to view our joined reflections. Her expression of languid surrender transcending any mask or disguise.

'There you are, my beautiful darling.' Despite her wanton expression, our joint reflection is fairly tame. She's still covered by her blouse, mostly, and my shirt still clings to my shoulders, the back of the chair hiding her lower nakedness. 'And there you are.' I twist her head to the side as we watch my cock, wet and glistening, sliding inside her body once more. I close my eyes against the heady sight, muttering a hard fuck as I grapple for control, hiding the room's multiple versions of us, our joining from a dozen perspectives, all of them fuck hot.

The pleasure is all consuming, the only thing anchoring me to reality is my hand in her hair as, with a vengeance, I bring myself between her legs like a blow. My thrusts are unyielding, the jut of my hips vicious. Her pussy is mine, and I'll leave my mark on it tonight. I know she feels it, my ownership of her body and heart, her cries echoing with the kind of pleasure only pain can provide.

I unravel my fingers from her hair, reaching for her hips again as my heart pounds in time with her internal pulse. With one more shift of my hips, my body is pure electricity, the hot pulse of my climax barrelling through me like a comet. Beneath me, Louise cries out, her heat pulsing around me as, deconstructed and dismantled, we both finally come undone.

Epilogue

LOUISE

I stretch, relishing the whisper of cotton against my naked skin. Sundays are the days I've come to love the most these past few months; Sundays following family Saturdays. Sometimes, Saturday evenings spent playing at the club. Naked weekends or weekends spent lunching, loving, and just hanging out with Dan and Hal. If I had to pick, I couldn't say which I prefer.

But, God, I love him, every dark, pale inch of him. Those indigo eyes.

As though sensing the weight of my gaze, dark, pale and dangerous stirs slowly from sleep. I'm not sure what to expect after last night—a night at the club. Sometimes, Dan seems hell-bent on punishing himself rather than me, yet other times, he wakes ready to torture me some more. So, as he stirs, I attempt to prepare for any awkwardness. Sometimes things that feel natural in the darkness sometimes bring discomfort into the light of day.

I take a deep, centring breath as I remember his arms pulling me to him during the silence of the night. Sleepy kisses, bodies connecting, his fingers woven with mine.

'Good morning,' Dan murmurs, his warm hand coming to rest on the curve of my hip.

'Hey.' I smile, thinking that the pillow creases his face wears make him look a little lived in. Not that I'd say so. Heaven forfend I tell him he's old!

'What time is it?' Jaw clenched, he arches his back through a languorous stretch. As he turns his head to me, his smile is breathtaking. *He's all mine these days.*

'I didn't think to wake you,' I reply. 'It's past eight.' He isn't responsible for collecting Hal today, is he? Hal had spent the night at a sleepover with one of his little friends.

'Not to worry,' Dan answers with a yawn, morning wood making its presence known as he rolls towards me. 'Charles is collecting Hal this morning. I thought we'd drink coffee and read the papers in bed.'

I like Charles. I can afford to. It wasn't my wife he was fucking, though it's hard to imagine he's the type. Affable and polite, Charles is probably just weak willed where Belle is strong. Strong and malice filled. Anyway, it seems as though my threats had hit a sore point. She no longer appears at the house, limiting herself to speak to Dan via phone. And to my relief, Charles had told me he and Belle are getting married next year. Dan is less inclined to believe it'll happen. But Belle is through torturing him. *Or else.*

Last week, I also began completion of my visa paperwork. I don't want to overstay my work visa, and Dan has begun talking about our longer-term plans. Engagement, marriage, the whole shebang.

He's coming to Thanksgiving with me next month. Mom is looking forward to meeting him. My dad not so much. A Catholic, divorced, single dad is pretty low down on his list of desirable couplings. Good job I'm a little too old to be sent to "camp" these days.

'An entire morning in bed,' I say happily. 'How heavenly. And perfect after last night.'

His responding smile is sleepy, sinful, and sexy, all rolled into one. Totally panty dropping, or it would be, were I wearing any.

'It's those reading glasses.' His voice is rough and sandpapery as his fingers reach out to touch my hip. 'I love having you in my bed wearing nothing but your spectacles.'

'Pervert.' It's not an insult. It's also true.

'And I can't seem to help myself when you come straight from the office, all straight-laced and gorgeous.'

'You can't seem to help yourself, period.'

'Come on, you love it when I play the boss who defiles his secretary.'

I snort. I love our role playing, even if it sometimes tweaks my feminist sensibilities. 'How can you be so perfectly well behaved with your staff, yet with me you're a knuckle-dragging Neanderthal?'

'Darling, what can I say? You bring out the beast in me. Not to mention, you just look so gorgeous crawling on your knees.'

My stomach takes the opportunity to point out its emptiness. Loudly.

'Hungry, love?' Dan chuckles.

'Well, yeah. Sunday means croissants. To enjoy the day fully, there has to be the correct calorie intake.' The café nearby has the perfect almond confections. Sometimes I even get to eat one while it's still warm before Dan rolls over me, crushing me and it into the bed. Though I do like how he follows the path of pastry crumbs. *With his tongue.*

'I believe it's your turn this week,' he says.

I twist my head to the window. It's raining. *Just for a change.* 'Don't make me,' I say, pouting as I take his half-hard length into my hand.

'Ah-ah. No distractions, now.' His eyes gleam with mischief as he reluctantly disengages from my fingertips.

'I'll get all wet,' I whine, snuggling into his chest to hide a cunning smile. 'Can't you just rustle up some scrambled eggs?'

'I like you wet, wanting, and desperate.' This man has the sexiest voice in the universe. 'But I'll settle for you looking like something the cat dragged in.' I pull back and stare up at him, my mouth half open, ready to protest. 'Unless you want to play me for it?' he purrs. 'Loser goes for coffee and breakfast.'

'I get to choose the game?' I reply a little huffily. He nods his assent. 'You're on,' I reply. 'And I choose *First In*.'

What follows in this warm bedroom in a leafy corner of London is a game we'd created for ourselves. A game involving a series of touches and strokes. Of heavy petting, the kind that leaves us both aching from the pleasure of it, yet desperately unfulfilled.

His cock is once more in my hand as he pushes my back flat against the bed, almost planking over me as his lips and tongue torture my neck.

'I was so hard watching you last night,' he whispers, his hips dipping, his cock brushing me. 'All those eyes on you, my beautiful girl.'

I moan, recalling how I'd sensed his eyes on me. His look from across the room was so hot, I'd worried he'd disintegrated my clothes. 'Tell me how you love to fuck me, Dan.' As I fist his cock, he thrusts into my hand, and as his hips dip again, I slide his satin hardness between my thighs.

'That's cheating,' he growls, a smile colouring his words. 'Hands aren't allowed. You deserve to be spanked.'

'Without hands? I'm not sure how that would work.'

'I'd give it a bloody good try,' he growls into my neck, a hot lick to follow. *A kiss to the forehead.*

'Maybe later,' I whisper in response. 'This girl needs feeding first.'

'I'll feed you all right,' he threatens. 'I'll feed you my cock.'

'Daniel, you're so bad!'

My exclamation drips with faux-astonishment, one hand touching his firm chest. Not even cheating, he takes the opportunity to lean over, sliding his length against my already slick entrance.

'Darling, spread your legs for me.'

'Oh, Dan,' I purr, 'you'll have to try better than that.'

But I have no words following, my breath catching as the ridge under his smooth head glides over my clit.

'Tell me you want this,' he demands.

And I do—as much as ever—but I'm also mindful of the rain. It ruins a girls' hair.

'I love a man who takes charge,' I whisper, my hips beginning to buck, though I'm careful not to be responsible for him sliding him inside.

'Let me hear you beg,' he growls.

'Buy me croissants.' I giggle. 'Feed me eggs!'

As he laughs a little, he inadvertently lowers himself, the head of his cock rubbing me again.

Later, I'd blame muscle memory. Later, I'd accuse him of underhandedness. But for now, I shift subtly, taking him inside.

I sigh as my body accepts him, admitting only to myself that I've lost to the man I love once again.

THE END

Acknowledgements

Thanks to my family. And I did hear you—honest! And keep sending the dick jokes.

To Natasha Harvey, the Queen of OCD, thanks for listening, OCD-ing, keeping me right, and listening to me panic and flap.*

To Aimee Bowyer, henceforth to be known as Aimee *Boo-yaah!* For spotting ALL the holes and not-so-desirable character traits. **

To hubby, thanks for not getting killed this year. That would've been problematic. And to my fuzzy mutt, Mr Sweep, for not snuffing it, too. *Twice.*
Seriously, the pair of you need to get a grip. You're not making my job very easy!

Thanks to the Lambs for bearing with me, reading, and all that good stuff.

* Must procure Natasha a crown.
**Ensure Aimee has a super hero cape.

About the Author

Donna Alam writes about exotic locations and the men you aren't married to, but wish you were. Escapism reads with heart and humour and, of course, plenty of steam.

Hailing from the North of England, she's a nomad at heart moving houses and continents more times than she cares to recall.

When not bashing away at a keyboard, Donna can usually be found, good book in hand, hiding from her family and responsibilities. She likes her wine and humour dry, and her mojitos sweet, and language salty.

Made in the USA
San Bernardino, CA
30 April 2019